# LOST
# WOMEN
## *of*
# MILL
# STREET

a novel

## KINLEY
## BRYAN

Blue Mug Press

The Lost Women of Mill Street

This is a work of fiction. All of the characters, organizations, and events portrayed in this novel are either products of the author's imagination or are used fictitiously.

Copyright © 2024 by Kinley Bryan

ISBN (paperback): 978-1-7379152-3-2

ISBN (ebook): 978-1-7379152-4-9

First edition: 2024

*Book cover by Jessica Bell Design*

# 1

## JULY 2, 1864

A wisp of cotton blew over loom number two and landed on Clara's brow. The lint, one of countless pieces that fluttered about the mill in a sweltering snowfall, stuck to her damp skin. She brushed it away absentmindedly, keeping the fibers from her nose and mouth, haunted by the news that had spread through the factory that morning fast as a cotton fire: Marietta had fallen. Not that any of the mill hands could claim surprise. Sherman's advance through North Georgia had been steady as a heartbeat, certain as one day turns into the next. And now Johnston's army would retreat again, this time leaving but sixteen miles of roadway between Sherman's troops and the weave room where Clara and her sister Kitty tended their looms.

Most townspeople with the means to leave had done so weeks earlier. When the Federals reached Cassville, thirty miles to the northwest, the "Roswell Royalty" had fled, their wagons piled high with furniture and trunks, cooking utensils and linens. But for a house slave left to stand watch, their grand homes now stood empty: Barrington Hall, Dunwoody Hall, Primrose Cottage (which was a cottage in the same way the last three years was a "neighborly spat").

It had been unnerving, watching them all leave. Clara had been reassured when the Roswell Manufacturing Company president boldly declared he would remain in town until the Yankees set a torch to his home. Despite his bravado, he, too, had left for locations further from Federal gunfire, leaving the mill workers to defend his property from the Yankee torch. He'd emptied the company store of its provisions, about two months' worth, and parceled them out among the workers. An act of charity toward his laborers or a means to keep food from the Federals, depending on whom you asked. Either way, Clara, Kitty, and four hundred others, mostly women and children with neither the means to leave nor a place to go, remained. Paid in company scrip, what wages they'd saved after rent and food were useless beyond town limits.

Clara shook the advancing army from her thoughts. Tried to, at least. There was nothing to be done. And losing your focus near the machines could be tragic, deadly even. The oppressive July heat, combined with the fetid broth of oil, sweat, and lint, seldom failed to make her lightheaded.

She stopped one of her power looms to remove the shuttle and replace the bobbin, which had run out of weft. Within seconds she'd threaded the new bobbin through the hole in the shuttle, putting her mouth to it to suck the thread through, and placed the shuttle in the box. From there, the shuttle would speed back and forth between the warp threads, simultaneously over and under the lengthwise strands of yarn. She'd made it into a game for herself, how fast she could replace the bobbin.

Her homespun dress clung to her sweaty skin, errant strawberry-blond curls to her temples. Though it was summer, she saw little more of the sun than she did in winter. Like all the mill workers but the slave men in the pickers room, her skin was pale as parchment year-round from working twelve-hour days, six days a week. But the sun's summer rays baked them all inside that factory, the mill like a giant brick oven, and they loaves of bread. The glazed windows remained closed lest any breeze break delicate threads.

A stocky figure appeared in the doorway a few feet from Clara. The Frenchman. He surveyed the weave room as if taking a measure of its activity. One hundred twenty power looms beat a frenetic, deafening rhythm. There were twenty rows of looms, three pairs of looms per row, each mill hand working a pair. An aisle between each pair of looms stretched the room's length.

Clara, in the first row, faced the door as she worked. She regarded the Frenchman, the temporary superintendent. This was a rare appearance, and no doubt had something to do with Marietta. Mr. Roche walked down her aisle, his chest puffed and his lips pressed together as if he were holding his breath, which he most likely was; you could get all stopped up from the lint if you weren't used to breathing it.

Clara exchanged a glance with her younger sister, who worked two looms across the aisle. Kitty playfully puffed out her chest and pursed her lips, mimicking the temporary superintendent. Clara smiled indulgently at her sister but shook her head. They had to be careful. Though their work was drudgery and the conditions poor, there were no better options for two unmarried women in Roswell, Georgia, three years into the war.

Kitty hunched over, barking out a deep cough. Clara's stomach pitted. When Benjamin returned, he would take them far from here. In the West, they would work on their own, better land and breathe fresh air. Kitty wouldn't suffer noxious mill fumes, they wouldn't be baked alive in these brick factories, and they would be free. Clara imagined cool autumns, and summers that didn't bring crushing heat. In the winter, when the fields lay quiet, she might make hats to sell in town in the spring.

She glanced over her shoulder. At the far end of the expansive weave room, Orton, the overseer, sat at his elevated desk. He rose as Mr. Roche approached. The temporary superintendent said something, and Orton nodded subserviently. Then he frowned. The superintendent gestured toward the front of the weave room and wagged a finger. *Yes, sir,* Orton said. She could tell by the movement of his lips.

No one knew how many days they had left at the mill. No one knew if the Federals would raid the town. It was the not knowing that kept Clara up at night. She recalled a newspaper article she'd seen in the company store weeks ago, the reporter's calamitous predictions sending a chill down her spine:

*An army of invasion will come down upon us, formidable in numbers and ferocious in its purposes of plunder and destruction. No man, woman or child will escape. One universal ruin awaits us all.*

For the benefit of her fellow workers, most of whom could neither read nor write, she'd paraphrased the reporter's predictions in less dire terms. Universal ruin or no, the mill hands would continue turning cotton to cloth for as long as those in charge kept the machines running, should they hope to make a living when the war was over.

When the factory bell tolled for the noonday meal, one hundred twenty looms stopped as the belts connecting each loom to the network above screeched to a halt. Clara told Kitty she'd meet her back at the cottage as Orton wanted to see her after her shift.

Clara hoped it had to do with her request. Some weeks ago, she'd asked Orton about moving Kitty to the dressing room, where the warp threads were prepared for the looms. An airier space, the dressing room was sheltered somewhat from the machinery's constant roar and the cotton fibers that hung in the air and stuck in your lungs. In the dressing room, Kitty's cough might improve.

She found Orton at his desk, which from an elevated platform overlooked the weave room. He wrote something in a notebook, and when he finally took notice of her, he grinned with one side of his mouth, revealing a chipped tooth partially hidden behind a thick mustache.

"You wanted to see me?" Clara said.

He made another mark in his notebook, then looked down at her. "That's right. Mr. Roche was just sharing his plans for if the Federals come."

"What kind of plans?"

"You let me see to that. What I want to tell you is, if the Federals raid us—and I reckon they will—as much as I'd like to stay and greet them with my shotgun, I see it as my duty, with your beau being gone and all, to offer you and your sister my protection. Eli

and I got a place in the woods where we can wait them out. You
and Kitty can come with us."

"That's kind of you, but we—"

"Now, don't be too hasty with your decision. I imagine
them Federals haven't seen this many women in some time. You
wouldn't want them taking notice of Kitty. We can protect you."

Kitty had turned fifteen last fall, and while her beauty was no
secret, it didn't sit right, the way Orton now commented on it.
He had paid Kitty no particular attention before. Yet now, out of
the hundreds of women working at the mill, she and Clara were
the ones Orton felt the need to protect? No, they would take their
chances on Mill Street. Certainly, the Douglas sisters were better
off among hundreds of other mill workers than alone in the woods
with the Enson brothers. Orton was harmless enough, though he
often acted like he had something to prove, to show he was as
tough as his brother. Eli was a different story. The sheriff and a
member of the Roswell Battalion, Eli would pick any job that gave
him a weapon and an excuse to throw his weight around.

"Kitty and I are staying at the mill with everyone else."

"You think that's wise? You don't have Benjamin here to protect you, and who knows when he'll come back." A pause. "If at
all."

"Of course he'll come back." How dare Orton suggest Benjamin had left her for good. It rankled that she found herself defending Benjamin's honor to the likes of Orton Enson.

"Just you think it over." Orton poured a clear liquid from a
bottle into a tin cup. Had he gotten so bold with his spirits? The
company president had a strict temperance policy in his town. Orton smiled, self-satisfied. "When the war is over, you and Kitty will

be glad of having the Enson brothers on your side." He gestured toward the door with his cup. "Now go on. Eat while you got time."

She stood unmoving a moment, then blurted a question about Kitty and the dressing room. *Not now*, Orton said. He took a biscuit from a pail and bit into it. Crumbs stuck to his mustache, which moved up and down with his chewing.

Clara hurried from the factory, her feet aching from hours of standing on the granite floor, the soles of her shoes worn practically to nothing. She passed the guard standing watch and trudged up the sloping path to Mill Street, where she and Kitty rented a cottage from the Roswell Manufacturing Company. Her mouth had gone dry. Kitty would have a cup of water waiting. She could almost taste its coolness, the way it would soften the sticky feeling on her tongue. The sun beat down, and her shoes kicked up dirt, and echoes of the weave room rang in her ears.

2

N ever before had Clara witnessed a stillness in the town as
complete as on that Sunday morning. The grand homes,
with their wide verandas and bold columns and tall windows,
stood eerily silent. It reminded her of the farm she and Kitty grew
up on, in the minutes before a storm: the way everything went
quiet, the squirrels and the birds and the livestock all finding places
to hide.

The cotton and woolen factories were quiet, too, but only because it was Sunday. That the mills continued normal production
as its landed gentry fled had surprised even the journalists covering the war. As Clara and Kitty walked to church that morning,
Clara recalled one evening weeks earlier when the fighting was
about seven miles outside of Marietta. She'd been approached by a
paunchy gray-haired man as she sat on her front stoop. A reporter
for the *Atlanta Southern Confederacy*, he'd wanted to ask her a few
questions.

"Do you have any plans to leave in advance of the Federals?" was his first. When Clara said she did not, the reporter shook his head. "I've been to nearly every home in Roswell, the grand ones near the square," he said. "Most are empty. Yet the factories are running like there's no enemy for hundreds of miles." The reporter squinted at her. "I'm curious, what do you and the other operatives plan to do?"

"Do?" she shrugged. "Keep working, same as always."

"Even if the Federals come knocking on the factory door?"

"It's not like we got wagons and horses to take us anywhere," she'd replied, unable to hide the irritation in her voice. "Or a place to stay if we did."

"You all must be frightened."

Clara shrugged again, unwilling to admit fear to this stranger, this man who had the luxury of observing the war as if from a great distance, even as he walked right up to its edges. The reporter thanked her and continued along Mill Street.

At church that morning, Clara and Kitty sat in the same pew they always had near the back, despite the many empty rows further up. Though the reverend gave a sermon as usual, his voice was changed. It could have been the heat. Even with the doors and windows open, the church was stifling, and the reverend periodically wiped a cloth across his brow without slowing his rhythm. The box pews blocked any breeze that might have found its way through the church's open doors.

Clara came to church less often than she used to, and when she did, it was for one reason: to feel closer to her mother. Some of her earliest memories were of going to church together. Leaning against her mother's arm while Kitty, still a babe, slept in their mother's lap, she'd close her eyes and let the rhythm of the reverend's words lull her. At the time, she'd had no sense of the words' meaning, but the way in which the reverend delivered them—the rise and fall of his voice, the conviction of his gestures—this, combined with her mother's closeness, had brought forth in her a profound contentment.

Today's sermon, however, brought Clara no sense of her childhood or her mother or contentment. It was the change in the reverend's voice. It wasn't the heat; this became clear as his sermon progressed. Though he spoke in generalities about courage and God's providence in war, the underlying message was that they must gird themselves for the onslaught of the enemy.

His forehead shiny with perspiration, the reverend addressed the women, who that morning comprised most of the small congregation. "While you may not fight on the battlefield," he said, "do not think you have no critical part to play! Cheer on your husbands, your brothers, your fathers. Brace them for the challenges to come. Bolster them with your love!"

Clara quietly cheered on her betrothed, though not for reasons the reverend would approve. Benjamin wasn't about to lay down his life for the benefit of the rich men who'd plunged them into war. When the Confederacy started drafting men into its army, he'd left for the Nebraska territory to stake his claim on 160 acres, courtesy of the federal government. Clara only wished he'd write and let her know how he was faring. And when he would return for them.

The reporter who'd asked her those dire questions weeks earlier had offered a decidedly hopeful view of their situation in his article, which Clara had read in the company store a few days later:

*This factory is of immense value to our government and is operating chiefly for its benefit, and the natural advantages surrounding will enable our forces to hold Roswell against overwhelming numbers should the enemy attempt a raid upon the place. We have sufficient artillery to command every approach and the heights are well fortified.*

Clara fanned herself in the humid church. The truth of that reporter's assessment could fit in a thimble, and they might all see for themselves soon enough how swiftly the town could fall. Up in his pulpit, the reverend grew more excited. Agitated, even. He entreated the women to shame into silence those among them who predicted the South's failure. At this, she glanced at Kitty, who widened her eyes and shrugged.

Raising his voice, the reverend called upon the congregation to pray for God's protection of absent loved ones and to bravely endure uncertainty. His words rose in volume and urgency—his whole head now shining with perspiration, his arms waving with frenetic energy—until, at last, his sermon reached a crescendo: "Strike till the last armed foe expires, Strike for your altars and your fires, Strike for the green graves of your sires, God, and your native land!"

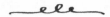

That evening, the whitewashed cottages on Mill Street trembled with talk of Marietta and the Union Army's ruthless general. In the mill workers' minds, General William Tecumseh Sherman had taken on a supernatural quality. He was the devil in the form of a tornado blowing his way across the country. A monster who bent iron rails into neckties, burned homes down to their chimneys, and left a howling wilderness in his wake.

The mill folk had debated with one another all afternoon whether or not Sherman would send troops to Roswell. Some said the Federals would attempt a river crossing there. Others thought they would cross further to the south and west. A woolen mill operative predicted a raid in two days' time. Others put it closer to a week. One thing was understood: The Union Army must cross the Chattahoochee somewhere, for the great river separated Northwest Georgia from Atlanta and the rest of the state.

The mill hands could only pray that Sherman chose somewhere else. If the Federals came to Roswell, it was certain the mills would be destroyed. The Federals would not leave standing a woolen mill and two cotton factories that provided the Confederacy with rope, candlewick, tent cloth, sheeting, and gray uniform cloth.

Despite the threat of a raid, or perhaps in defiance of it, the Summerhill men had promised to play their music, as they sometimes did on Sunday evenings. Clara looked forward to the fiddle and banjo as she and Kitty sat on their front stoop. They'd had their supper of rice and corn sprinkled with bits of smoked pork.

The worst of the day's heat had gone, though it was still hot and muggy. Like the Douglas sisters, other mill workers sat on their front porches in hopes of catching a breeze. Children played in the dirt road. Clara stitched a ribbon to a straw poke bonnet she'd made, and Kitty sewed a dress with the last of their homespun.

Kitty kept putting down her sewing to stare off down Mill Street, at nothing in particular as far as Clara could tell. Then she would pick up her sewing, a few stitches later putting it down again.

"What's troubling you?" Clara asked.

"It's nothing."

"Kitty."

"It's just—if Benjamin doesn't come back for us? Tell me we won't stay at the mill," she pleaded. "We could go back to Athens, or Macon."

"And do what?"

"You could work in a millinery."

Clara scoffed.

"Well, why not?"

"Benjamin will come back. Stop saying he mightn't. And this?" Clara nodded at the bonnet she was trimming. "I only do this for friends." Though she would be lying to herself if she said the idea of making hats for a living didn't fill her with a certain lightness. But that was only a dream, a dream that got her through long days at the mill.

"It's been near a year and a half and no word," Kitty said. Then, more softly, "Maybe it's time we make our own plans."

Clara finished stitching the ribbon to the straw bonnet, her stitches so small they were all but invisible. "Our plans *are* made!

We wait for Benjamin. Now I don't know why he hasn't written. Maybe he has, but you know getting letters through is difficult now. And he won't come get us till he's improved the land and is assured they'll give him the deed." Surely Benjamin would come for them within the year, if not sooner, and then she could set aside her worries at last. No other possibility deserved consideration.

Kitty sighed, tilting her head skyward. "Wish I was one of those ducks that nest down by the creek. Every summer they fly away. If I could fly away, I'd never come back."

Clara felt for Kitty, for the unhappiness she tried so hard to hide. Guilt at her own ineffectualness shortened her temper. "Wish all you want. It does no good. And run where? This is as safe as we get." Clara pointed at the forest beyond the gorge. "You want to wander out there with the ly-outs and deserters and stragglers?" Sure, it was easy for Kitty to say, *Do this* or *Do that*, when decisions weren't up to her.

When Kitty didn't respond, Clara softened. "It'll be all right." She put her arm around her sister. Kitty had never expressed much fear of the Union Army before. Now that the army was so close, the girl could no longer keep a brave face. "I know it's scary, an army coming and all, and everyone's worked up over Sherman, but"—here she lowered her voice—"the Federals are restoring the Union, as they should. As Mama and Daddy would say was right. Besides, there's a good chance they won't even come here." Clara hadn't a clue what the chances were, but she had to say *something*.

"It ain't the Federals."

Clara drew back. "Then what is it?"

"It's nothing." Kitty coughed, then set her sewing aside and stood. "I'm thirsty."

Clara watched her sister walk away, resisting the urge to tell her not to wander. Kitty had always been precocious and fun-loving. She used to sing to herself; she had the most beautiful singing voice. It occurred to Clara now that she couldn't remember the last time she'd heard Kitty sing.

Across the street, Nan Summerhill appeared on her front porch. Nan was a force: tall, broad-shouldered, and muscular, with an intensity of expression that dared anyone to cross her. She worked in the factory's dressing room. If she were a man, she'd be leading the battalion.

Nan crossed Mill Street and sat next to Clara with a grunt, placing a homespun bag on the steps. Clara had always found comfort in Nan's steady presence. A presence that helped calm her uneasiness amid the uncertainties of war and her worries for Benjamin and Kitty.

Clara now confided in Nan about her troubles with Kitty. "She keeps pestering me about what we'll do if Benjamin doesn't come for us. She knows he's got to secure a home first. Why does she act like he won't? I told her it's gonna take time."

"You know how the young are, always wanting to pick peanuts before the pods are filled. You must trust he's all right till you hear different." Nan placed a hand weathered with age and toil on Clara's knee. "And heaven forbid, if something happened to him, you can always stay here with us." Nan, her husband, and their two children all worked at the mill, just as Nan's mother had before her, and her sister did, still.

"Nothing's happened to him!" Clara squeezed the bonnet's brim. Then, loosening her grip lest she cause damage, she said more gently, "I fear the mill will be the death of Kitty."

"One day, she could move to the dressing room with me, ain't that what you said? Or even the store, one day. You both can read," Nan said, her tone changing slightly. "There's bookkeeping."

Clara doubted such a move would happen anytime soon. Orton had shown no interest at all when she suggested moving Kitty out of the weave room. Noting Nan's tone, however, she only nodded in agreement. She sometimes wondered if Nan resented her for having some education. She tried not to make a show of it. She'd once thought of asking if Nan wanted to learn to read but figured that if Nan wanted to learn, Nan would say so.

A cloth ball rolled toward them, stopping at her feet. She tossed it into a cluster of children playing barefoot in the dirt road. Alice, a girl of eight years, caught it in her four-fingered right hand. She'd lost the pinkie a year ago when she went to remove a loose thread from a spinning machine and her finger got caught in its moving parts. In an instant, her pinkie was gone. Clara had taught her some of her letters while she recovered.

"Good catch," Clara said. Alice smiled and went back to her game.

"They lined the bridge with cotton and straw," Nan said, wiping sweat from her temple.

Clara looked at Nan. "When?"

"A few days ago, Tom says."

About a mile south of the town square, the massive covered bridge spanned the Chattahoochee River. Six hundred feet from one riverbank to the other. The thought of it going up in flames was too terrible to think about.

"And there's a French flag flying at Ivy," Nan said, referring to the woolen mill that sat near the bridge.

"A French flag? Criminy!" Clara scoffed. "Who do they think that'll fool?"

Nan shook her head. "If that devil in blue comes here, heaven help us. He's gonna burn this place to the ground."

Kitty had returned from the pump and was talking to a neighbor when Nan reached into her bag. "Kitty!" Nan dangled a pouch attached to a length of yarn.

Kitty looked at Nan, then Clara, her eyes widening. "No, not that stinking gum!"

"Asafetida," Nan said. "Dipped in turpentine. Just hang it around your neck. Get over here so I can put it on you."

Kitty did as she was told. "Turn around," Nan said before lowering the pouch onto Kitty's chest and tying the yarn behind her neck.

Kitty twisted up her nose. "That's the awfullest smelling thing."

"But it works. And I have something else." Nan reached into her bag again and pulled out another small pouch. "Jamestown weed, dried and soaked with saltpeter. Smoke only a little at first, or it might could strangle you. After a time it'll loosen up your lungs and get rid of that cough." Nan handed Kitty a white clay pipe. "I'll need the pipe back."

Several nights before, Kitty had had another coughing spell. She'd been mostly asleep for the duration, or at least it had seemed she was. Clara, fully awake, had felt the cough in her belly, a caving-in feeling. It seemed the hacking would never stop, like Kitty would never again get a clean breath. And when the spell finally did pass, Kitty slept, but Clara lay awake, waiting for the next fit. She needed to be awake when Kitty coughed so she'd know when the

coughing ceased and that Kitty was all right. That morning when
Clara woke up, she had no recollection of ever falling asleep. She'd
gone straight to Nan's cottage to ask for more medicine.

Nan was known among the mill folk for her medicines and
cures. Her knowledge had myriad origins, including her Southern
Appalachian ancestors and the slave medicine practiced on nearby plantations. What she couldn't find by foraging, she acquired
through trade—with whom, exactly, she never said.

"Thank you," Clara said now, then nodded at the bonnet in
her hands. "I'm just about finished with the trimming." She had
made the straw poke bonnet in exchange for medicine Nan had
been providing Kitty in recent weeks. Nan had asked for a bonnet
to protect her from the sun. Clara had suggested the poke bonnet,
one with a brim exaggerated beyond what was typical. It might
have looked awkward on a smaller woman, but with Nan's height,
all would be in balance.

"You've got a real knack for that," Nan said in an unusual
display of admiration.

Clara looked up at her and smiled. Thinking about millinery
and creating bonnets and hair nets for others helped her through
the sameness of her days. That someone else thought she was good
at it, well, that made it all the better.

The truth was, there was a second reason Clara went to church.
The first was to call up memories of her mother; the second was
for the millinery. The beautiful bonnets the Roswell Royalty wore
were a delight to take in. From the church's back pew, she would
study them all. It was another sort of game: whose hat did she
like best, which hat might be better suited to someone else, which
colors flattered most, how might she rework a particular bonnet

to better suit its wearer. As the fighting wore on, however, there'd been few new bonnets to discover.

Across Mill Street, Nan's husband, Tom, appeared on the Summerhills' porch holding a fiddle. Tom Jr. followed from the cottage, a banjo in his hand. The father and son were two of the few men remaining in town. Many had left a month ago to serve in the Roswell Battalion, right about the time Marietta had come under attack. The Summerhill men were considered essential operatives at Ivy Woolen Mill and had been ordered to stay put.

Standing on their front porch, the men began to play. Clara relished these good-weather Sundays when they'd play music for anyone who wanted to listen. She and Kitty always did. Sometimes, if it wasn't too hot, there was dancing.

Today the heat kept Clara on the stoop. Inside her, however, came a flutter of excitement as the first notes hit the air. She closed her eyes. The banjo hopped, and the fiddle sang, and despite her fears over Kitty and the silence from Benjamin and the general dread pervading the town, a floating, peaceful sensation flowed through her. It was a delicious feeling that often came when the Summerhills played. She didn't understand how a song could make her feel things that weren't true, but it did, and what the music made her feel was this: that she was somewhere else, and something wondrous was about to happen.

# 3

In the twilight of Monday morning, Clara arranged her long wavy hair into a low knot and fastened a hair net over it. Though it wasn't as fancy as those worn by the town's wealthy women—who fashioned theirs with silk ribbon or chenille—Clara's hair net was well made. She had created it herself using her own hair and had adorned it with a sky-blue ribbon. The ribbon called to mind the bluets that grew in patches near the big oak on their old farm. It was a remnant of her mother's good dress, the dress she'd worn to church and been buried in. No one at the mill had ribbon in so lovely a color.

The Douglas sisters left their cottage as the sky to the east was waking up, although the sun had not yet risen over the silhouetted evergreens on the far side of Vickery Creek. In the semi-darkness, the sisters followed the steep and winding dirt road that led to the base of the gorge. Dozens of other weavers and spinners joined them. The rushing water grew louder as they descended the slope toward the mill, which stood on the banks of the big creek.

Kitty, usually wide awake and talkative within minutes of rising, was quiet, and that suited Clara's pensive mood fine. For the first time in a long while, when Clara looked to the weeks and months ahead, nothing took shape. Doubts and questions she'd kept at bay could no longer be ignored now that Kitty had spoken them aloud. Now that the Federals were closing in. If the Federals raided Roswell and destroyed the mills, what would they do? How would they survive? If the Federals didn't come, how long would Clara and Kitty have to remain at the mill before Benjamin returned? Would Kitty's health hold out?

Clara arrived at the mill with nothing settled but the belief they should have left with Benjamin despite his wishes to the contrary. The weavers passed the guard standing watch. Ever since the arson attempt a while back, guards had been posted at the factories. The fire had damaged the cotton house and pickers room and would have been worse had the mill hands not doused it with water from the creek. A new employee had confessed, claiming two men from Tennessee paid him to do it. He was tried and sent to jail in Marietta, and lucky for him. The factory workers surely would have hanged him if justice had been theirs to mete out. The mill was all that stood between most of them and starvation.

*The Federals might be on their way even now to finish the job.*

Clara and Kitty found their places in the first row. The warning bell had not yet rung when Orton rushed up and down the aisles, his bouncing steps making it seem like his heels never quite touched the floor. He tapped several weavers and directed them to the front of the room. The sisters exchanged a glance: What was this all about?

Orton stopped at Clara's looms. "Mr. Roche needs more weavers at Ivy for a couple days. He's in a mad hurry to finish a job before the Federals come." He nodded at the four weavers at the front of the room. "You go and join them."

Clara glanced at her sister. "What about Kitty?"

"She's staying here."

Clara hesitated. Since before the war, she'd worked side by side with Kitty.

"Go on," Kitty said. "I'm fine."

"There a problem, Clara?" Orton said, moving toward her.

Kitty nodded toward the door. *Go.*

The warning bell sounded.

"Clara!" Orton pointed toward the door.

"I'm going, I'm going." As Clara and four other weavers left the room, the network of belts that lined the ceiling and reached down to each machine screeched into motion, powered by the giant water wheel outside. Levers were thrown, and looms started dancing violently in place. Click-click-*clack*, click-click-*clack*, click-click-*clack*.

Clara glanced over her shoulder as she crossed the threshold. Orton stood close to Kitty, who focused on her work as if unaware of his presence, as if transfixed by the tent cloth forming before her. He spoke in her ear, but Kitty's expression gave Clara no clue as to what he said. Maybe it was something to do with the dressing room. But would Orton move Kitty out of the weave room today when he'd just sent five weavers to Ivy?

Kitty looked up and caught Clara's stare. The younger Douglas sister nodded toward the door and widened her eyes.

Clara had frozen. There was a hand on her arm. It was Nan on her way to the dressing room. "Kitty will be fine. You can leave her side for one day. I'll keep an eye on her."

"I have to go to Ivy."

"I know. Tom told me he needed more weavers."

Kitty doubled over, and several deep coughs barked out. Orton stepped away. Kitty's cough always was worse on Mondays, after the day off.

"Come on." Nan pulled Clara from the doorway. Then, with a wry grin, "You don't want to keep Mr. Summerhill waiting," she said.

Clara hurried to catch up with the others headed to the woolen mill. Her body shook as if she were cold. She hated leaving her sister—it was like leaving a part of herself behind. Clara couldn't help but see Kitty as the ten-year-old girl she'd been when they'd first come here.

They'd left the failing farm and come to the mill with their mother five years ago, before the war. It was supposed to have been temporary, a way to get by until their father could sell the rocky land he'd tried for years to coax a living from. He'd died of heart trouble before finding a buyer. Two years after coming to the mill, their mother died of a fever that had swept through the factory. As her mother lay on her deathbed, Clara promised she would always take care of Kitty. With no relations to turn to, the sisters had seemed destined for a life of lint and noise and fumes. Then Clara met Benjamin. A wagoner for the Roswell Manufacturing Company, Benjamin owned his own wagon and mule, and he had money saved and dreams of becoming a farmer. Not there in North Georgia's rocky soil, but in the West. In the Nebraska territory.

Clara clung to Benjamin's vision of a world beyond the mill. Weaving would not be a lifelong job for them, as it was for so many others. Not that she thought herself above her raising. But she and Kitty had skills and good teeth, and, thanks to their mother, they could read and write. To the extent that anyone belonged in that godforsaken factory, the Douglas sisters did not. Clara did her best to pretend, for the sake of getting along, that she did not know this.

"If that devil Sherman and his army of Lincoln-lovers comes here, he's gonna learn not to fool with us," said Temperance Enson, Orton's cousin and one of the five weavers sent to Ivy Woolen mill. Temperance's thin, wispy hair refused to stay in her hair net, and the humidity had already flattened her fluffy curls to her face.

"Amen to that," another weaver said.

"We won't make it easy for 'em," said another.

*He'll run this place through in minutes,* thought Clara.

"A shame, some of our own men haven't stayed to defend our town." Temperance looked pointedly at Clara.

"*Our* town?" Clara scoffed. As if they could lay claim to even the smallest piece of Roswell.

Temperance glared. "I always knew you were a Lincoln-lover."

"All right, girls, let's just get to Ivy." It was Mabel, a woman of about forty who lived in the cottage next door to Clara and Kitty with her elderly mother and two daughters. "No good in fighting among ourselves." She turned and spat snuff juice onto the road. Some swore by it, but Clara wasn't convinced snuff did much to protect her throat from the lint-filled air. And besides, she hated the taste.

Temperance's eyes continued to bore into Clara. She met her gaze only a moment before turning away, whistling a tune of indifference. About twenty minutes after they'd left the cotton factory, Ivy Mill, the Chattahoochee River, and the covered bridge came into view. Members of the Roswell Battalion stood guard.

The muffled din of machinery and the shouts and whoops of doffer boys tossing rocks into the water greeted the small group of weavers. Above Ivy Mill's doorway flew the French flag, just as Nan had described. *What folly!* The mill was no more French than Clara was—and she was Scottish all the way to the backbone. And despite there being a Frenchman currently in charge, the woolen mill still made gray cloth for Confederate uniforms. Had they stopped weaving the letters "CSA" into every bolt of it?

"Bonjour," Clara said as she nodded to the guard posted outside. He looked at her oddly and she continued with the others to the weave room on the first floor. The overseer, Tom Summerhill, assigned them to their looms.

The mill operated uneventfully, but the day felt different, and not just because she was at Ivy. All day long, the weavers were on tenterhooks. Clara sensed it in the furtive glances toward the door, in the fretful faces, the chewed fingernails. She got caught up in the collective trepidation. At times she almost wished the Federals would storm into the factory, just so she wouldn't have to anticipate it any longer. She especially hated being apart from Kitty at a time like this.

—— *ele* ——

When the bell tolled at the workday's end, she rushed from the woolen factory and ran, as fast as her tired feet would allow, up the hill to town. Clara arrived, panting and sweating and miserable, at their cottage. She swung open the door. "Kitty!" The front room: hearth, rug, table, chairs, bonnets hanging on pegs. No Kitty. In the back room, the beds were undisturbed, still made as neatly as they'd been this morning. Clara's legs weakened, and she collapsed on her bed. She tried to collect her thoughts.

Kitty should have been home by now. *Could it be she worked late?* Clara took the winding road down to the cotton factory. The night guard stood watch. The factory was empty, he said, and he wasn't to let anyone inside.

As Clara stood outside the factory, she recalled something she'd seen that morning, only now she saw it in a harsh new light: Orton standing close to Kitty. Too close, she now realized. *Had he brushed himself up against her?* Clara pleaded with the night guard to let her see the factory for herself, and at last, he relented and stepped aside.

Finding the weave room empty, she checked the other floors, calling for Kitty all the while.

No response. Clara cried out in alarm, imagining terrible things. This was what happened when she left Kitty's side. The girl needed watching over.

She dragged herself up the gorge to Mill Street and stood in the Summerhills' doorway. Inside, Nan was preparing dinner.

"Kitty's gone!" Clara cried between gasps for air and while pressing a stitch in her side. "You were supposed to watch her!" Somewhere in the back of her mind, it occurred to her that she'd never raised her voice at Nan before.

Nan's eyes widened. "I did watch her. I walked home with her."

"She's not at the cottage!"

"But I saw her go in." Nan pointed with a wooden spoon. "She said she wasn't feeling well. That she was gonna rest till you got home."

Clara steadied herself against the door frame. "I fear it's something to do with Orton. He brushed up on her this morning, and I knew it, deep down, I knew it. I should've said something. I never should have left her there—"

"I'm sure she's fine."

"What if he sent me away so he could get to Kitty? Why didn't I see that? It's all my fault!"

"Clara—"

Her heart racing, Clara nearly shouted: "I swear, if Orton's laid a finger on her, I'll kill him myself!" As she said this, she checked the street again. No sign of Kitty, but there was Temperance, not ten feet away in the middle of Mill Street. Temperance was staring at Clara, her steps slow and deliberate.

Nan only chuckled at Clara's threat of violence. "Maybe Ida Mae needed her help with something. Did you ask her?"

"No, I—" With a glance across the street, Clara saw Ida Mae, her next-door neighbor and Mabel's mother, sitting in her rocker on her front porch. Clara rushed over to her.

Ida Mae was a former weaver now too old for mill work. "She was here, but then she left," Ida Mae said, looking toward the gorge when Clara asked about her sister.

"When? How long ago was that?"

Ida Mae frowned, remembering. "A half-hour, could be."

Children played in the road while their mothers fixed supper, and Clara made her way back toward the gorge, searching for Kitty's tall, thin frame, for her straight ash-blond hair slipping out of its braid as it did by this time each day. Upon reaching the edge, she looked down toward Vickery Creek and the mills. She called out for Kitty.

The world spun, and she fought for clarity. What if Kitty was in danger? Where should she look next?

She would find Orton if only to rule out the possibility this had anything to do with him. She turned in the direction of The Bricks, where he rented an apartment, and—

A short distance away, Kitty carried a pail of water as if nothing were the matter.

"Oh!" Clara cried out, rushing toward her. "Where *were* you?"

"Down by the creek," Kitty said calmly. "Then I went to fetch water." She lifted the bucket as if her sister required proof.

"But you told Nan you were ill. That you were going to rest."

"I did, but then I decided it was the heat bothering me, so I bathed in the creek." She set down the pail and stretched her arm. Her hair hung in a single braid brought forward over her shoulder, tied at the end with a sky-blue ribbon matching Clara's.

"By yourself? Kitty, it's not safe! We don't know how close the Federals are." A pause, then, "Orton didn't do anything, did he?"

Kitty frowned. "Do anything? Like what?"

"I saw how close he stood to you this morning. And just now, I thought— Did he say anything? Bother you at all?"

Kitty looked at Clara as if she was a simpleton. "He was being real nice, in fact. Says he might have a job for me in the dressing room."

"Oh," Clara said, still upset and unsure what to do with the feeling. "That's...good."

Kitty stifled a cough, and when she stopped, she studied her sister's face. "Were you crying?"

"No." Clara sniffed and wiped her nose with the back of her hand. "I mean, yes. I was concerned, is all." Clara squinted. "You sure he didn't bother you?"

"Clara, it's *Orton*. The same chucklehead who begged to be kept at the mill so he wouldn't have to fight."

Clara let out a tight laugh. "You're right—but we're not supposed to know that, remember? My imagination must've got the better of me. Listen." She grabbed Kitty's shoulder. "I don't want you going off by yourself anywhere from now on, you hear me?"

Kitty tugged herself free of Clara's grip and continued toward their cottage with confident steps. "I can take care of myself. I'm not a child anymore. I'm fifteen. Mama was married at my age."

"And that was too young," Clara said, catching up. "You think she'd have made the same choice at twenty? Give up teaching to come out here and try to live off this barren land?"

Kitty stopped, throwing up her free hand. "You're fixing to do the same thing with Benjamin!"

"I ain't fifteen! And it'll be different in Nebraska. The land is better. You'll see." Clara took the pail of water from Kitty. "Let's get some supper. It's been a long day, and I'm tired as anything."

That night, Clara woke only once. It must have been well after midnight, and as she lay awake, it occurred to her that she'd fallen asleep without hearing her sister cough. She closed her eyes, breathed in a stuttered breath as she often did when waking in the wee hours, and exhaled long and slow, satisfied in the knowledge that Nan's remedies were helping. Kitty may not have wanted to wear the asafetida around her neck or smoke the Jamestown weed, but see? Her cough was improving. Clara allowed herself to fall back asleep, pleased she'd been able to help mend her sister's health.

# 4

As they ate porridge in the dimly lit cottage the next morning before dawn, Clara studied her sister: Kitty's long, thin fingers gripping the spoon; her delicate nose; her apple cheeks without color; her pale blue eyes; her downturned mouth.

"Why don't you stay home?" Clara suggested. "You don't look well." Clara felt guilty for so hastily congratulating herself on mending Kitty's health.

"Then I won't be paid, and besides, I'm all right."

"You look poorly."

"I didn't sleep well, is all."

"But you weren't coughing as much. Or did I sleep through it this time?"

"No, it wasn't my cough. Reckon it was the heat got to me." Kitty looked at Clara. "Whatever you're fretting over, stop it. You think I can't manage anything."

Kitty pretended to be tough, but Clara knew better. She saw her sister's downcast eyes and quivering hands. The usually happy-go-lucky girl was uncharacteristically quiet.

"Suit yourself then." They ate their breakfast in silence. Maybe it was best Kitty went to work today, after all. Better than being alone at the cottage with the Federals not far off. The sisters finished up and went outside.

"Clara!" Nan called from her front stoop in the twilight. She met them in the middle of the road, all restrained excitement and grim determination. "Did you hear what happened?"

Kitty's eyes widened. "What is it?"

"Jack came by last night." Jack was Nan's younger son, currently serving with the battalion on picket duty at Willeo Creek. "Said a Federal raid is coming soon. Today, could be. They sighted a detachment of Union soldiers well east of Marietta."

"Is he sure they're coming *here*?" Clara asked. Anticipation of the Federals' arrival—and the dread that went along with it—had been part of their daily lives for so long that it was strange to think the anticipating part was near over.

"Sure as I'm standing here."

"Terrifying, isn't it?" It was Mabel from next door. She was helping her mother onto her rocker on the front stoop where the old woman spent her mornings. "We've all heard the stories."

Clara warned her sister to stay close to the other weavers, not to wander anywhere alone.

"I ain't scared of a Yankee," was all Kitty said.

"It's not just a Yankee. It's an army of men," Clara urged, her exasperation getting the better of her. "We should all fear that." Had Kitty no idea how dangerous it might be, an army of invaders?

What the men might be capable of when their officers weren't watching?

Clara found her place at her looms at Ivy Woolen Mill, and as she waited for the bell, she regarded the women and girls around her. Some appeared nervous and quiet. Others seemed unbothered as they chatted and laughed in small clusters. Temperance was looking at her. Clara turned around to avoid her glare.

The bell sounded and they took their places, and the machines whirred into motion with a roar.

Clara tended to her looms, replacing bobbins as they ran out of weft, her thoughts on the advancing army. Hours passed, and gray wool cloth formed on the looms before her, and then it happened: The bell tolled, far too early to signal the noonday break. A warning bell. The blood rushed from Clara's hands. This was it. At first, the overseer kept the looms running, so Clara and the other weavers kept at their work. But not long after the bell tolled, a noise reverberated from somewhere outside, layered on top of the din and tremble of the power looms.

Clara regarded the others; her own wonderment reflected in their faces.

Seconds later, several doffer boys from the spinning room rushed in, shouting and pointing toward the river. A new scent mingled with the oil and sweat: woodsmoke. Clara exchanged a look with the woman across the aisle. She'd smelled it too. The overseer hurried down a long aisle toward the stairwell. The looms were still running. He returned moments later, his expression inscrutable.

Clara was anxious to see for herself what the doffers had witnessed. The machines kept running, and though she risked reprobation, she left her place and hurried to the stairwell. Several others crowded around her at the window. She let out a cry, and her hand flew to her mouth. Even though she'd suspected what it was, still it was hard to believe the sight.

Flames consumed the covered bridge. Even at this distance, the heat warmed her face. Large planks fell to the river with an unholy crash and sizzle.

A soldier in blue ran past Ivy Mill toward the bridge. The sight of Union troops was like the realization of a dream. More soldiers followed, racing down the road from town toward the river.

The Union soldiers yelled and pointed their guns across the river. On the far bank, the Roswell Battalion fired back.

"Get back inside!" the guard shouted to several doffer boys who'd run outside for a closer look at the fighting.

The day had taken on a dreamlike quality. Their mills and this sleepy town, this isolated place of hard work and no small amount of suffering, had become a battlefield. After three long years, the war had found Roswell.

The gunfire stopped.

Clara peered from the stairwell window. The overseer hadn't come to reprimand her for leaving her looms. Then again, it was Tom Summerhill, and he likely wouldn't make a fuss. Most of the Federals now moved back up the hill toward town. Several remained at the river crossing as the bridge burned. The Union soldiers were stranded on the north side of the Chattahoochee

River—for now, at least—along with the town and the mills and the workers.

The bridge was destroyed. What came next? The clashing of armies frightened her, and men traveling in packs would always be cause for alarm. Clara returned to her post where the looms clacked frantically—a thread had snapped in her absence. She fixed the thread and went back to work like nothing had happened. The girls around her had not left their posts, for they had the fear of punishment beaten into them, if not by the overseer, then by their own parents who could not abide a loss of wages.

That evening, the end-of-day bell tolled, and Ivy Mill dispensed its anxious mill hands into the hot and sticky July air. They clustered outside Ivy, speculating as to their fate, sneaking nervous glances at the soldiers posted at the river crossing. Clara did not stop to join in the speculation, eager as she was to get to Kitty. Upon cresting the hill, out of breath from the climb and her pace, she found more Union soldiers amassed on the town square. She gave them a wide berth as she approached Mill Street.

On a normal day, everyone retired straight to their cottages for supper. Today Clara found dozens of mill hands knotted in the road. She pushed through the crowd, searching for Kitty.

Ah! There she was, sitting on a neighbor's stoop, deep in conversation with a drawing-in girl.

Word of the skirmish and burning bridge had traveled fast. Many from the cotton mill had smelled the smoke that morning during their break. The Ivy Woolen Mill workers, privy to the day's terrible excitement, described what they'd seen: the burning bridge and the battalion across the river firing back at the Federals. The bridge destroyed. Other mill workers anxiously traded snippets of knowledge, gossip, and speculation about what the invaders had done and what they might yet do.

Kitty caught Clara's eye and joined her in the cluster of people on Mill Street.

Clara put her arms on Kitty's shoulders. "Are you all right?"

"I'm fine," Kitty said.

"How was your cough today? Orton didn't move you to the dressing room yet, did he?"

"It was all right. And Orton wasn't there."

Clara drew back. "Wasn't there? He didn't come to the factory today?"

"I never saw him." Kitty shrugged. "Some are saying he went off to fight with the battalion."

"Orton Enson?" a weaver standing nearby interjected. "More like he went for the hills. It's always the men who talk the toughest who are the most coward."

"Reckon that's why the owners are long gone," someone else said to murmurs of agreement.

"Shut your mouth." Temperance spat into the dirt. "Orton's no ly-out, and he's tougher than any of you."

Temperance was mostly ignored—everyone knew she had a temper like nobody's business—and anyhow, Lou, a fixer in the cotton mill, was waving his arms to get the crowd's attention.

Lou was a little older than Clara, a clever man who was maybe a bit arrogant, but not maliciously so. He began to speak from the nearest stoop. He'd seen and heard much that day. The factory bosses, headed by Mr. Roche, had gone to talk to the Federals where they were camped at Willeo Creek. The mill representatives had claimed neutrality, hoping to convince the Federals not to destroy the factories.

"Mr. Roche says to them"—here Lou imitated the Frenchman, puffing his chest and gripping imaginary lapels—"vee are zee subjects of Great Britain and France, and vee are under zee protection of zees nations."

Nervous giggles bubbled among the crowd.

Lou paused as his audience, many of them hard of hearing after years in the mill, some of them excellent at reading lips, leaned in to learn what came next: "The general told Mr. Roche that the Federals had no direct orders to burn the mills. We are free to travel around Roswell!"

Cheers rose from the group. The mills would not be destroyed! Everyone would have work and a place to live when the Union Army moved on. Clara felt a tremendous weight lifted from her shoulders. Greatly heartened by the news, she promised herself she would ensure Kitty was moved to the dressing room. This time, she wouldn't let Orton refuse her.

Lou warned the workers to stay close to their cottages that night, not to leave Mill Street. "Don't let your kids wander near the square. The Federals are setting up camp there." Sherman himself had not come to Roswell, Lou said, to murmurs of relief. It was a general named Garrard. A glance toward the town square and then, with a trace of suppressed glee, "I hear he's moving into Barrington Hall."

# 5

At a little before six the next morning, the mill hands followed the winding dirt road that descended to the creek. Clouds like cotton slivers stretched themselves thin, tinted pink and lavender. The mill workers' footfalls were quieter than usual. Some had fled in the night. Others remained in their cottages. The evening before, they'd been abuzz with the enemy's arrival and the brief skirmish, but this morning they were somber as if marching into battle themselves. No one knew what the coming hours would bring.

The job at Ivy complete, Clara walked with Kitty to the cotton mill, half expecting to see a soldier in blue at the mill's entrance, blocking their entry. But it was the usual guard, and he didn't stop her or anyone else from going inside and finding their places at the carding machines, spinning mules, power looms, and drawing-in frames. Clara stood ready at looms one and two. The warning bell sounded, and the workday began.

For the first hour, Clara watched the doorway, certain the Federals would appear at any moment. It wasn't until late afternoon that one of their officers darkened the doorway. Mr. Roche stood beside him, his chin lifted in defiance. The officer wore a smart blue jacket with gold buttons and stood just a few feet from Clara, whose looms were nearest the entrance. The warning bell rang. The weavers threw the levers, and the belts overhead slowed to a stop. All went still. The room was quiet but for the ringing in her ears.

The Frenchman and the Federal officer approached. The officer leaned over Clara's looms and studied the newly woven cloth. He frowned beneath a bushy red beard. She held her breath.

He asked Mr. Roche what it was the women were making. Mr. Roche did not tell him it was tent cloth; he said only that this was a French mill and not loyal to the Confederacy.

The officer looked up from the cloth and met Clara's eye. "What type of cloth is this?"

Clara could smell his breath: pipe smoke. She looked to Mr. Roche, then to the officer. Through the pounding of her heart she heard herself say, "Tent cloth, sir."

"And whom do you weave this for?"

Clara couldn't speak. Mr. Roche wanted her to lie. But she was a terrible liar, and the officer wouldn't believe her. And even if he did believe her in this moment, eventually he would discover her lie, and then what would he do?

Clara looked again to Mr. Roche, whose face had turned red as pinkroot. He was angry with her. She would pay for this. Her delay in answering would cost them everything. She was supposed to have immediately said, *I weave this for the French owners of the mill to be sold overseas,* but she wouldn't have convinced anyone. The officer eyed her expectantly, but she remained silent, the lie caught in her throat. Never had the weave room been quieter.

The Union officer addressed Mr. Roche instead. "We have orders to destroy the mills. Command your operatives to leave at once."

Clara's stomach dropped to the oily, tobacco-spit-covered floor.

The red-faced Mr. Roche waved his arms. "You cannot do this! These are French mills! There will be repercussions if anyone destroys property belonging to France!"

The Union officer ignored him. Mr. Roche, still protesting, followed him out of the weave room.

Clara looked at Kitty, who was almost smiling. She'd be free of the mill at last. Never mind that they might starve now. The weavers stood at their looms, staring blankly at one another, frozen by the enormity of the situation. Once they stepped away from their looms, they could never step back.

It was only a minute before the officer with the gold buttons reappeared and ordered everyone out of the building. Jolted into action, the women and children—and two male second hands—filed past him and outside. Clara startled at the sight of the Federal soldiers lining the bank of Vickery Creek. There were so many of them! The soldiers watched the mill workers, and the mill workers watched them back.

Workers from the spinning and carding and drawing-in rooms followed the weavers outside, and soon the factory was empty of people. Clara and Kitty and all the mill hands stood on the sloping path that led up to Factory Hill where they lived.

Mr. Roche feverishly ordered them to move away from the building. He held up his hands, palms out, motioning for the horde of mostly women and children to move further up the hill. When the mill workers had retreated, the soldiers went inside.

The soldiers emerged from the mill carrying bolts of tent cloth. These they carried past the mill workers and up the path. At the top of the hill, they went in the direction of The Bricks, the apartments where the boss men lived.

This emptying of factory goods went on for a time. As the final soldier passed them, carrying the last bolt of tent cloth, Temperance spat, just missing his boots. "Lincoln-lovers!" she yelled. "God will punish you for this!"

The soldier, untroubled by Temperance's fury, continued up the hill without a glance in her direction.

Temperance sneered at Clara. "Well done, Miss Milliner."

Clara started to defend herself, to say that, of course, the officer must have known the answer to his question before he had asked. That lying would not have saved them. But what was the use? Temperance had never liked the Douglas sisters. She thought they considered themselves above everyone else on account of their knowing how to read, for one thing. Clara decided to do as the Federals did and ignored her.

Sitting beside her sister on one of the large rocks lining the path, Clara watched the mill. On the fourth floor, the topmost one, the picking work was done. This was where the slave men had worked, some of them owned by Barrington and others hired out from nearby plantations. Clara noticed none of these men were present today; she silently wished them safe passage to wherever they'd gone. The top floor was the most prone to fire, filled as it was with highly flammable, loose cotton fibers. Because the mill was built into the hillside, the fourth floor opened onto a village street, making it easier to take in the cotton bales arriving from places like the Smith plantation a mile up the road. The bales were picked apart, bits of twigs, leaves, and other debris removed, and picker machines transformed the raw cotton into heavy, rolled-up sheets.

It was the top floor that exploded first. Windows flashed white-yellow. Glass panes burst. A collective gasp from the crowd, and Clara shrunk back. In no time at all, black smoke escaped from the fourth-floor windows.

The third floor was where carders fed the sheets of cotton into machines. The machines' metal teeth tore the cotton apart, cleaning and disentangling the fibers and forming the cotton into a loosely compacted rope that was then combined and twisted into roving. Now the third-floor windows lit up as if a bolt of lightning were trapped inside. More breaking windows, more smoke streaming out and pouring upwards into the sky.

Awestruck, Clara watched the top floors burn, almost giddy with the terror, the unrealness of it.

Next came a burst of light on the second floor, the spinning room, where the roving became yarn. And finally, the Federals set ablaze the ground floor weave room, where Clara had spent six days a week for the past five years. Black smoke now flowed from every window. Individual streams joined with the smoke that rose from the burning roof.

The inferno heated their faces, and so Clara and Kitty retreated with the others further up the hill. They watched, transfixed, as fire consumed their factory. The windows glowed bright orange, the brick building lit from within like a jack-o'-lantern.

It was beautiful. Terrible. There was no going back to what had been.

Some of the women were sobbing.

A spinner cried out. *We'll starve without the mill!*

A carder feared the Federals would burn their homes, too.

Clara was afraid. The mill, awful as it had been, was supposed to be their refuge until Benjamin returned. Now the mills were gone, and she had no idea where Benjamin was. Had he even made it to Nebraska? Had he chosen a different territory? Her fear turned to anger. Where were the mill owners? Somewhere in Savannah, she imagined, sipping tea on grand verandas. Expecting the mill hands to protect their mills from the Union Army. The owners would blame the workers for the mills' destruction. Maybe they'd do as Temperance had done and blame Clara, specifically, for not being a better liar.

Temperance pointed at Clara. "Finishing what Benjamin started! This is what you wanted all along."

At first, Clara thought she had misheard. It was a strange thing to say, even for Temperance. The woman was just making things up now. Things that would hurt Clara and Kitty and Benjamin. What had they ever done to her? "That's a lie, and you know it!"

"You think you're better than us. Always have. It's nothing to you if the mills are gone."

"That's not true! I never wanted them destroyed."

"Go on, git," Kitty said. "Go make up stories about someone else."

"Kitty—" Clara wanted to stop her from antagonizing Temperance further, but Temperance was already retreating up the hill.

The Douglas sisters sat on the side of the road that led down the rocky gorge to Vickery Creek and the burning mill. They watched the fire for a long time without speaking. At last, Kitty said, "We could go to Athens."

Athens was several days' walk from Roswell. A dangerous walk for two young women on the road alone in the middle of a war. And what would they find when they got there? There were too many things she didn't know, and so she gave no response.

The factory burned, and Clara was mindlessly picking the bluets near her feet when there came an awful crashing sound. She looked to the burning factory: The top floor had given out, its picking machines crashing onto the third floor, a large section of exterior brick wall falling with them.

Then the third floor collapsed, and the carding machinery—and fourth-floor picking machines—fell through to the second floor. It was only moments later when that floor, too, succumbed to the fire and the weight and the spinning frames and the carding machines and the picking machines all plunged onto the ground floor weave room with the most fantastic, horrendous sound. Like a thousand thunderclaps at once. It made a lump in her throat and tears prick her eyes, and she almost laughed from the horror of it.

Through the flames, Clara caught glimpses of machinery. Every so often, a section of brick wall crumbled and fell to the ground or into the creek.

Some people were saying there was nothing to do but stay in their cottages and wait for the soldiers to leave. Then the owners might come back, and they would make sure their operatives didn't starve, even if there was no weaving or spinning or carding to be done until the mills were rebuilt.

Others disagreed, saying that with the mills destroyed, the owners had no use for them and would do nothing to help. After all, the owners had abandoned them to face the dangers of war alone. And years ago, when a fever swept through the factory, leaving several dead, including the sisters' mother, and sickening enough workers that production shut down for two months, it was these same owners who had offered no medical care. Nor had they paid any wages during the shutdown. It was foolish to think they would do anything to help the workers survive until new factories were constructed.

Clara wasn't sure what to do. Kitty would keep pestering her about Athens. But there was safety in staying with the others, and most people were planning to stay put. Because the company president had distributed the store's provisions among the mill hands before fleeing Roswell, there was enough food to last a month or two—as long as the Federals didn't raid their homes.

Clara decided she and Kitty would stay. Survive until Benjamin came back. Surely she would hear from him soon.

It was near supper time, and the Douglas sisters were among the few stragglers on the hill, still watching the mill burn, when Lou, the fixer, came running down the path behind them. There was a terrible look in his eyes, and Clara's thoughts raced with horrors the Union Army might have already committed. The Federals must have raided their homes while they sat there stupidly on the hill, watching their livelihood destroyed. Now what would they do? How would they survive?

Lou stopped, panting and sweaty, a few feet from Clara and Kitty.

"What happened?" someone shouted as Lou caught his breath. "What've they done?"

"It's not them. It's Orton. He didn't flee." Lou pointed upstream. "They found him by the dam."

"Is he all right?" someone asked, although they must have known by Lou's expression that he wasn't.

Lou shook his head. "Orton was lying face down in the creek. He's dead."

## 6

Thursday morning, the mill was a brick skeleton, still smoldering. Massive machinery lay in a heap on its granite floor. Clara stared at the ruins, her mind knocked sideways by two new truths: The mill was gone, and Orton was dead. A half-empty bottle of spirits was found by the dam, Lou had said last night. The bottle sat on the ledge of the observation platform built on the dam's near side. Evidently, Orton would go there at night to drink, under cover of darkness and rushing water. It must have been Monday night that Orton, skunk-drunk, fell from the ledge thirty feet to Vickery Creek below, landing on the creek bed armored with rocks.

It was a grisly death, and yet Clara could summon no feelings of sorrow. Orton had always made her a little uneasy, she could admit to herself now. Over the years, there'd been rumors about him and some of the female hands, including Mabel—although Mabel remained tight-lipped on the subject. Despite Orton having done nothing to harm her or Kitty, she felt something like relief that he was gone. He would certainly be mourned by Temperance, however, who adored her cousin and seemed to regard him as the father she never had, even though he wasn't much older than she was. Clara hadn't seen Temperance since the day before and wondered how she'd taken the news of his death.

Back at the cottage, Clara made corn pone while Kitty slept. She mixed the corn meal with boiling water and, once it'd cooled some, formed the dough into small circles. Having cleared a corner of the hearth, she placed the dough circles there and covered them with a cloth, topping the cloth with hot coals from the fire. While the pone cooked, she collected up their provisions. There was a loose floorboard in the back room where they slept, underneath which some previous occupant had dug a hole. Into the hole, she placed what food they had: strawberry preserves, salt pork, corn meal, rice.

Surely the Federals would waste no time crossing the river and moving toward Atlanta. They'd have to build some sort of bridge first. How long would that take? Clara glanced at the door to reassure herself it was locked. If they left the mill workers alone and didn't raid their homes, the sisters would have enough food to last them a couple months, provided they were careful.

The pone had just finished cooking when a sharp noise pierced the morning quiet. Clara jumped, nearly dropping the small cakes onto the floor, and hurried to the window. In the middle of Mill Street, a Federal soldier sat astride a horse, a strange-looking horn at his side. Cottage doors opened, and mill workers slowly emerged. Clara woke Kitty, and they joined the crowd gathering outside.

When most had assembled—the adults with their arms crossed, the children peering from behind their parents' legs—the soldier spoke. "You are to report to the town square within the hour. Collect your things, including food and other necessities, but only as much as you can carry yourself." The soldier circled his horse slowly as he spoke, commanding the mill workers gathered around him.

Murmurs arose from the crowd. "We ain't going nowhere," Nan said, her hands on her hips.

The soldier turned to face her. "You will not remain in your home under any circumstances."

"Where are you taking us?" someone asked.

"Report to the town square within the hour," the officer said. "You'll receive more information there." He circled his horse once more, eyeing them all with indifference, and rode toward the square. Soldiers posted themselves at intervals along Mill Street.

Clara felt a rising panic. If the Union Army forced them from Roswell, how would Benjamin find her? She glanced next door at Ida Mae, sitting in her rocking chair, worrying the folds of her skirt. Mabel gripped the back of her mother's rocker, behind which her own young daughters hid. Her mouth was pressed in a thin line. Ida Mae could barely stand; to move from bed to porch, she needed help. She was not fit for a journey of any sort. Where did the Federals expect Ida Mae to go?

"Get inside." Clara pulled Kitty by the arm. Swallowing hard to suppress the lump in her throat, Clara told herself she must be strong for Kitty's sake, and so she focused on the task at hand. She directed Kitty to fetch her homespun sack and fill it with the provisions she'd just hidden under the floorboard.

Into their bags went strawberry preserves and smoked pork, a change of dress and undergarments, hair nets, and a tin cup.

Twelve pennies, the only money they had that wasn't scrip. A
blanket each. She reached for her favorite bonnet, the one that
provided the most protection from the sun. She would have to
leave the others behind, and the thought of it nearly caused her
tears to spill.

"Where are they taking us?" Kitty asked.

Clara cleared her throat, searching for a confident tone.
"Could be they just want us out of the way. I can't imagine they'd
send us far. Marietta, maybe? Reckon we'll be back before long."
Donning the wide-brimmed bonnet, she tied its ribbons under her
chin. She wrapped the corn pone in a cloth and placed it in her bag.
"Don't forget the asafetida and Jamestown weed for your cough.
And Nan's pipe." The medicine might last them two weeks, three
if they were lucky.

From their front porch, Clara took a last look at Mill Street.
After five years, it didn't seem real that they were leaving. This
wasn't how it was supposed to happen. They were supposed to
leave with Benjamin. A hollowness clawed at her insides.

"I don't care where we go," Kitty said as she closed the door
behind them. "I hope we don't never come back."

"Kitty!" Clara stared.

Kitty stormed off a few steps ahead of Clara, forcing her into
a jog to catch up. The sisters made their way toward the town
square, passing burned-out buildings as they went: the gristmill,
cotton houses, storehouses—even the president's and the superintendent's offices. Only the company store remained, perhaps
because it was empty. Smoke hung in the thick July air.

Roswell had been especially quiet in recent weeks, with little
that stirred beyond leaves rustling in a summer breeze or squirrels

darting among the trunks. Now the town swarmed with invaders. Blue uniforms moved in and out of deserted homes, up and down streets, and through the square. What would the Roswell Royalty think to see the Federals marching into their homes as if they were the inhabitants?

Army tents crowded half the town square all the way to Barrington Hall, which sat across from the square at the end of a long, cedar-lined path. Barrington Hall was Roswell's version of a Greek temple. Its tall white columns wrapped around three sides. A captain's walk on the roof allowed the company president, Barrington King, to look out over the mills and the creek and the river—like a real king surveying his domain. But not today. Today a Union Army general was making the mansion his headquarters.

On the town square's other half—the two halves separated by a great black walnut tree—mill workers were gathering. Clara and Kitty claimed a shady spot beneath the central tree's sprawling canopy. Nan moved her sack of foodstuffs to make room. Even out of the sun, even this early in the day, it was sweltering. Shady places filled up fast, then the sunbaked areas, and eventually, little empty grass remained visible. Hundreds of women and children sat, red-faced and sweating, in the July sun. Those unfortunate ones without bonnets shaded their eyes with their hands.

"Look at us, sitting outside on a Thursday morning. Haven't done this since the wheel flooded," Clara said. "I've a right mind to thank Mr. Sherman," she said dryly.

Nan was looking toward the far end of the square. "I'll be damned if they don't plan on carting Ida Mae away with the rest of us!" She pointed at two soldiers carrying the old woman, still in her rocker, down the street and into the church. Mabel followed close behind Ida Mae, bent forward with the weight of three knapsacks filled with her mother's and children's things. Her two girls trailed her like ducklings.

Soldiers walked past the town square, some of them eyeing the women with a vulgar curiosity. Clara moved to block Kitty from their view. The square was nearly full when the Federal officer who'd ordered them from their homes trotted over and blew that awful horn of his again.

"Attention, mill workers! Attention!" After waiting for the crowd to settle, "By the order of the Federal Government of the United States, you are hereby placed under arrest," he announced.

A collective gasp rose from the crowd. Clara and Kitty looked at each other. The officer continued. "Every man, woman, and child employed in the production of cloth for the Confederate Army is hereby charged with treason."

Now it was more than a gasp that rose from the crowd: confusion and shouting and a few cries. "Quiet!" A raised hand, a pause, and then, "You will be sent to Marietta by wagon to await further decree," the soldier said. "Until then, you are to remain on the town square, where you will be provided with food and water."

Treason! It was impossible to fathom. Most of these people—Kitty and Clara included—had worked at the mill years before the war, long before the mills were commandeered by the Confederate government. It wasn't as if the workers got to choose their customers.

"Why are they doing this?" Clara asked no one in particular. What was the point of locking up hundreds of women and children in Marietta anyway? The mills were destroyed. There would be no more sheeting or candlewick or gray wool cloth in any case.

Clara wondered if she would be blamed for this somehow, for not lying to the Federal officer.

Nan paced beneath the black walnut. "It was that French ruse that done it." She cut a glance at the Federal officer, who conferred with two others. "Tom said their general was inspecting a bolt of wool, and when he saw the 'CSA' on it, he got this awful look on his face. Like he wanted to kill someone."

Clara was relieved a lie on her part would have done nothing to help them.

"And now our mills are gone," Nan said, "and they're sending you all to Marietta."

*You* all? "You're not coming with us?" Clara noticed then that Nan was alone. "Where's Tom and Tom Jr.?"

"Making other plans. Tom won't go with the Federals. He'd die first. And I won't go without Tom." Nan said they were going to set up camp in a rock cave overlooking the Chattahoochee River. Tom had gone to secure it. "You can come with us, you and Kitty," she said in a low voice. "We'll go after dark."

Clara didn't answer. She was watching Temperance, who sat cross-legged on the grass, chewing on a fingernail, bouncing her knee, and glaring at the Federal officer. She looked like she wanted to slit his throat.

When Clara looked back a while later, Temperance was gone.

By evening, more army tents had appeared, like an infestation of mushrooms spreading from the town square to the front lawns of the mansions surrounding it. Clara had never seen so many men, so many strangers, all at once. For supper, a soldier gave them each a hard, cracker-like biscuit and a piece of salt pork. Kitty dangled the meat in front of Clara's face. "Tell me this isn't the nastiest piece of meat you ever saw! Stinks like the devil, and look—hairs still on it!"

Clara made a face and told her in a low voice she didn't have to eat it if she didn't want to but that she ought to try to eat the biscuit. Though they'd brought some of their own food, she didn't know how long they would need to make it last.

As the mill workers were eating their supper—or quietly discarding it—wagons were lining up along the north and east sides of the square. More wagons than Clara had ever seen all at once. With her focus on the wagons, she didn't see Temperance come up behind her.

"Missing your ribbon, *Miss Milliner*?"

Clara turned. It was strange, seeing Temperance holding a length of Clara's sky-blue ribbon, the same as what she'd used to trim her hair net, the remnant of her mother's favorite dress. Temperance needed to get her grimy fingers off it.

"Where'd you get that?" Had Temperance gone into her cottage just now and removed it from her hair net? In her haste, Clara had left it behind. Why would Temperance even want the ribbon?

"As if you don't know." She shoved it at Clara.

"It's dirty." Clara held the ribbon between her fingers.

"Yeah, that'll happen when it lands in a muddy creek." Temperance leaned in close, poking her finger into Clara's shoulder. "I know it was you. You pushed him off the dam!"

Clara leaned back. "What? You're cracked!" She pushed Temperance's hand away. "Why do you keep accusing me and Benjamin of things we haven't done? You know Orton drank too much. He fell all on his own."

"Then what was your ribbon doing in his pocket?"

"That's not Clara's ribbon," Kitty said. "It's mine. Orton took that from my hair a few days ago. Said I needed to come and see him later to get it back, but I never did. He liked to tease me, but I didn't want the ribbon that bad."

Clara stared at Kitty. "Why didn't you tell me?"

Temperance narrowed her eyes. "No. He didn't fall on his own. He sat on that ledge many a night and never fell." Then, to Clara, "I know you're behind this. You didn't think he was good enough for your little sister. I heard what you said. If he touched your precious sister, you'd kill him yourself, I—"

"I didn't know—"

Nan stepped between them and, towering over Temperance, "You ought not accuse people of things you know nothing about," she said.

Temperance lifted her chin. She was looking for a fight, and she couldn't fight the Federals, and she would make up a reason if one didn't exist. She snatched the ribbon from Clara.

Clara reached for it. "Give it to me."

Temperance pressed the ribbon to her chest. "When Eli gets back, you'll hang for this."

Along the edge of the square, more wagons had lined up. Clara looked from Temperance to the wagons and back. People were crowding the wagons. Some had already climbed aboard. Clara had been so focused on Temperance that she hadn't noticed all the families fleeing the square.

"Keep it then," Clara said, grabbing Kitty's hand and standing. "Get your bag. Come on." She pulled her sister toward the wagons. They went quickly to one of the closest. There was only a short line, but by the time it was their turn to climb in, there was no more room. They hurried to the wagon behind it, only to find that it, too, had filled up. By now, it seemed everyone was racing to find a seat. At the fifth wagon they tried, a soldier said it could fit one more, and Kitty said Clara ought to go first and Kitty would stay behind, but Clara wouldn't hear of it, and while they stood there and argued, someone else scrambled past them and took the spot.

They went from wagon to wagon all the way to the end of the line. All were full, the first few already pulling away from the square. Clara and Kitty returned to the black walnut. Temperance was gone.

"You can come with me," Nan said.

Clara thanked Nan but said she and Kitty would get a wagon with the next group. The hatred in Temperance's eyes had frightened her. She could not safely remain, not when Temperance thought her responsible for Orton's death. And she didn't want to be anywhere near Roswell when Eli Enson returned.

*7*

Outside the privy behind their cottage, Clara waited, sweaty and itching, while Kitty took her turn. They'd spent the night on the town square, along with the two hundred other mill workers who'd been left out of the wagon caravan. Others, like Nan, had slipped away after dark. Throughout the night they'd been soaked by the rain that filtered through the leaves of the black walnut tree. Red bumps dotted her arms. She pressed each mosquito bite with her fingernail, though it relieved the itching only for a minute, if at all. Clara urged her sister to hurry. They would not miss the next wagon caravan to Marietta, whenever that might be.

On their way back to the square, the sisters passed dozens of soldiers camped on the front lawn of a grand home. The men were mostly idle at the moment: shaving, playing cards, drinking chicory. Clara held Kitty's hand and put herself between the men and her sister. She tried not to look at them directly, but even a sideways glance revealed the prurience with which the soldiers watched them. One of the men, clean-shaven with sandy hair and full lips that held a pipe, leaned back in his chair. His head tilted back so that he looked down his nose at them. A checkerboard had been carved into the table next to him, and another man sat in a chair opposite. Clara wasn't surprised when he spoke.

"You girls would be even prettier with smiles on them faces." The man cast a glance at his checkers opponent and grinned.

Clara's left cheek burned where the soldier watched her, and she almost raised her hand to her face to block him from view, but she didn't want to give him the satisfaction.

"Pay them no mind," Clara said softly to Kitty. She squeezed Kitty's hand and quickened her pace. The soldier laughed as they walked away.

By midday, the wagons still hadn't returned from Marietta. The Douglas sisters left the shade of the black walnut and brought their belongings to an empty patch of grass closer to the north and east sides of the square, where the wagons had lined up the evening before. They would be ready. They would not spend another night outside, surrounded by all these men.

But afternoon came and went, and still, there were no wagons. Clara considered asking a soldier when the wagons would return but could not muster the courage to approach one of them. When Kitty said she'd do it herself, Clara convinced her to refrain, not wanting to draw any of the men's attention to her. Meanwhile, Orton was buried at the church cemetery, the funeral presided over by the reverend, one of the few local gentry who'd not fled. A couple dozen mill hands attended the service; Clara and Kitty weren't among them.

That evening, resigned to another night on the town square, the Douglas sisters spread their blankets on the grass. Clara covered herself with a second blanket for protection from the mosquitoes. She hoped it wouldn't rain again.

Kitty fell asleep quickly, but Clara lay awake fretting over Benjamin, hoping he had staked a claim on a good piece of land. Hoping that he would write to her soon. Or better yet, show up in Marietta to take them away. If she had a nagging sense that something was not right, she ignored it. Benjamin could handle himself. He'd gotten away, and soon he'd take her and Kitty away, too.

"It's a rich man's war and a poor man's fight." That's what Benjamin had said when Eli Enson questioned his loyalty, his decision to leave Georgia rather than be conscripted. "You want to die for these men who call themselves royalty," Benjamin said, "that's your business. Me, I got no use for this one-horse barefooted famine-stricken Southern Confederacy."

Eli had called Benjamin all sorts of names, said he ought to have at least served in the local battalion, but there was nothing Eli could do to stop Benjamin from leaving.

And while Kitty may have likened Clara and Benjamin's plans to what their parents had done, it wasn't a fair comparison. Their father had given up his carpentry business in Athens to fulfill his dream of being a landowning farmer without knowing anything about farming. Their mother, young and in love, had followed him. The farm's rocky soil hadn't grown enough to live on, and he was too stubborn to admit it. But Benjamin was prepared, having once supported himself as a hired hand on nearby farms. And, he said, the land would be better. As for Clara, she wasn't basing such an important life decision on whimsical ideas of love. Yes, she had a deep fondness for Benjamin, and they had a solid friendship, but love? Clara wasn't sure. It might come later. She might grow into it. The important thing was to make this move to better all their futures. Benjamin needed her, and she needed him. And Kitty needed to get out of that mill.

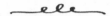

A noise woke Clara. At first, she thought she'd dreamed it. Or it might have been distant thunder. The night was black as pitch—no campfires were allowed after dark—and Clara fought a slight panic when she couldn't see Kitty sleeping beside her. She reached out in the darkness. When her hand found Kitty's shoulder, she exhaled in relief.

Somewhere a horse whinnied.

Distant gunshots broke the quiet. The gunfire—coming from the direction of the river—continued for several long minutes.

A moment of quiet, then shouting. Faint at first, then growing louder, rising up from the ravine.

Silence again.

Kitty coughed in her sleep. Clara felt a stab of dread. Though better for a few days, Kitty's cough had returned after last night's rain. Between the gunfire, Kitty's coughing, and the fact that they were sleeping exposed on the town square surrounded by soldiers who considered them the enemy, it was a long time before sleep returned.

Someone's hands gripped her arms, shaking her. Clara, groggy with sleep, squinted in the daylight. Kitty was leaning over her, wearing a halo of cloud. "They're here!" Kitty pointed.

Clara blinked twice and then followed the line of Kitty's finger. The first wagons were pulling up alongside the town square. Awake in an instant, Clara bolted upright. She surveyed the other mill workers. Though their numbers had thinned, too many remained for the wagons to hold them all.

Clara rolled up her blankets, stuffed them in her bag, and followed Kitty, who'd already run toward the caravan. She felt a rush of relief when they'd climbed into a covered wagon and secured a place on a bale of hay.

The small thrill of having boarded washed through her, leaving exhaustion in its place. Her mind fuzzy from a lack of sleep, she watched, somewhat dazed, as other workers scrambled aboard. A woman lifted her son onto the wagon and then wobbled on the wooden box as she tried to climb in. A girl in braids reached out to steady her.

The gunfire from the night before now seemed like a dream, and Clara wondered if Eli had been among the men fighting. How close was he to where they now sat? He might be just across the river. Even so, she assured herself, he would not return to Roswell while it was occupied by the Federals.

When the wagons could hold no more dank and miserable mill workers, the mules pulled them away from the square and toward the road that led to Marietta. Mercifully, the covered wagons were open at each end, allowing a breeze to pass through.

Clara, sitting at the front, startled at the sight of Temperance, who leaned against a tree lining the path to the Barrington estate.

Temperance was watching them. As they passed, she left her post and approached, slow and steady, until she was only a few feet away. Clara drew back.

"The Federals can't save you," Temperance said, her eyes fixed on Clara. "Eli will come for you."

"Pay her no mind," Kitty said.

"I didn't kill Orton," Clara said in a low voice. The others in the wagon looked at her. "I had nothing to do with it."

Temperance kept pace with the caravan, walking backwards to face Clara. "You keep saying that, but that don't make it true."

The wagon turned onto the road leading to Marietta. As the mules carried them further away, Temperance slowed to a stop, spat, and yelled, "Lincoln-lover!"

Clara turned to Kitty. "I know she never liked me, but this?"

"Some people are so full of hate it's got nowhere to go," another weaver said.

Kitty placed her arm around Clara. "Let's never come back."

Through the opening at the back of the wagon, she took a last look at Roswell. Temperance was gone. The grand homes grew smaller in the distance. Clara could hardly believe they were leaving.

If Clara had had a set of paints and a canvas and the talent to make good use of them, and if she were asked to paint a picturesque Georgia town, her painting would resemble Marietta. Wide, tree-lined streets. Stately homes. A spacious and verdant public square surrounded by merchants of all kinds. That's how she recalled Marietta from the several occasions she'd accompanied her father there on business.

Today, however, the pretty town was covered in a layer of Union Army. As the wagon caravan arrived there in the early afternoon, Clara pointed out the changes to Kitty. The three-story brick hotel was now a Soldier's Home, and the grand pillared courthouse a military prison. The millinery shop whose window she'd peered through years ago, full of wonder at its treasures, now bore a sign declaring it the "U.S. Christian Commission." Beneath the awning of the tannery, a sign read "Army Post Office." The dry goods store, where her father once let her buy some ribbon, was now the Medical Purveyor of the Department of the Tennessee.

Kitty, who'd never been to Marietta before, listened politely but couldn't have felt the same sense of disorientation Clara did.

The wagon caravan rolled through town, past the Western and Atlantic train depot and the limits of Clara's experience. Elegant homes she'd never seen, now serving as army hospitals. A new view of Kennesaw Mountain. A mile or so down the road, the mules turned onto a gently sloping path. When they crested the slope, the view became a wide grassy hill, at the top of which sat a grand brick building with four white columns and a brick tower on either side. Along the hillsides at slightly lower elevations were smaller buildings and garrisons. White tents dotted the rolling landscape, and the expansive grounds stretched as far as she could see. Someone said it was the Georgia Military Institute.

The caravan stopped at one of the smaller buildings. The mill workers disembarked, and soldiers led them inside. They were led down a long hall, past classrooms filled with rebel prisoners, some of whom Clara recognized from the mill, many she didn't. She spotted Ida Mae's rocker in one room, the old woman lying on a pallet beside it. Mabel and her daughters sat nearby. Near the end of the hall, a soldier stopped and pointed to an empty classroom, and they filed inside. Pallets lay on the floor. There weren't enough for everyone, but Clara was quick and claimed one for her sister.

Weary from two nights on the square and the hours-long ride from Roswell, the sisters lay down to rest. Kitty fell fast asleep. Clara, curled up on the floor beside her sister, used her bag as a pillow. She wondered how long the Union Army would keep them there. Did they really mean to arrest them and send them to prison? Was this the prison? What sort of threat were the mill workers to the Federals anyway? She feared Temperance would lead Eli to Marietta once the Federals moved on. If she and Kitty were lucky, Benjamin would come for them first. He would hear the news of what had happened and find them.

They were sixteen miles from Roswell. It was the farthest from home she'd ever been.

## 8

It was just before dawn, indigo dark, and a dense fog obscured the grounds. Clara could scarcely tell where they were. It was only the slant of the ground that hinted the military institute building was one way, the main road the other. "Summer fog for fair," Clara said, an attempt at levity. The path beneath their feet disappeared into the haze as they waited.

Minutes earlier, a soldier had appeared in the classroom where they slept and ordered them to collect their things. They were being sent to the North. Now Clara and Kitty stood outside in the foggy twilight with the others. The last of the Roswell mill hands had arrived several days ago, followed by workers from the nearby Sweetwater Creek mill, a hundred or so of them, who'd suffered the same fate they had.

Soldiers on horseback hovered in the mist at the edges of the crowd. When one of them confirmed the classrooms were empty, they started down the path toward the road. The mill workers moved with them, quiet with sleep and fatigue and apprehension.

They had long since lost control over their lives. They didn't yet know the true nature of their new overseers.

The procession had nearly reached the road when, through the mist to the left of the path, Clara spied an officer sitting astride a magnificent horse. He sat several feet back from the path, so still that he might have been mistaken for a statue. Something in his countenance made Clara unable to look away.

As they drew closer, her breath caught in her throat.

The man was a general, she could tell by his long blue frock coat, the gold buttons in three groups of three, the stars on his lapels. Whispers scattered through the mass of weavers and spinners. Not wanting to stare but unable to help herself, Clara studied the general: his stern look, his unkempt hair, his ill-tempered mien.

Her heart beat faster as she was nearly upon him. He watched them closely.

At the last moment, she cast her gaze downward, as fearful of looking him in the eye as one might fear looking directly at the sun. She followed the worn-out shoes of the person in front of her.

When they reached the main road, Clara dared to look back, catching a last glimpse of General Sherman as the mist closed around him.

The fog had lifted, and the sky brightened by the time they arrived in town a half-hour later. Upon reaching the public square, the soldiers on horseback came to a halt. Up front, the soldier raised his hand, and everyone stopped.

The depot was off the square to their left. Clara pulled Kitty toward the edge of the crowd for a better view. They'd never ridden a train before. Just beyond the depot building, a freight train waited on the tracks, a soldier posted at each boxcar.

The soldier who'd raised his hand said they were to board at any car and that they were to do so in an orderly manner. Clara grabbed Kitty's arm and hurried to one of the cars. The converted freight cars had, at most, one window per side. She would ensure Kitty sat by one of them.

It was bedlam as the workers, now fully awake and no longer quiet, crowded the railway cars. Clara and Kitty were the first to arrive at theirs. A stool had been placed on the ground by the door. A soldier standing next to it handed them each a sack of rations, and they stepped up into the former freight car, which stank of animals and sweat. Rows of benches crossed the straw-covered floor. In the back corner was a toilet—a privacy curtain hung open to reveal a square box with a hole in it. Clara hurried to a bench closest to one of the two windows and told Kitty to sit there, where the fresh air might help her cough. They only had a little more medicine and, without Nan, were unlikely to find more. Nan had been kind enough to let Kitty keep the pipe.

Clara exhaled, feeling a little relieved as she watched Kitty look out the window. She inspected the sack of rations: hardtack, salt pork, dried potatoes, beans. A good amount. How long would they be on the train?

"Look," Kitty said, pointing out the window. Clara leaned over. Two soldiers were lifting Ida Mae, rocker and all, into the car ahead of theirs. Mabel and her two daughters followed.

The converted freight car became more crowded and humid by the minute, and no one had bathed in a week. Clara was anxious for the train to start moving. Once the car could hold no more, the soldier who'd handed out the rations took a seat at the front, facing them. He was a young man who couldn't have been more than twenty, despite the beard and mustache he may have grown in an attempt at appearing older and tougher. He looked upon them with no malice, and for that, Clara was grateful.

Someone asked where they were going, and the soldier said Louisville, Kentucky. *How far was that?* This same question was asked aloud by Kate Terly, one of the Terly twins, who were Clara's age and had also worked in the weave room. The reply: four hundred miles to the north.

Clara felt sick to her stomach. Four hundred miles. Another country, it might as well have been. And in a way, it was. What would happen to them when they got there? Kitty, strangely enough, seemed untroubled.

"I never thought they'd take us all the way to Kentucky," Clara said, her heart beating faster. "How will Benjamin ever find us there?"

"We'll be all right—" Kitty coughed with her mouth closed as if trying to contain it.

"But he won't know where—"

"We can manage, the two of us together."

Clara frowned at her younger sister. Why was Kitty placating her in this way? Treating Clara as if *she* were the younger one? Then, a realization: Kitty didn't *want* Benjamin to find them. Kitty didn't like Benjamin. Maybe she never had. How had Clara not seen this before? "You don't care for Benjamin."

"That's not true."

"But it is true, isn't it? Tell me, what is it about him you find disagreeable?"

"Benjamin's all right. But we can take care of ourselves. We have done for a long time now."

"Until he comes for us."

Kitty looked out the window. "Yes. Until then." She started coughing again. Clara asked the soldier for water, and he pointed to a barrel near the depot building and told her to hurry. Clara took her tin cup from her bag, rushed outside to the barrel, scooped up water, and brought it back for Kitty.

Kitty drank gratefully, and her cough subsided.

Despite Kitty's confident words, Clara knew she didn't mean it. No one could feel brave in a situation like this. She tried to be calm, for her sister's sake. But everything roiled beneath the surface: the uncertainty of the coming days, weeks, and months; Kitty's health; Benjamin's progress.

The whistle blew, and Clara nearly fell backwards as the train jerked into motion. Slowly, the train picked up speed. The car swayed, and every now and then, the window caught a breeze, momentarily wiping out the stench of livestock and providing some relief from the heat.

The train moved at a speed she'd never known. Outside, the world sped by, strange and war-torn: plundered fields and deserted towns and burned-out houses with only the chimneys left standing. Sherman's sentinels.

The sky grew dark that afternoon. Lightning lit the window in rapid bursts, overlapped with booms of thunder. A young boy—a doffer from Ivy Mill—started to sob. He was terrified of torpedoes.

The soldier sitting up front assured the boy that the track was clear, that the Union Army had made sure all the torpedoes were gone. The noise was only thunder. The boy's sobs slowed to a sniff as he accepted the soldier's words as official and true.

Night one: Chattanooga. The train pulled into the station at dusk. Beyond the small tin-roofed depot rose a hillside strewn with white tents. Beyond that, a mountain. Kitty had fallen asleep, resting her head and arm on the windowsill. Clara studied her face. Her skin was so white it was almost translucent. Blue veins crisscrossed at her temple. Her skin sunk between cheekbone and jaw.

Kitty stirred when the train whistle blew. Clara stepped off the railroad car and approached the depot. She peered through a window; inside were cots laden with sick and wounded men. Using the tin cup from her bag, Clara fetched water from a barrel near the depot and brought it to her sister.

Night two: Nashville. The rail yard was a frenzy of activity. Train whistles blew, engines hissed, tracks veered off in multiple directions. The mill workers disembarked by an expansive, two-story brick building that dwarfed Chattanooga's tin-roofed depot. Federal soldiers led them through the depot and onto the street.

As they walked down the street, bystanders stared as if they were a traveling circus. Clara spotted a familiar figure a short distance ahead: the Frenchman. Mr. Roche walked alone and carried an old valise. He walked freely, without a provost guard. Why was he allowed to go free, and they were not? She soon lost sight of him.

They were taken to the courtyard of a prison, where they were given beef liver and bread. Kitty couldn't stomach the beef liver, so Clara gave her some of the preserves and pone she'd brought from home. That night in the Nashville prison, lying on her blanket on the dirt floor, Clara hardly slept at all.

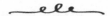

Night three: Louisville, Kentucky. Earlier that day, the train crossed a river so wide there was an island in the middle of it. Clara had thought the Chattahoochee a big river, and it was, but this was something else. As they crossed the bridge, the railroad car swayed, and Clara stilled her body for fear any ill-timed movement would cause the railroad car to rock right off the bridge and into the water far below. It was the most terrifying part of that day's ride, the second most being the two tunnels they'd sped through in such close succession that Clara had barely recovered from the first one—the sudden darkness, the smell of wet rock only inches from the window—when once again the light and heat of a Tennessee summer became damp and dark as the train entered the second tunnel.

When they arrived in Louisville, the train whistle blew long and loud as if proclaiming exhaustion from its journey from the South to the North. The depot was all soot and gray. On railway sidings, families peered out from boxcars. Clara wondered where they had all come from—and how long they'd been there.

The mill workers were herded off the platform and onto Broadway, a muddy street crowded with soldiers and beggars, horses and wagons. Standing at the group's edge, she lost her balance as two hogs darted past in the dusky twilight. This was a far cry from their sleepy mill town. The noise and activity assaulted Clara's senses, and she withdrew into herself. One of the mill hands, a churlish woman known for tattling on coworkers and other bootlicking behavior, pointed further down the road at two Negro men in army uniform, muttering angrily at how *didn't that just beat all*. Clara, exhausted, hungry, sore, and more than a little apprehensive, found herself fascinated by this foreign place.

They'd walked only a short distance before stopping at a large building surrounded by a high fence. The prison spanned an entire city block. A gate opened, and several soldiers appeared, escorting four male prisoners. The knot of mill workers shifted away from the prison toward the other side of the street. The Confederate prisoners were marched down Broadway, turned onto a side street, and then they disappeared from view. At first, Clara thought the mill workers would be put in that prison, but of course, it was for men.

The provost guard shouted for their attention. Pointing to a building opposite the prison, not as large but surrounded by a similar tall fence, he said this was where they would be kept. The building was meant to be a hospital for the prison across the street, but construction was only just finished, and it was still empty.

The hospital gate opened, and a soldier emerged. He glared at them, then turned his head and spit. He said something to the provost. Clara heard the word *secesh*. The word was new to her ears, but its meaning was plain enough: *Secessionist. Traitor.* The provost guard replied loud enough for the mill workers up front to hear, saying their only crime was trying to make a living at a cotton mill, and, turning to the Georgians, said whoever took the oath of allegiance would be allowed to look for work in the city immediately, or they could wait until arrangements were made to take them across the river to Indiana. There was a mill in Cannelton where they might find work. Or they could choose to remain at the hospital.

*The sooner they send these people to Indiana, the better*, the second guard said, in a voice meant to be heard by the lot of them. Louisville was overrun as it was with *that class of people*, and why on earth did Sherman send all this *secesh* here?

One of the mill hands shouted, *Beats us!*

A third guard led them inside the hospital building and through its darkened halls. Gas lamps hung on the walls, unlit. As the building was only just finished, the water and gas weren't ready yet, the guard said almost regretfully.

He led them into a large, high-ceilinged room. Clara and Kitty found an empty corner and spread their blankets on the floor. Soldiers carried Ida Mae and her rocker into the room and helped her down onto a pallet near Clara and Kitty. Ida Mae's daughter and two granddaughters lay next to her. Halfway across the room, eight-year-old Alice, whom Clara had taught to read as the girl recovered from the accident that had severed her finger, sat with her mother and several other spinners.

The soldier, tall and thin and bearing a kind expression, apologized for not having enough pallets for everyone, explaining that they weren't prepared to receive so many people all at once. He placed several water buckets and dippers throughout the room and then left.

The women huddled in small groups, working out their plans: who would sign the oath immediately, who would go to Indiana, who would stay there. Clara, unsure what was best, listened more than she spoke. The conversations didn't last long. Fatigued by their journey, the mill workers quieted after less than an hour and the entire room soon settled into sleep.

As Clara lay down, a train whistle sounded, low and forlorn. Moonlight angled through the windows along one wall of the cavernous room, casting silver light on the clusters of women and children. The few men from the Roswell and Sweetwater Creek mills had been taken to the military prison across the street.

Clara wondered if it would be better to take the oath immediately or to remain at the hospital. The prospect of wandering a foreign city searching for work filled her with dread. They had no money other than their twelve pennies. If they didn't find work right away, where would they sleep? How would they be safe? On the other side of the river, in Indiana, there was a mill. But with Kitty's health as it was, how could Clara let her work there?

"I'm well enough for mill work," Kitty had said when they'd spoken of it earlier that day.

"Not with your cough. And your medicine will only last another week at most, and I don't know how we'd get more."

"My cough is better today. And they say the northern mills aren't as bad."

"But what if they are? Can we take that chance?"

"I can."

But Clara knew that Kitty was just acting brave, not wanting to be a burden. Clara made up her mind: They would stay in one place for now. They would be fed there. It was a new building, relatively safe and clean. Benjamin could find them more easily if they remained. If they wandered from the rest of the mill workers, how would he ever know where they'd gone?

*9*

S ome women left as soon as arrangements were made to ferry them across the Ohio River to Indiana. The Terly twins, who had worked in the weave room, were among those who signed the oath of allegiance and said goodbye and left to seek work in a Cannelton, Indiana cotton mill. Clara watched the twins pack up their bundles, wondering if she'd ever see them again. A persistent nagging feeling had settled in her middle, swelling each time she reconsidered her choice to stay. But every time, staying seemed the lesser of two evils.

And so the Douglas sisters remained in the hospital prison. Life was tolerable at first. Some guards treated them with kindness, most with indifference. They spent much of their days in the fresher air of an enclosed courtyard. The building was shaped in a V, with two long corridors that overlooked the triangular courtyard, a tall fence forming its third side. They heard train whistles blast and wagons rumble by but saw nothing of what transpired on the other side of the high fence. A tulip tree grew in the middle of the courtyard, and sometimes a bird would perch on its branches and sing as if there weren't a war going on.

On Sunday afternoons, a little bit of the outside world came in. Well-dressed ladies bearing gifts visited the refugees in the court-yard. They brought ginger biscuits and fresh apples, clean blankets and cotton stockings. Some mill workers had refused their charity on principle, certain the women had come looking for orphans to pluck as servants. But Clara and Kitty welcomed the Sunday Ladies—as they called them—and their bounty.

Clara had taken a liking to one Sunday Lady in particular: Mrs. Hopewell, a woman in her mid-twenties who offered her gifts with an apparently genuine interest in the women, and without a trace of self-satisfaction that she was *doing a good deed*. When, during her second visit, Mrs. Hopewell discovered the Douglas sisters could read, she subsequently brought them issues of *Putnam's Monthly* and *Godey's Lady's Book* and *Ladies' Home Journal*. "I shall be pleased if they are read by someone else," Mrs. Hopewell said. "I never throw a single issue away. Mr. Hopewell will be glad to see them gone. He thinks they are too much clutter." Kitty read the magazines' short stories to the children. Clara studied the illustrations of bonnets and hair nets.

Clara inwardly appraised every hat the Sunday Ladies wore and, with little else to do, thought upon them days into the week. When she first met Mrs. Hopewell, she admired her beautiful black hat, trimmed in violet and dipping in a V at the center of her high forehead. A cluster of silk violets perched on top, and a black bow draped behind her head. Though it was well-made and lovely and likely cost more than Clara and Kitty made in a month, for some reason, it didn't suit the woman.

Later that day, as Clara ate a little plum cake another Sunday Lady had brought—sweet yet tart, juicy yet crumbly, the high point of her week—it occurred to her what it was she didn't like about it. The hat sat too high on Mrs. Hopewell's head, the pile of violets perched atop adding unflattering height to the woman's elongated face. Clara considered the ways in which she might improve upon the bonnet. If she were to design a bonnet for Mrs. Hopewell, she would make something with less height and more brim. As it happened, the following Sunday, Mrs. Hopewell wore a style much like Clara might have chosen for her: a straw bonnet with a moderately wide border and a large bow to one side.

"There are heaps more hats on the outside," Kitty said when Clara shared her appraisals. "You could look at them all day long if you want."

Clara's stomach pitted. "We're safe here. Benjamin will find us. We just have to be patient."

But by early August, conditions at the hospital compound began to worsen. New prisoners arrived every few days, and the building could scarcely fit more. There was little food. More families crowded in the room where Clara and Kitty had stayed since mid-July, the increase in bodies combining with the sweltering summer heat to make conditions unbearable. Refugees seeking some measure of security from the guerrillas, army deserters, and stragglers roaming the countryside poured into the city at such a rate that there were rumors of another female prison planned for further down Broadway.

Days blended together in a dank and dreary plod. Clara languished, stuck between a past she had tolerated and a future that crept ever further away. In the waning daylight one August evening, in their corner of the cavernous room, Clara lay on her side, suffering from a stomach cramp, a result of the awful meat she'd been given earlier. Lying on her side, she waited, eyes clenched, for the pain to subside.

A girl cried out. A terrible, wrenching cry.

Clara recognized the voice. She raised herself on an elbow and saw that it was Alice, the girl she'd taught to read as she recovered from losing a finger to a spinning frame. A woman hurried from the room and returned with two soldiers. The soldiers knelt where Alice wailed. The men lifted the limp body of the woman who lay there. Alice reached up her hands as if to pull her dead mother back to her. The soldiers carried the body from the room.

Only eight years of age and no family left. It broke Clara's heart. Alice's father, conscripted by the Confederate Army, had died in the fighting somewhere in Tennessee the previous year. Holding one arm to her stomach, Clara hunched through the clusters of refugees and sat beside Alice. Suddenly quiet, the girl looked at her, sniffled once, and fell into Clara's arms.

Clara whispered words of comfort and asked if she would come and join her and Kitty. Alice nodded. Back in their corner of the large room, Clara rubbed her back until her sobbing slowed, first to stuttered breaths and then calm and smooth ones.

The damp night air of August made it difficult to sleep. Odors pressed in on them; odors from so many bodies in one place, from sickness, from the night buckets kept in a corner of the room. Though her stomach pains had finally lessened, Clara woke so many times throughout the night that it hardly felt like she'd slept at all.

Before sunrise the next morning, a faint moaning rose up in the darkness beside her. She placed her hand on Alice's forehead; it burned with fever. When the girl shivered violently, Clara put her own blanket on her. Alice started to cough. In the darkness, someone yelled for the child to be taken to the sick room. A guard marched in and took her away. Not wanting Alice to be alone and scared, Clara tried to go with her, but the soldier refused.

Clara lay down again, exhausted and hungry. At daybreak she surveyed the room, alert for signs of sickness, recalling the fever that had spread through the factory a few years earlier. Her mother had been one of the first to fall ill. She'd complained of a chill as they ate their noonday meal one late-summer Saturday, but nevertheless returned to the factory that afternoon. Clara, filled with foreboding, had watched as her mother's pale face turned red with fever as the hours passed.

That evening, her mother's fever raged. Hour after hour, Clara sat by her bedside. She stayed home from work the following Monday so that she could care for her. The sickness spread to others, and later that week, the factory shut down. Clara and Kitty both developed a milder illness. Clara recalled walking in a feverish stupor to get water from the pump so that she might cool her mother's brow. Mill Street had been all but deserted.

Now Clara shook Kitty awake, shocked at how bony her sister's shoulders had become. It was time to leave this awful place. The prospect of trying to survive on their own in a strange land still terrified her, but the possibility of contagion scared her more.

The sisters collected their belongings and hurried down the main hall to an office near the building's entrance. Sitting behind a desk, a grim soldier spoke in hushed tones with a towering man who wore a long coat and black tie. The sisters waited in the hall. Minutes later, the civilian left.

Clara led Kitty into the office. "We want to sign the oath of allegiance."

"Not today," said the soldier at the desk.

Clara looked at Kitty, then back at the soldier. "But we were told we could leave if we signed the oath. And we want to look for work."

"No one's leaving today." The soldier stood. "By order of the city of Louisville, everyone inside is under quarantine, effective immediately. There's been an outbreak of measles in the building."

Clara cast a worried glance at her sister, her alarm reflected in her sister's countenance. Kitty, unlike Clara, had not had the disease. "But we're not sick!" Clara took a step toward the door. There'd be a guard posted outside. And a gate beyond that, with more guards.

"You may not show symptoms now, but you've been exposed to the disease and could develop symptoms at any time." The soldier came to the front of his desk. "No one except medical personnel is to enter or leave this building for three weeks."

"But—"

"Follow me," he said impatiently. "Those who aren't exhibiting symptoms will be kept in an area separate from the sick."

That night, Kitty went to bed early, complaining of fatigue. With growing dread, Clara watched her sleep restlessly, furious at her own helplessness. Kitty woke the next morning with a fever and cough. It wasn't long before a guard appeared. "I'm going with her," Clara said.

"Do you have symptoms?"

"Yes," Clara lied and feigned a cough. She'd had the measles before Kitty was born and knew she was unlikely to get it again. In any case, she would not leave her sister. Together they helped Kitty walk to the measles ward at the end of the long corridor. The room was as large as the one they'd left, with tall, whitewashed walls that harshly reflected the sun. There were two long rows of cots, half of them tenanted by sufferers, their sharp frames visible beneath white sheets. Some slept while others lay awake, gaunt and glassy-eyed with fever. Clara, trying not to shudder, squeezed Kitty's hand.

The guard led them to two vacant cots along a row of windows. Kitty lay down, allowing herself to be covered by the white sheet despite the ward's oppressive heat. In the cot opposite them, Alice's racking cough jolted the poor thing awake every few minutes.

Clara ached with guilt. If she hadn't been fearful of trying to find work in Louisville or elsewhere, if she had for once dared to do something on her own, then Kitty wouldn't be sick. She lay in her cot, feigning a cough, when a nurse first came by not long after their arrival. The nurse, slightly older than Clara, regarded her with intelligent eyes and a downturned mouth, and introduced herself as Nurse Kemp. With a studied efficiency, Nurse Kemp felt Clara's forehead, looked into her eyes and throat, and asked about her symptoms. The nurse frowned but said nothing more and then turned to Kitty. "She's my sister," Clara said.

Nurse Kemp nodded slowly and, after her evaluation of Kitty, left them momentarily, returning with a rag and a bowl of water. Placing the cloth and water on the chair that separated the two cots, she asked Clara if she might tend to her sister "so long as your strength allows." Without waiting for a reply, she moved on to the next patient.

Clara wet the cloth and placed it on her sister's forehead, hoping it provided some relief. The rest of the day, she lay on her cot and watched Kitty, who grew more listless with each passing hour and moved only when she convulsed with a cough.

The next morning, Kitty's eyes were crusted shut. Clara gently wiped her sister's puffy eyelids with the damp cloth. When Kitty opened them, Clara recoiled at the sight: red veins crisscrossing her eyes in such a frenzy that there was little white to them. Still feverish, she drifted in and out of sleep.

The morning silence of the measles ward was broken only by coughing. As the day went on, more stricken refugees arrived, soon filling three quarters of the beds. Clara remained by Kitty's side, placing cloths on her forehead, reading her stories from Mrs. Hopewell's magazines, and feeling mostly useless. Kitty spoke little, only to ask for a sip of water or a cloth for her forehead. In one fleeting moment of recovered strength, she declared bravely, if weakly, that she would fully recover, after which she immediately fell asleep. Clara kept a vigil all afternoon and into the evening hours until she fell asleep herself.

Kitty, on the third day of her illness, felt strong enough to sit up in bed. Red dots freckled her forehead and temples. A few had spread to her neck and arms. When she complained of a headache that morning, Nurse Kemp made a poultice and applied it to her forehead. As she did so, she turned to Clara. "Collect your things. It's time for you to go." Clara started to protest, but the nurse would brook no challenge to her authority. "You aren't sick. I suspect you had measles years ago. I allowed you to stay because she's your sister, but now we need the bed."

"Can I at least visit her?" But the answer was no, the measles ward allowed no visitors. Kitty turned slowly to Clara and told her not to fret, that the worst was surely past. Clara kissed her on the forehead, gathered her sack, and returned to the room where they'd stayed upon their arrival. It was even more crowded than when she'd left. No open spaces remained by the walls or windows. She squeezed into a spot in the middle of the room where she was surrounded by strangers.

The next day, when a soldier appeared at the doorway—the amiable lanky one who, upon their arrival, had brought them water and apologized for the lack of pallets—she inquired after Kitty. He returned minutes later with the distressing report that the spots had become bumps and her fever had returned. Clara felt almost nauseous with dread. The soldier, whose drawn features hinted at his own suffering, said the nurse assured him Kitty would be all right, but Clara didn't believe him.

That evening, as she lay on the floor, Clara closed her eyes and prayed Kitty would recover. *If she gets better, I will take her from this place. I will find a way to support us. We won't wait here for Benjamin. Please just let her live.*

Kitty survived that interminable night and all the next day. The day after that came the soldier's hopeful report that her spots were fading, although she was very weakened from the disease and could barely lift her head. Another day passed and when by late afternoon the soldier hadn't come, Clara, nearly mad from anticipation, went to the measles ward herself. The door was ajar, and she peered in. Her heart grew weak at the sight. The room resembled a sepulcher, every cot filled with a listless body. Kitty lay in her cot, asleep. How was it possible that the girl had gotten yet thinner? Nurse Kemp fed broth to a patient and, upon noticing Clara, came to the doorway. "You shouldn't be here."

"Will Kitty be all right?"

"She's weak but she will recover. You must be patient. By-and-by she will return to you."

A week passed—although it might have been more, might have been less, for time stretched and shrunk inside the prison hospital—and the kind soldier returned to the room not with Kitty but with Alice, newly an orphan. He sought someone to watch over her, and Clara volunteered. "And my sister?" Clara asked, as she did every day. The soldier smiled and said he expected Kitty to be discharged from the measles ward very soon.

The next day, as Clara brushed Alice's long black hair, the girl suddenly squirmed and pointed at the doorway. Clara looked where she pointed. Kitty! She dropped the brush, ran to her sister, and held her startlingly thin frame in a tight embrace, refusing to let go. Kitty told her that was quite enough, and that Clara needn't be so fretful. But she was hugging Clara back just as tightly.

The morning after the quarantine was lifted, a different soldier appeared in the doorway. Standing beside him was a woman wearing a black robe and a strange white bonnet. The soldier pointed to a group of girls sitting nearby, plaiting one another's hair and reciting rhymes. Among them was Alice.

The woman nodded, and the soldier approached Alice, calling her name.

Alice, her back to the soldier, didn't look up from her doll. Her hearing had suffered since her recovery. One of the other girls tapped her on the knee, then pointed at the soldier behind her. Alice turned.

The woman with him was Sister Frances, the soldier said, and she was going to help Alice find a new family.

Sister Frances told the child to collect her things. Alice said nothing. A pause, then she hugged her friends and put her doll and blanket into a small bag. Clara went to her, tears shimmering in her eyes, and told her that all would be well, that she would get a nice family who would love her very much. She feared the chances were small, that Alice would most likely be put to housework, but hoped that saying it would make it come true. Kitty gave Alice a tiny dress for her doll; she'd sewn it from remnants of a dress belonging to Alice's mother. The girl's lips moved up at the corners, almost a smile. The sisters held Alice in a long embrace.

"Come now, Alice." Sister Frances reached for the girl's hand, pausing a moment upon noticing her missing pinkie. "We've other children to collect."

The bravery of little Alice going off into the world alone was almost too much for Clara to bear. She wished she could take her with them, but what future could she offer?

"Do you feel strong enough to leave?" Clara asked Kitty that same morning.

"I do. Is it even still August?" Then, with a dip of her chin, "Still 1864?"

Clara smiled. She, too, had lost track of time. "Maybe they'll tell us on our way out."

They sponged their bodies with tepid water and rubbed themselves dry with a coarse towel. Sufficiently clean, they said goodbye to Ida Mae, who sat in her rocker facing the window that looked onto the courtyard and the high fence beyond; and to Mabel, who sat cross-legged on the floor beside her, sewing. Mabel said they planned to leave once her daughters were released from the measles ward.

With one last look at the room, a wave of pity washing over Clara for the scores of refugees remaining, she and Kitty carried their bundles down the main hall toward the entrance. It was not without some trepidation that Clara told the guard they were ready to sign the oath of allegiance. But once she'd pledged her oath, she was pleasantly surprised to find the nagging feeling in her middle, a feeling she'd grown so accustomed to she'd almost forgotten it was there, was gone.

As they stood before the tall fence, Clara exhaled with a heavy sigh. A guard moved to open the gate, and she squeezed her sister's hand. How right a thing it was, uncertainty and all, to be leaving.

# *10*

The gate thudded closed behind them. In front of them, a flurry of wagons and livestock and soldiers and draymen passed by on Broadway. In her hand, Clara clutched their signed oaths of allegiance, dated the 29th of August, 1864.

Lightheaded from overwhelm, she leaned against the high fence, feeling both conspicuous and invisible. Everyone in this overcrowded city was a stranger. Back home in Roswell, she'd known everyone she came upon, day after day. And they had known her: She was Clara, who can read and write; Clara, who can make beautiful bonnets and hair nets; who is an older sister; who has seniority in the weave room. In this crowded, martial-law city, she was a foreigner. *Secesh.*

Clara put a hand to her bonnet, grateful both for its protection from the sun, already bringing sweat to her underarms and brow, and also for the respectability it afforded her. At the very least, she and Kitty wore bonnets that were well-made, if somewhat soiled.

"We might could look for work," Kitty said when, after a minute, Clara still hadn't moved.

"Here in Louisville?"

"Why not?"

Because they didn't know the city. Because it was bursting with refugees needing work. Because she was scared. Not wanting to disappoint her sister, she said, unconvincingly to her own ears, "Won't hurt to try."

As they headed eastward, Federal guards marched a group of Confederate prisoners down Broadway toward the prison, their hands bound behind their backs. Clara could not have been more surprised to see among them a face she recognized.

Quickly she pulled Kitty behind a dray loaded with barrels.

"Oh!" Kitty exclaimed when Clara pointed to Eli Enson. His dirty trousers were ill-fitting and threadbare, and his dark beard had grown long and was tinged with dust. His eyes were hollowed, but his capture had not muted their malevolent gaze.

Kitty asked in a whisper, "You reckon he saw us?"

"No," Clara said, although she wasn't sure.

The guards led Eli and the other Confederates into the prison, and the gate closed behind them.

Kitty wondered aloud if Eli knew about Orton's death. Clara said no, again more wish than certainty. "He must have got captured somewhere south of Roswell." A pause. "Come on then."

They followed Broadway a while, passing tobacco factories and tradesmen and the depot that marked their arrival in the city. The aroma of baking bread wafted from a bakery, causing Clara's stomach to growl. What a loaf of bread could do to improve her sister's frail condition. Turning away from the scent, she led Kitty down one of the numbered streets, which they understood would take them closer to the river. Now and again, they paused under the shade of an awning or one of the trees lining the street to escape the heat. They came upon Market Street, which, as the name suggested, held the largest concentration of the city's shops.

*Are we going to walk past them all, or am I going to go inside?* Clara chided herself. At last, she stopped, resolute, in front of a dry goods store. This was as good a place as any. She stood on the wide sidewalk, conscious of the drabness of her appearance. She grabbed Kitty's hand. "Come on then."

When Clara asked for the proprietor, a clerk pointed to a serious-looking man with close-set eyes and bushy brows. He was unrolling a bolt of cloth while a customer waited. When the customer left, she approached.

Clara had barely gotten a full sentence out when the proprietor barked that he didn't hire rebels. She said she was no rebel and showed him her oath of allegiance. He wasn't at all interested in what oaths they'd pledged. She rushed from the store with Kitty close behind her.

The blood pumping faster through her veins now, it was less daunting to walk into a grocer's further down the street. The grocer, who wore spectacles and a neatly trimmed beard, was more sympathetic, if no more helpful. Even if he had a place available, he said, he couldn't hire Clara or Kitty. The city had prohibited the employment of rebels as clerks. Clara tried to explain that they weren't rebels, that they had pledged their allegiance to the United States, but even as she said it, she knew that as far as anyone else was concerned, their pledge of loyalty meant nothing. The grocer only shook his head, and her shoulders drooped under the weight of disappointment.

"Wait," he said as they turned to leave. He nodded at a container of apples. "Take one for you and your sister."

Emboldened by this kindness, Clara thanked the grocer, selected two apples, and walked out the door with her head held high.

At each shop they tried, it was the same result; all that varied was the degree of hostility with which they were met. "The city is overrun with your kind looking for work," one merchant said. As the day wore on and Kitty began holding onto Clara's arm for support, she looked for a place to rest. They came upon a massive gray building with wide front steps leading up to a grand portico.

"I'm tired," Clara said, leading her sister to a corner of the steps where they would be out of the way. "We should rest." This was too much for someone recently recovered from measles.

"I know you're saying that on my account. I'm fine."

But they'd only just sat down when a provost guard told them to move, and they walked until they found a cemetery. The trees and grass offered a welcoming place to rest. With her pennies, she bought them nuts from a vendor, and they sat in the shade among the gravestones. Together they sat in silence, both too exhausted and hungry to speak. Clara studied her sister. Kitty wasn't coughing as much, but the disease had weakened her. Her hands were almost skeletal. It hurt to look at them, the bones as visible as if covered only by a thin sheet.

Now that they'd stopped walking, the fullness of Clara's exhaustion made it difficult to imagine getting up again. She stared at the gravestones. It was no use, this city. She resigned herself to trying the Cannelton mill. Maybe it was her fate, mill work. If only she had made this decision weeks ago, Kitty never would have gotten sick.

"We'll go to Indiana," she announced after a time. "Maybe I can support both of us. You need more time to recover. Tomorrow we'll cross the river."

"A fresh start is just what we need," Kitty said.

Clara was too tired to argue this was not the start of anything, that this was just a temporary way of getting by. Sooner or later, Benjamin would trace their path to Louisville, and somehow he'd learn that the mill workers were sent across the river to Indiana, and from there, he'd find the cotton mill. She could not contemplate the alternative, that Benjamin would never find her, and she would spend the rest of her life breathing lint-filled air in a deafening factory. She said nothing.

The sun had dipped behind the buildings when, not knowing where else to go, they found their way back to the train depot where they'd arrived more than a month ago. They sat on a bench inside for a while. When the station agent realized they hadn't bought a ticket, he kicked them out. In the growing darkness, the sisters leaned against the side of the building. From boxcars stranded on sidings, refugees watched night settle in.

"I'm starving," Kitty said.

Clara's stomach growled. She regretted having spent the day exhausting themselves looking for work. They could have been in Indiana by now. She opened her bag even though she knew there was nothing in it to eat. She'd long ago given what rations she'd had to Kitty. "We'll rest here for the night," Clara said. "Before sunup, we'll go to the dock. They're supposed to let us cross the river to

Indiana free of charge if we show them our oath." Clara kept both
oaths folded up inside her bonnet for safekeeping.

Clara's spine pressed into the brick building, making it difficult to get comfortable. At some point, she would have to lie down
in the dirt.

"Look at all of them. It's no wonder crime has gotten terrible."
Above them, a man's voice. A well-dressed couple cast glances at
the boxcars filled with people fleeing the war.

His companion clucked her tongue. "It's a certain class of people that have come up from the rebel states. Rather than find honest employment, they'd prefer to steal or prostitute themselves."

Were she less tired and hungry, she might have cared about this
calumny. She was no thief, no prostitute: She was Clara, who could
read and write and make beautiful bonnets.

A gruff male voice jolted Clara awake.

A man wearing dirty trousers towered over them. He pointed
at Kitty, who lay sleeping on Clara's shoulder. "I said, 'How much
for the girl?'" The man took a step closer, the stink of alcohol
attending his words.

Clara put an arm across her sister, that she might shield her
from his view. "You got the wrong idea," she said evenly, not
wanting to anger him. "She's not... what you think."

Another step. "Surely she is. Or will be, she gets hungry
enough." He reached into his pocket.

"No!" Clara yelled. Kitty awoke. The man frowned threaten-
ingly, and she softened her voice. "We're waiting—"

"Girls!" A woman's voice called from somewhere nearby. "Where have you been?"

Clara found the source of the voice, a woman in one of the boxcars on the sidings. A too-thin woman in soiled, torn clothing. Clara looked around to see if there were other girls the boxcar woman might be calling to. But, no, the woman was calling to them.

"Yes, ma'am!" Clara stood up and pulled Kitty to her feet. Together they rushed to the boxcar. Standing at the boxcar door, Clara glanced over her shoulder. The man had turned away.

Five sleeping children lay on blankets at one end of the boxcar. At the other end, a family of six. The woman bid them to come inside.

Clara's hands were shaking. "Thank you," she said in a low voice as she and Kitty climbed into the car. "That man... We're not—"

"One night," the haggard woman said, offering them the empty space at the center of the boxcar. There was just enough room for the two of them to lie down. "Then you got to move on."

"Yes, ma'am. I only have eight cents to pay you." Clara reached into her sack.

The woman, who spoke in a voice that sounded like home, told her to keep her pennies, that she would need them. "You best leave the city tomorrow. It's no place for two pretty girls on their own." She closed the door, all but a crack, sliding it slowly so as not to wake the children.

The next morning, Clara and Kitty followed Ninth Street all the way to the steamboat landing, a bustling expanse at the city's edge where the land sloped down to the Ohio River.

Clara almost regretted their decision the instant the Ohio River came into view. Never had she imagined a river could be so vast. The Chattahoochee had always seemed wide, even more so when she crossed its covered bridge. And they'd passed over some wide rivers on the train coming north, like that one with an island right in the middle of it. But what spread before her now was something else entirely. There ought to be another name for a river this wide. Just as a pond was not a lake, and a lake was not an ocean, this was more than a river. She squinted at the buildings and trees on the opposite bank. They were so distant they appeared small and flat like they were part of a landscape painting. This river, she thought, could be a *mile wide*.

"A shame there's no bridge," Clara said nervously as they stood on the wharf at the foot of Ninth Street. She'd never crossed a river by boat.

Kitty only laughed and looped her arm through Clara's. Together they wandered the busy landing, where steam whistles sounded, and hucksters called out, and wagons rumbled past in all directions. Steamboats lined the wharf. One of them must be the ferry to cross the river, but which one?

Kitty spotted a soldier walking near a riverboat, and they approached. When Clara asked him about the ferry, the soldier pointed to a row of buildings at the top of the landing and directed them to the provost marshal's office. They were to get their tickets there.

Clara started to ask which building he meant, but the soldier had already moved on, so she and Kitty made their way up the landing and hoped to find it themselves without too much trouble.

"Look there!" Kitty pointed. On a sidewalk in front of a two-story building, Ida Mae sat in her rocker. Her two granddaughters played with dolls on the sidewalk beside her.

"I signed the dratted oath," Ida Mae said, pointing a thumb over her shoulder to the provost marshal's office. "My granddaughters won't die in a Yankee prison. They were mighty sick... Mabel's inside, getting our tickets. Reckon I got a few more miles in me."

"You're going to Cannelton?"

Unable to speak for a moment due to a raspy cough, Ida Mae shook her head. Then, when she recovered, "Cincinnati. Indiana don't want any more of our kind."

Above Ida Mae's head, an announcement was posted in the window:

*Refugees, male and female, are to be forwarded at the expense of the United States, if unable to pay their own way, to Cincinnati or St. Louis by water or to any point not over 100 miles by railroad.*

"Lots of Roswell and Sweetwater folk went to Cannelton," Ida Mae said, wiping her mouth with a handkerchief. "Can't be enough work for everyone."

"Let's go to Cincinnati!" Kitty looked up from the sidewalk where she'd sat with Ida Mae's granddaughters.

Clara squinted at her. "You seem awful excited about a city we know nothing about."

"Think of Eli," Kitty said. "What if he comes looking for us once he gets out of that prison? If lots of Roswell folk went to Cannelton, he's like to try there."

"But I had nothing to do with"—she lowered her voice—"that."

"But Temperance is set on it, and if she convinces Eli it was you..."

They hadn't seen Temperance since leaving Roswell, and Clara suspected she was hiding in the hills surrounding the town, like Nan's family, waiting for the Federals to leave. It seemed unlikely that Temperance could get word of Orton's death to Eli in the Louisville prison, if she even knew he'd been captured. However, the male second hands and a few overseers from the mill were imprisoned there, and if Temperance had poisoned their ears, they might well spread the lies to Eli. And it would take Eli no time at all to find them in Cannelton.

She turned to Ida Mae. "I didn't kill Orton."

Ida Mae held up a thin, veined hand. "Far as I see it, he had it coming."

Clara took a step closer and with a glance over her shoulder, as if Eli might walk up behind her, "What do you mean, 'he had it coming'?"

But Ida Mae didn't answer, only watched her granddaughters play beside her.

Clara returned to the issue at hand. It was the most momentous decision of their lives: Cannelton or Cincinnati. In Cannelton, there was a mill where they could find work. Maybe. Who knew what they might find in Cincinnati? Benjamin had warned her against cities once when she mentioned Kitty's desire to go to

Athens or Atlanta. "You're a country girl, through and through," he'd told her. Country life was all she knew, after all. And if they chose Cincinnati, would Benjamin be able to find them there? On the other hand, she didn't want Kitty near another textile mill. The weight of their future pressed upon her.

"All right." Clara decided that despite its unknowns, there had to be more opportunity in a larger city, further from the many refugees looking for work around here. "We'll go to Cincinnati."

Kitty smiled. Clara bit her lip. She knew nothing about Cincinnati, and now she was taking her sister there.

"Biggest city west of Philadelphia," said the man inside the provost marshal's office as he checked their oaths of allegiance and wrote something in a logbook. He handed them two pieces of paper. "Take these to the packet *Bluegrass Belle* and get in line. They'll be loading her now. These tickets give you girls deck passage, including meals, all the way to the Queen City. Good luck to you." Then, as Clara stood there holding the tickets, "Now don't dawdle, or all the best spots will fill up before you get there."

The Douglas sisters made their way down the bustling wharf, careful to avoid the carriages and stagecoaches bringing travelers to and from the riverfront.

"Isn't it beautiful?" Kitty said as they reached the packet docked near the water's edge.

Shielding her eyes from the bright sky with her hand, she tilted her head back to take in the steamboat. Her sister was right. It *was* beautiful, like a fancy layered cake, three decks stacked atop one another, the outer edges frosted white with swirls and garnishes. Two smokestacks rose in the center like giant candles. To use her late father's expression, it was *some pumpkins*.

# 11

Clara and Kitty waited on the landing with other impoverished folk while the cabin passengers boarded the *Bluegrass Belle*. They reminded her of Mrs. Hopewell, with their fine hats, each a little work of art. Brims wide and narrow, crowns low and high, various types of ribbons, ornamental feathers, and artificial fruits and flowers. As usual, Clara could not resist a sizing up: this color combination flattered, those feathers were too tall, that bonnet shape complemented its wearer's features.

As the well-dressed boarded at the bow, roustabouts loaded cargo near the stern. Some wore vests and shirts; others wore coats and vests and no shirts. All of them carried the freight on their head and shoulders. It looked like backbreaking work.

Once the cargo and livestock were loaded and the cabin passengers had boarded, the scores of deck passengers were directed to cross the long board laid from shore to boat and to claim a place on the deck. A cot if they were lucky, and if not, then a box or bale would be their berth. "Look for a crate with a destination further than your own," was one man's advice. There was much jostling and commotion as the horde narrowed into a single file line to cross the stage.

Once aboard, Clara hurried to the starboard deck—the side for women and families, said a man in a straw hat—and fought her way through the crowd, farther and farther toward the stern as the people in front of her claimed the empty cots, dozens now already claimed. The main deck rose only a few feet above the water. To her left was a meager railing; to her right was an interior wall. Clara kept as close to the wall as she could, but the deck wasn't very wide. They had walked half the deck's length when they found a lone cot unclaimed.

"You take it," Clara told Kitty. "I'll find something."

Clara made a berth out of hay bales, which were stacked in rows along the deck's edge. The deckhands shouted at them not to move any of the cargo. With Kitty's cot pushed next to the hay bale, the two sisters had adjoining berths. "It's not so bad," Clara said.

Toward the interior of the main deck, sheltered from the elements by the upper decks, cargo holds housed livestock, mostly sheep and pigs. A few horses. There were barrels and boxes and burlap bags. On the upper decks, Clara imagined fancy staterooms, a luxurious dining area. All of it was as unreachable to her as the moon. No matter. Even with the stench of livestock, a bale of hay on an open deck was better than where they'd been.

When a whistle blew suddenly, loud and deep, Clara jumped. The engine sounded its low, steady breathing like the drawn-out snores of a drunk man's sleep. As the riverboat pulled away from the dock, the wharf slowly retreated, and she watched with a mix of fear and excitement as the stretch of water separating them from land widened. The wharf grew smaller in the distance, and soon Louisville, with its train depots, tobacco warehouses, miles-long streets, and more people all in one place than she'd ever seen, disappeared behind a bend in the river.

For much of that morning, the river was smooth and quiet. Kitty slept on her cot, and Clara, for the first time in weeks, felt herself relax. It would be two days before they arrived in Cincinnati. Until then, there were no decisions to be made. For now, they had a place to sleep and food to eat. Three meals each day! Cincinnati was many miles upriver, and she would think about their arrival later. Maybe she would talk with Mabel and find out what they planned to do. They might face Cincinnati together.

As the riverboat paddled up the Ohio, the passing scenery was mostly forest. Clara fell into a sort of reverie, watching some small thing—a fallen branch or a duck—drift by. Now and again, her peace would be interrupted by a deckhand rushing past, cursing at the deckers to get out of the way.

To her relief, the river had narrowed since Louisville. At one especially narrow point, their progress had slowed when the boat had difficulty maneuvering around a submerged tree, the tree's upper branches bobbing at the surface.

Every few hours the *Bluegrass Belle* would stop at a river town to load sacks or barrels or livestock. Later that afternoon, when the boat docked at a farm, Clara made her way to the bow, where soldiers had placed Ida Mae's rocker under cover of the deck above. Mabel was talking with a Union soldier while her daughters leaned over the railing, watching the loading.

Clara knelt by Ida Mae. "I never expected they'd send us this far."

"Don't imagine we'll ever go back." The old woman looked tired, as if the journey had taken the last of her strength.

"What about your grandson?"

"Danny." Ida Mae's voice softened, and her eyes closed. "All sorts of a boy, he was. Never gave his mama any trouble."

"'Was'? What happened?"

Ida Mae held a handkerchief to her mouth. It was a minute before her coughing ceased and she could speak again. "They told us, when we was in that refugee prison, they told us Danny died near Atlanta. One of the mill girls stayed in Marietta, see, and she got work in a Union field hospital. She saw Danny before he died, and he begged her to find his mama and tell her goodbye."

Clara put her hand on Ida Mae's. "I'm so sorry."

"Danny's father left when he was young. Danny had this idea that if he found glory in battle, his father would come back." Ida Mae scoffed. "Glory," she said bitterly. "They say that so boys like our Danny think there's something in this war for them."

Clara was quiet for a time, and then, "Ida Mae? What did you mean when you said Orton got what he deserved?"

Ida Mae pulled her hand from under Clara's. She pointed at her granddaughter, the younger one. "Orton's her father."

"What about Paul?" Mabel's second husband was a farmer and the father, or so Clara had assumed, of both of Mabel's girls. Clara wasn't sure where he was now.

"You think Paul had a say?" Ida Mae frowned. With a veined hand, Ida Mae shooed a fly off her skirt. The old woman had never looked so weary. "Now go on, and let me rest. I'm tired."

Ida Mae was coughing again as Clara left the bow. When she returned to her hay bale, Kitty was asleep on her cot. This was the most she had slept in weeks. A strand of her ash-blond hair had fallen across her nose. Clara tucked it behind her ear and pulled the blanket up over her shoulders.

At dusk, a deckhand carried a long-handled iron basket filled with burning fuel. He secured the handle in a socket on the deck near the bow, and the basket of fire at the handle's end extended out over the water. It cast a flickering light on the water and the riverbank and the trees. On occasion, a spark leapt from the basket and sizzled as it hit the water.

Clara couldn't relax. Not with the sheep bleating in the cargo hold. Or the great unknown that lay ahead in Cincinnati. During the day, it was easier to fight back thoughts of the uncertain future or the woeful past. But at night, the present moment faded and her thoughts were defenseless against yesterday's regrets and tomorrow's problems, which rushed in with a vengeance.

Here, at least, mosquitoes did not number among her troubles. Smoke from the basket of fire kept them away. As the night grew darker, the fire's effect became both eerie and enchanting. Tree trunks glowed in the firelight. Branches extended out over the water and, in the flickering light, appeared to shift to and fro. The engine's exhalations kept a steady rhythm. Wrapped in her blanket, Clara drifted off to sleep.

She awoke the next morning just before dawn, startled awake when the steamboat's forward motion stopped. She checked on Kitty, who slept peacefully on her cot. The *Bluegrass Belle* docked on the riverbank. But there was no cargo piled on the shore waiting to be loaded, no livestock herded by a farmer.

There was movement near the bow. In the twilight, two soldiers carried a coffin from the boat onto the dock. A woman and two children followed, and at the end of the small procession, a third soldier carried Ida Mae's empty rocking chair.

# 12

Shortly after sunup, someone yelled, "Grub pile!" and Clara and Kitty hurried to the bow, along with other deck passengers and forty-odd deckhands and roustabouts. There they found pans of food deemed unfit to serve on the upper decks: broken meat, jellies imperfectly molded, broken bread and cake, over-boiled potatoes. They served themselves on tin plates they'd bought from a huckster at one of the landings. After all the salt pork and hardtack, the riverboat food was a welcome change.

Clara sat on her hay bale with a plate of currant jelly and mushy potatoes. They would have four more meals, courtesy of the *Bluegrass Belle* and the federal government, before they arrived in Cincinnati. Kitty, lounging on her cot, devoured a chunk of cornbread. It was good to see her eating so well. The girl had yet to utter a concern about Cincinnati. Clara almost envied her; it was like she wasn't bothered at all.

When Clara told her Ida Mae had passed in the night, and that Mabel and her daughters had disembarked while Kitty slept, Kitty was solemn only a moment before remarking wryly that that was just like stubborn old Ida Mae, choosing to die rather than live on Yankee soil. Kitty either didn't realize or didn't care that with Mabel's disembarkation, they'd lost the last of the people they'd known. There was no one else from Roswell on the *Bluegrass Belle*. Whatever came next, they would have to face it alone.

Clara needed a plan. Sometime tomorrow, they would arrive in a city unthinkably large: a hundred and fifty thousand people, someone had said. For the first time in her life, Clara had no one to advise her on what to do. Not her parents. Not the mill bosses. Not Benjamin. Everything she and Kitty did would be up to her. It was at once terrifying and thrilling.

She hadn't expected the latter. But the thrill of this new freedom was overshadowed by thoughts of all the ways things could go wrong: They wouldn't find shelter, and they would freeze to death come winter. They would be assaulted. They would starve. What if the people of Cincinnati, upon hearing her voice, considered her the enemy? Who would be inclined to help them, if anyone at all? The questions and fears whirled ever faster, a tornado of foreboding until she clamped her hands over her ears and shut her eyes to make them stop.

The sun was high when the *Bluegrass Belle* pulled close to the riverbank. Just beyond a small dock stood a shack surrounded by piles of corded wood.

"Up! Up, you!" a man barked at the sisters.

"What is it?" Clara asked. "What's the matter?"

"What's the matter is the boat's near out of fuel!" The man was missing a front tooth and smelled worse than the livestock. "You don't think she runs on me good looks, do you? We're wooding up." He thumbed over his shoulder at the piles of corded wood near the riverbank. The crew were laying the stage from the bow to the wood-yard's dock.

"You want us to carry wood?"

"All deckers who's able must help with the wooding."

"I'll go. My sister's not well."

Kitty put down her reading. "I can do it."

"Save your strength. You'll need it when we get to Cincinnati."

Kitty rose anyway, and Clara decided not to argue. They followed the others off the boat to the wood-yard. A shingle nailed to a stick read, "$2 soft wood, $2.75 hard wood." A clerk deposited money into a box, and the mate directed the laborers. The deckhands, roustabouts, and other deck passengers carried wood from the wood-yard and stacked it on the bow.

The mate oversaw their labor, shouting at them to move faster, carry more. "Here, now! This ain't no frolic! It's a wooding, not a napping! Get on with it, then!"

Clara, carrying a small stack toward the boat, glanced at the upper deck. Well-dressed cabin passengers leaned against the railing to watch the spectacle. Clara's cheeks burned. *Now see this! Watch as the feeble-looking mill girls perform incredible feats of strength!* Oh, to be one of those women with their lovely hats and their staterooms.

A woman wearing a pretty bonnet of pale yellow silk gripped the upper deck railing with gloved hands, watching the activity with casual amusement. Clara imagined her life: a tidy two-story house on a tree-lined Cincinnati street. Upon the woman's arrival at the wharf, there would be people waiting to welcome her home. She had a fashionable milliner who designed her custom bonnets. What cares or concerns could that woman possibly have?

Clara slowed her pace to match that of her sister, who, carrying her second armful of wood, was breathing heavily. Kitty would not look at her. Surely it was because she wanted to pretend she wasn't struggling.

Kitty deserved better than this. In Cincinnati, things would be different. Kitty would not have to do any heavy labor or factory work. How Clara would manage this was a mystery. But watching her struggle—Clara bent to pick up a piece of wood her sister had dropped, all while the mate yelled at them—nearly broke her heart. Clara would take better care of her so that by the time Benjamin found them, Kitty would be strong enough for the journey westward.

On their third trip back from the woodpile, Kitty's pace had slowed. "Here, give me some of those," Clara said. "That's too much for you."

Kitty turned her armful away. "Stop! I can do it."

"You go sit after this. I'll tell them you're not well."

Kitty's protests were cut short by a cough. The mate yelled at her to go lie down, that he wasn't having her die of consumption on his boat. Clara continued with the wooding. Sweat trickled down her back. This far north and still, the late-August heat was stifling. They might as well have been in Georgia.

After an hour spent dockside loading wood, the packet left the small dock and continued up the Ohio River. The sisters spent their second afternoon aboard reading Mrs. Hopewell's old magazines. Clara felt uplifted by the illustrations of hats and bonnets and hair nets, each more beautifully trimmed than anything she'd ever seen, even among the Roswell Royalty. In looking at them, she felt a world of possibility. What she might create, if only she had access to such fine materials! She would make bonnets of her own that would rival the ones on these pages.

"Look at this one." Clara pointed to an illustration of a ruffly headpiece. "Says it's a 'fancy dinner-cap, made of figured illusion, point applique lace, and violet ribbons.' What do you reckon a 'figured illusion' is?"

Kitty only shrugged. She was admiring embroidery patterns. "Five dollars for a dozen patterns." She showed Clara the advertisement for *S.P. Borden's Celebrated Embroidery and Braiding Stamps*. "Imagine having five dollars to plank up on embroidery!"

"When we get to Cincinnati, I'll find work, and one day I will buy you all the embroidery patterns you want!"

"Maybe I'll get a job myself," Kitty said.

Clara put down her magazine. "I'll support us both, somehow. You're gonna rest and recover and get stronger. You'll need strength for the journey west."

"What if I don't want to go?"

"I ain't leaving you behind! And what else are you going to do, find a husband? I thought you didn't want to marry as young as Mama did."

"Maybe I don't want to marry at all."

"Then you'd certainly better come with us to Nebraska!" Clara gave her sister a serious look. "You *will* need to find a husband one day." Then, when Kitty only shrugged, "Maybe you don't want one *now*," Clara said, "but you're only fifteen. You'll change your mind when you're nineteen or twenty. Why wouldn't you? A husband is many things: a constant friend, a protector, a provider."

"Maybe for you."

Clara paused. *Of course, she can afford to think that way when I am the one doing all those things for her.* "You're young yet. You'll see."

"I want to be free to do what I please."

"And what is that?"

"Oh, it changes. But I don't want someone else deciding it for me."

A deckhand took several hay bales near the one Clara was sitting on. "You don't know what it's like, to carry the burden of responsibility. Of duty. How hard it is."

Kitty was silent, then, "You have no idea what I can do. You think because I'm younger than you, I don't know anything. Or that I'm weak on account of my cough. You're no better than Benjamin."

"What are you getting at? Kitty?"

"Nothing. I don't want to talk about it." Kitty lay on her cot, facing away from her sister.

Clara called her name again but was met with silence. She stared out over the water, wondering how in the world their conversation ended up there.

Just after supper, the riverboat pulled up to a landing where the crew loaded several hundred crates of apples. It was incredible how much freight they'd taken aboard in the past two days. The vessel couldn't possibly hold more. And yet, a few hours after that, the *Bluegrass Belle* stopped to take aboard five horses and several dozen hogs. While the horses were corralled with little trouble, the drovers and roustabouts had to chase several wayward hogs, which slipped into the river again and again. The sisters laughed at the sight, and Clara was grateful to see Kitty's good humor return. Once the hogs were secured in a pen on the main deck, the stench and squealing were much less amusing.

"All that noise, I'll never sleep," Kitty said that evening as she lay on her cot.

Clara yawned. "There's one good thing about the hogs." Then, when Kitty gave her a questioning look, "Now I can't smell the sheep."

The first of September dawned with a mild morning that led to a sunny afternoon, and the Douglas sisters saw Cincinnati for the first time. As they neared the city, deckhands scurried about to ready the cargo and livestock for unloading, and so Clara and Kitty had gone to the bow to get out of their way.

As the riverboat rounded a bend, the Queen City came into full view on the left bank. The land jutted out into the river, as if the city had pushed the water into a southward-bending U. The land angled up from the riverbank to a row of tightly packed buildings. And from there, Cincinnati spread north: buildings and factories and a haze of coal smoke, and then row houses that stretched all the way to the bluffs skirting the city.

Clara felt a fresh wave of wonder, then terror. It wouldn't be long now before the boat docked. What then? There were no soldiers leading them anywhere. No other mill workers to band together with. They were on their own.

As the riverboat neared the landing, it passed between two massive stone towers on either bank. A bridge, unfinished. Just past one of the towers, the steamboat docked at the busy river port. Not far away, passengers boarded another riverboat, one with wheels on either side. Beyond that steamboat was a row of long flat-bottomed boats. Elsewhere were cigar-shaped boats and towboats pushing barges. Like the water, the landing teemed with activity. Sailors, soldiers, merchants, roustabouts. Passengers embarking and disembarking. People moving in every direction.

Kitty leaned over the railing as if she couldn't wait to get off the boat, while Clara searched the activity for some clue as to what they should do. In all the bustle, no one looked like them: two lost women from Roswell, Georgia. These strangers would be of no help. Ridiculously, she considered staying on the boat and sailing back to Louisville, putting themselves back inside the prison hospital until the war ended.

She lifted her chin. A hundred and fifty thousand people. An astonishing number.

*A good choice. You'll find lots more opportunities here. Good factory work.*

Clara would pretend to be brave, for Kitty's sake.

# 13

The cabin passengers descended the grand staircase by the dozens and disembarked at the bow, which had become cramped and claustrophobic as they funneled onto the stage bridging the water at the river's edge. At the stern, roustabouts unloaded barrels and boxes and livestock. Between these two streams, the Douglas sisters were kept waiting on the main deck and warned to stay out of the deckhands' way.

Out went the horses and the sheep. Out scurried the hogs, squealing and grunting. Drovers waited on the landing for the livestock, and Clara watched as one man herded the hogs, with less difficulty than she'd have predicted, through the crowd and down a street.

Finally, it was their turn, and they disembarked with the other deck passengers onto the public landing. Kitty squinted in the late-summer sun. "Where to now?" She said this as though the question had only just occurred to her, as if Clara hadn't been fretting over this very moment for days.

As far as the federal government was concerned, it had washed its hands of them. They'd been given tickets out of Louisville, but no instruction on what to do or where to live in Cincinnati. The only people they'd known on the *Bluegrass Belle* had been Ida Mae and Mabel, and the latter had disembarked with her daughters and Ida Mae's coffin back in whatever river town that had been.

Clutching her homespun bag to her chest, Clara stood on the landing, wide-eyed, searching the crowd for someone in uniform. A provost marshal or other soldier. "Keep your bag close," she warned her sister. "A city this big will have thieves—and worse."

Everywhere she turned was a face she didn't recognize. She looked from one stranger to another. This was to be her new home, and yet it was utterly foreign. The landing felt unsteady beneath her feet. Something rammed into her leg, and she lost her balance and fell onto the dirt-covered landing. A wayward hog snorted and ran past. A hand appeared in front of her face, and her sister helped her up.

Clara brushed herself off and was about to settle on a direction when a middle-aged woman stood before them wearing a cheerful blue hat trimmed with white ribbon. "Girls," the woman said with a warm authority. "Smile for me. A little wider? Ah, yes, good. You two look hungry. Would you like something to eat?" She reached into a bag and produced two bread rolls.

"Thank you," Kitty said, accepting one.

Clara's stomach grumbled, but she took none. "Who are you?"

The woman ignored the question, only told them to come with her and that she would explain more when they got to where they were going.

Something wasn't right. Clara didn't move. "We—we're wait-ing for someone." She looked worriedly at Kitty, who was eating her roll and had already moved ahead, willing to follow the woman with no hesitation.

The woman, who'd begun walking, confident the girls would obey, stopped and raised an eyebrow. Clara again searched the crowd for a uniformed official, someone who could help them. But it was hot and crowded and dusty, and when the woman resumed walking, they followed her up the landing.

When they came to a street, another woman, this one plump and smartly dressed in a matching burgundy bonnet and dress, stood in the first woman's path. "Let's give these girls a chance to find honest work first," said the woman in burgundy. Then, to Clara and Kitty, "You are refugees, yes? Just off the *Bluegrass Belle*?"

Clara nodded, wondering what the woman wanted from them.

The first woman, whose interest in them Clara now fully un-derstood for what it was, turned away without a fight. Her little blue hat disappeared into the crowd. The woman in burgundy introduced herself as Mrs. Helen Holmes, a volunteer with the Cincinnati Refugee Relief Commission. There was a place they could stay for free if they came with her.

The sisters exchanged a look. The weight of responsibility pressed on Clara's shoulders. What if this Mrs. Holmes wasn't who she said she was? Then again, they had no money for a board-inghouse, and to sleep on the docks or in some warehouse where they'd be easy prey seemed riskier than following her.

Despite having no evidence, apart from the interaction with the first woman, Clara felt that Mrs. Holmes was a woman of good character. She would trust her instincts. "We'll come with you."

"Very good." Mrs. Holmes led the sisters along Front Street, talking all the while, her gait as brisk as her speech. It was as if she'd been saving up words for a week and couldn't hold them in a minute more. "You may stay at Longworth House while you look for work. We'll help you with that. And if you can't find work in the city, we'll help relocate you to the country. There are plenty of rural folk needing a hand, what with their men off fighting. And many of the refugees who come here soon discover a life in the city isn't for them."

Clara wondered if she would be one of them. The streets were so crowded, and everyone seemed to be in a terrible hurry. She recalled Benjamin's warning about the destitution and filth of city life.

"What work experience have you— Look out!" Mrs. Holmes threw an arm in front of Kitty, who'd almost stepped into the path of a speeding carriage.

Clara grabbed Kitty's hand—the girl was clearly not heeding the dangers all around—and told Mrs. Holmes they'd worked in a cotton mill.

"Splendid! Cincinnati's garment industry is thriving. We've a number of manufactories west of Vine Street and throughout the business district. It's harder than usual to find work in the city, I'm afraid, with the war going on. Many people have come here looking for work. There's other factory work, of course. Shoe factories, all sorts of food production, soap and candle factories, I could go on."

And go on she did, explaining how soap and candle making were big business, thanks to the pork industry. "Outsiders like to call us *Porkopolis*, but the fact is our meatpacking business is first rate. You'll see a few hogs now, but this is nothing. Autumn is just around the corner, and that's when hogs will fill the streets. Breweries are big business, too, although I wish it weren't so. It's the influx of German immigrants. A hardworking people, yes. I'm simply not fond of their choice of industry. People need fewer opportunities for vice, not more. Beer on Sunday—heavens! Ah, here we are."

Mrs. Holmes stopped in front of a brick building. It had once been a school, she said, but earlier that year, the school board had permitted the Refugee Relief Commission to use it. Since April, they'd taken in more than four hundred refugees. Most were from East Tennessee, although some hailed from Georgia and a number of other states besides. At the moment, the Longworth House sheltered about five dozen. Men and women stayed on separate floors and a third floor housed families.

Mrs. Holmes led the sisters to a small classroom on the women's floor, which they were to share with two Tennesseans. The room was clean and bright. They were each given a pallet and bed-tick, freshly laundered sheets, and a pillow.

Having shown them their living quarters, Mrs. Holmes disappeared into the hallway, returning minutes later with a stack of folded clothing. "These should fit you girls," she said, placing the stack on Clara's bed-tick: a nightgown, chemise, and a dress for each of them.

A clean, comfortable place to sleep and new clothes: Clara could hardly believe their good fortune. She collapsed on the bed-tick, which was stuffed with straw. This was heaps better than sleeping outside on the steamboat. In fact, this was the cleanest place they'd been since leaving home. She wondered how many new beds she would sleep in before she called another place home.

Kitty lay down, and, seeing her now, Clara's joy dampened. Kitty looked so frail. Her hair had thinned, and her eyes were dark and sunken. The measles had taken its toll. And though she was better, she was not fully herself. Within minutes, both sisters, exhausted from the long journey, were asleep. They slept all afternoon, through the night and into the next day.

—ℓℓ—

"Where will we look for work?" Kitty asked the next morning. She lay on her back and looked up at the tin-tiled ceiling.

"I'll try the factories. You stay and rest. Like I told you, I'll work for both of us, at least for now."

Kitty frowned. "I feel all right. I can work."

"You need to rest. This is the most comfortable place we've been for weeks, and you're still recovering." Then, seeing Kitty's disappointment, "Maybe you can take in piece work," she said.

"Why do you want to keep me shut in here?"

"I just want you to be well." While they could certainly use two incomes, this city presented a raft of dangers to a young, trusting girl like Kitty. Better that Clara found work while Kitty regained her strength. A few weeks from now, when they knew the city better, Kitty could look for work. In the meantime, Clara would fret less, knowing her sister was here in the schoolroom, watched over by women like Mrs. Holmes.

And Kitty would not be alone, as they shared the room with two other women who, until last week, had been living in a warehouse near the river. Only one of them spoke, a young woman not much older than Kitty from Scott County, Tennessee. What an ordeal she had endured. Her parents had died before the war, and she was left to care for her two younger brothers. When war broke out, one brother left to fight for the rebels, despite her pleading for him to stay. The other joined the Union Army. It wasn't long before, as she put it, "rebel hordes descended like so many vampires." Her home was pillaged, her lands laid waste, and she was driven to seek refuge wherever she could. She was on the road, alone, for weeks, walking the entire time. Clara asked if people along the road had treated her kindly. "Some did, but others did not," she said. "To relate all my sufferings since the morning I left my home would require volumes." As soon as she regained her strength, she planned to travel further inland to seek an honest living. She could not accustom herself to city life.

The woman was young and stout, and Clara felt optimistic about her chances. The woman's companion would have a harder time of it. She lay on a pallet facing the wall, a thin blanket covering her skeletal frame. Weeks earlier, she had given birth in the warehouse. The infant had died a day later.

Clara wondered how many more women and children were out there, barely surviving in stables and warehouses and abandoned buildings. Living in boxcars on sidings. It would only get worse when the weather turned. How fortunate Clara and Kitty were to be at Longworth House. She would not waste this opportunity. Unlike the Tennessee women, she did not want to be sent into the country to work on someone's farm. Were that to happen, she and Kitty might be separated, and Benjamin might never find them.

One way or another, their future depended on the Queen City. Even so, as she looked out the window at the row houses opposite their building, the houses seeming to go on forever, this vast city made her feel small and inconsequential in a way she'd never felt in Roswell. What would Benjamin say if he knew she was here in the city? He'd warn her to be careful. Not to trust anyone. He might say she wasn't up to it. And he'd probably be right.

# 14

Mrs. Holmes gave Clara a scrap of paper upon which were written the names of garment and other manufacturers where she might find work and a small handwritten map to help her find them. If she lost her way, Mrs. Holmes advised her to ask a shopkeeper or soldier for help. "And mind the carriages and horses when crossing the street," she warned. "Some folks here go full drive like they're the only ones on the road."

Clara stepped outside and took a deep breath. It was a bright and crisp fall morning with a nip in the air. A few wispy clouds dotted the blue sky. If ever there was a more optimistic morning, Clara could not recall it.

She glanced over her shoulder at Longworth House, where Kitty remained despite her pleas to come along. Though she regretted having to leave her sister behind, it was the safest place for her, and besides, it was best that she not tire herself out by wandering all over the city.

Pausing to check Mrs. Holmes's map, turning it a quarter turn so that Longworth House was at the bottom, she got her bearings and headed east. A right turn on Race Street and left on Third, and, continuing along that street for some time, she began to fear she'd missed her destination. She stopped at a most unusual-looking building to check the address. Three long arched windows stretched more than half the building's height, the upper part of the windows shaped like dollops of whipped cream. Between each of these, a flower was carved into the building's exterior. A Federal officer descended the curved staircase and told her this was the Soldiers' Home. He was kind enough to direct her to the garment factory she sought.

It was only a short walk down the street. Her heart pounded as she worked up the courage to go inside, unaccustomed as she was to looking for work. The mill didn't count, for her mother had arranged it. And Mrs. Holmes had reminded her that morning that their stay at Longworth House would not be indefinite. "I'll do my best to help, but if you're unable to find work in the city, we'll find you a situation further inland," she'd repeated. "I'm afraid I can't guarantee you and your sister will stay together. In fact, it's almost certain you'll have to split up."

Clara could not let her sister be sent to some godforsaken farm to spend her youth washing other folks' undergarments. No one else would look after Kitty's health as Clara did. She mustn't fail to find employment.

Cincinnati ought to have opportunities, but what if her experience didn't compare to that of others in this crowded city? Benjamin had always said the expenses of living in a city were enormous, and employment uncertain. It was one of the reasons he'd wanted to live off the land. In cities there were always more workers than jobs, he'd said. And that was without considering the aggravating effects of war, all the refugees fleeing the ravaged countryside seeking a new means of survival.

She stood outside the shirt and collar manufacturer, newly aware of how her voice sounded. She talked differently than the people here. They might look at her as the enemy, a foreigner taking jobs from the locals. She opened the door and went inside to a showroom. It was a long space, maybe two hundred feet by thirty, all wood counters, glass cases, and the scent of wood polish.

A genteel-looking sales clerk pointed her to a door at the far end of the showroom. She walked the length of the room, on both sides of which were shelves of crisp shirts stacked all the way to the ceiling. Upon reaching the door, she paused, gathering the nerve to knock. Before she was ready, the door opened, revealing a man wearing a white shirt and vest, and leaning on a cane. He took one look at her down his nose and said the factory wasn't hiring. Clara nodded and quickly escaped through a second set of doors at the end of the long showroom opposite where she entered. She exited onto a different street, of course, and it took her a minute to figure out where she was. She wanted to get back to Third Street but did not want to go through the shirt and collar store again, so she went the long way around the block.

After crossing the street with caution, for it was crowded that Friday morning, she followed the map and found her way to a wholesale clothing manufacturer on Walnut Street. A female clerk led her to the top floor of the four-story building, where an over-seer took Clara's name and address and said that while they weren't hiring operatives in ready-made clothing at present, he would contact the Refugee Relief Commission if he had an opening.

Back outside, and with a growing apprehension, Clara referred to her list and set off again. The city housed a seemingly endless variety of shops. With such a number of stores, she was certain there was nothing you couldn't buy in Cincinnati if you had the money for it. Duhme Jewelers, with its chatelaines and cameos and mourning jewelry of jet and black glass, and Wheeler and Wilson, where she paused to gape through the window at the sewing machines and wonder how to operate them. A sign outside E&T Fairbanks Scale Manufactory boasted its scales could weigh one-thousandth part of a grain *or* loaded canal boats weighing five hundred tons!

Despite the city's bustling wealth, it seemed there was no place for a mill worker from Georgia. By late afternoon, with sore feet and deflated spirits and still no work, Clara made her way to the last employer on Mrs. Holmes's list, a wholesale dry goods business on Fourth Street.

The luxuries of Fourth Street made Clara all too aware of her plain attire. The storefronts, with their large windows offering colorful displays of capelets and bonnets and jewelry, were as elegant as the women who passed through their doorways. Even the Roswell Royalty hadn't dressed as fine as some of these women, who brushed past her as if she weren't even there. It was at one such storefront window that Clara stopped abruptly, her eye drawn by the beauty inside. "Madame Murphy, Fashionable Millinery" was painted in white on the glass. Clara peered through the window. Bonnets bursting with flowers and feathers perched atop brass stands. Landscape paintings adorned the walls, and leather settees offered well-heeled customers a place to rest. A woman who worked there, perhaps Madame Murphy herself, spoke to one such lady.

*You should go in*, Clara told herself. *Be brave. Maybe they're looking for help.*

Clara glanced at her cotton dress, a donation from the refugee commission. It was the nicest article of clothing she owned. Yet it hardly made up for the rest of her attire: straw bonnet in need of bleaching, plain collar, marked-up shoes with worn heels. She wasn't well dressed enough to enter a shop like that. She'd be laughed right out of it!

She stood there another minute, hating herself for her cowardice while recognizing the truth of her assumptions. A shop as fine as this would never hire her. What was the point of humiliating herself?

Just then, the woman Clara took to be the proprietor noticed her peering through the window. Feeling almost as if she'd committed a crime by simply standing there, she resisted the urge to flee, as it would only prove her guilt. Instead, she knit her brow, making a show of studying the hat in the window (a white silk bonnet trimmed with violet ribbons and pink roses, perhaps the loveliest bonnet she'd ever seen, with its pretty net of ribbons at the back, in lieu of a curtain). Clara regarded the hat as if—as if!—she were considering a purchase, and with a thoughtful look, as if to say, *perhaps another time*, she turned from the window and continued along Fourth Street.

Ten minutes later, Clara rushed out of the dry goods wholesaler, hoping to get to the street before tears spilled down her cheeks. The man inside had been so hateful in his rejection of her, sneering and calling her *secesh*.

What a miserable day it had turned out to be. The sunny skies, which only this morning had cheered her on, were now discordant with her mood. Clara hurried along the sidewalk, head down, crumpling the paper Mrs. Holmes had given her. She tossed the balled paper into the street, where it was immediately flattened under a horse's hoof.

Several blocks later, she stopped, wiped her cheeks, and set her shoulders back. She couldn't let Kitty see her so upset. She would go back to Longworth House and figure something out. This was a tremendous city; surely there would be more places to try tomorrow.

But which direction was Longworth House from where she stood? Clara retraced her steps and searched the street where she'd thrown the crumpled paper and its map. It was gone, carried along with the dust and wind and horses' hooves and carriage wheels. Well, didn't that beat all? Tears welled again.

Clara leaned against a storefront window to figure out what to do next. Mrs. Holmes had said to ask a shopkeeper or a soldier for directions if she got lost. Well, here was a shop. In the window behind her was a trunk, and quite a lovely one, made of pine with wide red slats, a domed top, and leather handles. The trunk next to it was open, the lid's interior sporting a colorful lithograph of a serious-looking bearded man seated in a chair. Beneath it were the words "Abraham Lincoln, Sixteenth President of the United States." Next to the Lincoln trunk was one half its size, lined with pretty floral fabric. A sign in one corner of the window read "Dugan Brothers Trunks – Manufacturers and Dealers in Trunks, Carpetbags, Valises, and Satchels – Wholesale and Retail."

There was something soothing about the simple, elegant beauty of these trunks: the smooth pine, the solid hardware, the lovely linings. Perhaps the Dugan Brothers could point her in the right direction.

Inside the shop, she smelled leather and wood. Two rows of large trunks filled the center of the floor from the front to the back. Shelves stretching to the ceiling on either wall displayed smaller trunks and carpetbags. Some trunks were covered with leather, others with metal. There were trunks with flat tops and domed tops, some with wood slats crossing their lids, some without. Brass hardware gleamed from the corners and edges of every trunk, large and small.

There was a man wearing a leather apron and missing the lower half of his right arm, the empty half-sleeve pinned near his shoulder. He looked to be in his late twenties. There was kindness in his blue eyes, and he smiled at her as if they were old friends. "Can I help you, miss?" His voice was deep yet soft.

Certainly, he didn't view her as a customer. These trunks must cost a fortune. Despite her new checkered dress, she didn't present the image of someone who could afford one. "I'm a little lost, is all. I'm staying at Longworth House on, well, Longworth Street. It used to be a school, I think?"

"Of course," he said, nodding. "You're not too far. Out here is Pearl Street." He pointed to the storefront window. "Go right and head that way several blocks until you get to Race, then take a right, and it's, oh, a half-dozen blocks, and you'll arrive at Longworth."

When she thanked him, he introduced himself as Mr. Hauley Dugan, co-owner of Dugan Brothers Trunks. "I'm guessing you're not from around here?"

"It's obvious, isn't it?"

"Tennessee?"

"Georgia."

"This war has made plenty of refugees."

"My mill was burned, and we were forced to come here…" She didn't know what else to say.

"I'm sorry you were sent so far from home. It seems there's no end to the suffering war causes. And, as ever, those who wage it are the most immune from its effects."

"You're a veteran?" Clara asked, glancing at his arm, where it ended at the elbow.

"I am." Then, when he saw her noticing his arm, "It could've been much worse," he said. "And learning to write left-handed has been an amusing challenge."

Clara smiled. "Your trunks are beautiful. I've never seen anything like them."

"Thank you," he said, looking her right in the eye.

Clara's cheeks warmed. Quickly, before he could notice her blushing, she thanked him for the directions and left the store.

Kitty was in good spirits that evening. Mrs. Holmes had brought her piece work, allowing her to earn some money without leaving Longworth House. Not enough to live on, but it could be added to whatever Clara brought in. It was good to feel useful, Kitty said. Clara told her she'd had no luck, and that she'd even gotten lost at one point, and that maybe the city was a bad idea. The only bright spot had been a friendly trunk-maker who'd pointed her in the right direction. Kitty begged her not to give up on the city, that she would have better luck on the morrow. Clara didn't see Mrs. Holmes that evening and was grateful to be spared the embarrassment of recounting her failure.

That night, as Kitty and the Tennessee women slept, Clara gazed out the window until her thoughts stopped racing. At last, she went to her bed-tick. She lay down and covered herself with one blanket. The other blanket she rolled and placed under her chin, like a scarf. Her mother used to do this for her when she was ill. There was something soothing in the way the rolled-up blanket filled the space beneath her chin. It always made her feel safe and at peace, like everything was going to be all right.

## 15

The next morning, as the Douglas sisters ate breakfast in the common room at Longworth House, Mrs. Holmes asked Clara if she'd had any luck the day before. When she admitted to having had none at all, Mrs. Holmes nodded as if unsurprised and wrote the names and addresses of several more potential employers on a piece of paper, urging her to make the best impression possible. "We can have you here at Longworth for one month at most," Mrs. Holmes said with a sigh. "There are just too many refugees in need of a place to stay, and we're expecting more as the weather turns."

Clara hated the thought of Kitty going to work for a strange farmer somewhere in the hills of southern Ohio. "I'll find something today. You can count on it." She chewed a bite of biscuit; it stuck in her throat, and she swallowed hard.

"Forget the factories," Kitty said when Mrs. Holmes had left. "Think of all the millineries there must be here. You've got right smart of talent for making hats. Why work in a factory when you could be a milliner?"

Clara put a hand on Kitty's shoulder. "I love that you think so well of me. But what millinery shop is going to hire a refugee from Georgia who's never sold a hat in her life? I have no real experience. Not the kind they care about. And you should see the millinery shops here! I'm hardly fit to step inside."

"There must be more modest shops." Kitty sipped her tea.

"I make hats for family and friends," Clara said, pushing back her chair. "And that's enough for me."

The morning went as poorly as the day before. Feeling very low, certain no one was going to offer her a position, Clara paused at a crowded intersection, and for a moment, her thoughts clouded over from the overwhelm of it all: the carts, the horses, the shoppers, the fruit cart vendors. All around her, people were going about their day, knowing their purpose and where they belonged. For Clara, it was as if she stood at a great window, and all the activity transpired on the other side of it, and she could not get there from here.

She inhaled slowly, pulled back her shoulders, and turned onto Fourth Street. At one point, Clara paused in front of a dry goods store, struck by its colorful window display. Across a framework six feet square were drawn ribbons of various widths and colors. Ribbons had been woven vertically through them, creating a giant, colorful checkerboard that filled the window. Never had she seen this much ribbon all at once. The Roswell Company Store might have had a few colors to choose from any given month—before the war, at least. But nothing like this. The indulgence of it almost made her a little uneasy. Such riches, all in one place.

She imagined herself walking inside to gape at all the colors and fabrics, to feel the different textures. But she was not the type of person to walk into a store like that, just on a whim. And the welcome she received from the last dry goods store she dared to enter was hardly an encouragement. And besides, she only had a few pennies to her name. She couldn't buy anything. This store was for other people.

She was still thinking about that beautiful, giant checkerboard of ribbon as she started down a side street and passed a saloon. A commotion erupted behind her. Turning, she witnessed a man stumble out of the saloon and land in the street, narrowly missing a carriage. Another man followed him out, yelling, "Butternut scum!" The first man stood up, dusted off his pants, and looked ready to fight as he moved toward the saloon.

The man who'd tossed him out stood mere inches from his face. "Only loyal Union men in here."

The Butternut growled. "You all are fools! Fighting to free them—"

"And you're a coward, staying at home and talking treason." The Union man raised his hand as if to hit him. "Get outta my sight!"

"Lincoln-lover!"

At this, the Union man punched him in the jaw. The Butternut stumbled a few steps back, and once he'd regained his footing, he pulled out a bowie knife.

Clara gasped, retreating to a safer distance, yet unable to take her eyes off the altercation. The Union man took a step back, away from the knife. She wondered if he might draw a gun.

At that moment, two uniformed soldiers appeared from around the corner and ordered the man to drop his knife. He hesitated but ultimately complied, and they put him in handcuffs and marched him down the street, and it was over.

For the rest of the day, she took care when passing a saloon. The fight had brought to mind Temperance and the sight she'd made, standing on the roadside holding the sky-blue ribbon and yelling *Lincoln-lover* as the army caravan took them from Roswell. Temperance had never been an agreeable person, and while she'd never been particularly friendly to Clara, she'd become downright hostile in recent weeks. The longer the war dragged on, it seemed, the more ill-natured the woman got and the more she'd directed her churlishness at Clara. Perhaps Temperance sensed Clara's loyalty lay not with the Confederate cause but with those who would put down the rebellion. Temperance may have noticed she'd never uttered one word in support of Jefferson Davis or slavery or the Confederacy. Clara Douglas had never been one to speak what wasn't in her heart.

It was mid-afternoon when Clara stood in front of Jeffras, Seeley, & Company, a wholesale millinery and dry goods business. She felt a flutter of excitement at the word "millinery." At seven stories tall, it was the largest manufacturer on her list so far.

She hesitated outside the building, reluctant to go in and face yet another rejection. She would forestall it as long as she could. After a few minutes, however, she began to feel conspicuous, standing there in front of the building, the first floor of which appeared to be a salesroom. Soon, someone would step outside and ask her to keep moving. She paced in front of the window. It had been a mistake to come to Cincinnati. They should have gone to Cannelton, to the cotton factory.

Clara wiped her sweaty palms on her dress. How tempting it was to flee to Longworth House, to give up this mad quest. The thought of her separation from Kitty kept her there, pacing in front of the imposing building. *It will be over, one way or another, in ten minutes*. She could survive the next ten minutes. When two women carrying parcels emerged from the building, chatting beneath their matching high-brimmed hats, she hurried inside before the door closed and she lost her nerve.

The first-floor salesroom stretched all the way to the next street. A clerk pointed her to a passenger elevator that took her to the sixth floor. In a workroom as big as the Roswell mill's weave room, maybe bigger, rows upon rows of women sat hunched over sewing machines. Her first impression of the expansive room was that it was much quieter than the weave room at the cotton mill. And no lint floated in the air.

A man approached Clara where she stood in the doorway. He introduced himself as Mr. Loomis, the floor overseer. Upon learning she sought work, he boasted that Jeffras, Seeley, & Company was one of the most complete establishments of its kind in America. They were Cincinnati's leading millinery house, he said, specializing in the manufacture of ladies' cloaks, suits, and undergarments. He asked about her experience, and after she'd told him about her years at the cotton mill, he said he could use an operative in undergarment production.

At last! After so much rejection, she could not believe her luck. Now that she'd found work, she laughed at her earlier self, who'd nearly given up hope. She would be able to support herself and Kitty, and they would have some measure of security until Benjamin came.

Mr. Loomis asked if she knew how to use a sewing machine. When she said no, his silence sent a shiver of panic through her. He was about to dismiss her. Clara could not let that happen. She needed this job. She'd had it and would not lose it now. This was the job she was going to get. Before Mr. Loomis could send her on her way, she squared her shoulders, jutted her chin and, recalling Mrs. Holmes's instruction to make a good impression, said, "I may not know how to use a sewing machine today, but I'm a fast learner. When I started at the Roswell mill, I didn't know how to use a loom, and soon I was one of the fastest hands in the weave room."

Mr. Loomis waved a hand. "We will teach you," he said grandly, and stated her weekly salary.

A wave of relief washed over her. In a moment of boldness brought on by joy, she dared to ask about the millinery room. She pointed to her hat and said she'd made it herself. The straw hat she'd worn since Roswell was simple but well structured, with a lilac ribbon tied under her chin. Though it was her finest work, it needed a good cleaning after their long journey.

Mr. Loomis smiled patronizingly. Seventh floor, he said, pointing to the ceiling. "There are no jobs available in millinery. It's our highest paid position, and it's what all the girls aspire to."

"I see." At least she had tried. She could tell Kitty that.

Mr. Loomis led her to a stairwell and told her to return the next morning at seven. She would work until six-thirty. She was not to use the elevator when the store was open, as it was for customers only.

Clara thanked him and left Jeffras, Seeley, & Company. Outside, she smiled and drank in the crisp September air. With a great burden lifted, she felt like she could breathe again. And though it was a factory job, the working conditions were far better than what she'd endured in Roswell. The workroom was not nearly as hot, there was no lint floating around, and no stench of oil and grease. And Mr. Loomis didn't seem the sort to bother the women. Though her salary would be more than what she'd earned in Roswell, Clara wasn't certain if it was enough to support both herself and her sister, as she did not know what their expenses would be once they were compelled to leave Longworth House. But if things went well, then once Kitty's strength returned, maybe Mr. Loomis would have a job for her, too.

# 16

Early Monday morning, Clara set out for Jeffras, Seeley, & Company, grateful to have a job to go to. Like the Cincinnatians she passed on the sidewalk or who sped by in carriages, she had somewhere to go, somewhere she was expected. No longer was she on the outside of all this activity, looking in.

A boy on the corner held up a newspaper and shouted, "Atlanta captured! Rebel army cut in two!" Clara paused to read the headline. If Atlanta had fallen, then the end of the war would be near. Things would be better, then. Once the war was over, Benjamin would find her. Somehow, she had connected in her mind the end of the war with Benjamin's return.

Upon her arrival at 99 West Fourth Street, Clara hurried to the stairwell, as Mr. Loomis had instructed, and climbed to the sixth floor. There were scores of sewing machines set up in long rows, many with women already sitting in front of them. No one had started to sew yet. A few women glanced her way, but apparently seeing nothing of interest, returned their attention to one another.

She hung her bonnet on a peg and waited for someone to tell her where to sit. There was a simmering excitement among the women, and Clara caught snippets of their conversations: *now the war would end* and *wasn't Sherman a genius,* and *soon their brothers and husbands and sons would come home.* Not knowing anyone as she did, her kindred feelings found no expression.

That morning, Clara was instructed by a senior operative on how to use a sewing machine. The small machine was easy to operate, a tame animal compared to the beastly spinning frames and looms. Once she understood the basics of how the machine worked, the operative showed her how to sew the simplest of undergarments. She worked on making pockets of various sizes that would be sewn into women's day dresses, skirts, and mantles. For eleven hours that day, she sewed pockets. And eleven hours the next. And every day until Sunday, her day off. An ache seized her neck, and the detailed work strained her eyes. Still, she reminded herself as loneliness and tedium weighed on her those long days, the conditions were far better than at the cotton factory.

On her way to and from work each day, she passed Madame Murphy's Fashionable Millinery on Fourth Street, where still displayed in the storefront window was the white silk bonnet trimmed with violet ribbons and pink roses, the loveliest bonnet she'd ever seen.

As September wore on, Kitty said she felt stronger and wanted work outside of Longworth House. She was less than happy with staying in their room all day doing piecework. *Soon,* Clara told her. *Be patient.* With the money Kitty earned, combined with Clara's salary, the sisters moved out of Longworth House in late September.

They moved into a boardinghouse at 221 Elm Street upon a recommendation from Mrs. Holmes. The boardinghouse keeper, Mrs. Bell, was a kind yet stern woman whose boarders included young salesmen and male clerks, married couples with children, and some single women, several of whom had once been Longworth House residents. The boardinghouse was a former row house with rooms partitioned by thin walls to allow for more tenants. Clara and Kitty rented one of the least expensive rooms, a small upstairs room at the end of a dark hall. It had one bedstead, one window, and no closet. The sisters hung their clothes on nails hammered into the wall. They each had two dark calico dresses from home, as well as a new dress apiece from Longworth House. Upon their departure, Mrs. Holmes had also given them each a donated winter coat, scarf, and pair of mittens, warning them the winter to come would be "treacherously cold, quite unlike what you're used to."

There was a tiny stove for heating and two chairs for sitting—shackly things, for one chair was missing several spindles, and the other had a mended leg. Clara and Kitty ate with the other boarders in a common room on the first floor. The cook, a woman named Charlotte, a freedwoman from Tennessee, prepared their meals. Mrs. Bell provided laundry service with the help of two servants.

The morning after they moved into the boardinghouse, Clara gave in to her curiosity. Shortly before her workday started, she peered into the seventh-floor millinery room. The day's millinery work had already begun. Women somewhat older than those in the sewing room were grouped at tables. Each table appeared to be making a different hat. One table made winter bonnets. At another table, mourning bonnets. Fancy silk bonnets at yet another. Everyone at a particular table followed the same pattern and made the same hat over and over.

When two women came up behind her, Clara moved out of the way to let them in. Embarrassed, Clara hastily returned to the undergarment sewing room, where the work was just about to begin. She found her seat at her sewing machine.

"Forget about up there," said Polly, an operative at the sewing machine beside her. She looked up at the ceiling, indicating the millinery workroom above them. "You'll be forty before you got the seniority."

Clara shrugged as if to say she didn't care. She wasn't certain she liked Polly. The woman wasn't unfriendly, and in truth, she was one of the few women who paid any attention to Clara at all, but she was rather disagreeable.

Emboldened by her peek into the millinery workroom, on her half-hour break that day, Clara did something she'd been contemplating for weeks. She went into the dry goods store she'd first noticed a month ago, the one with a giant, colorful checkerboard of ribbon displayed in its window. Inside was everything a woman would ever need to clothe her body or adorn her hair: cloth, shawls, wraps, ready-made garments, handkerchiefs, hosiery. Fabrics of all kinds: braids of silk, cotton, wool, and mohair. Something called Agra gauze, a cobwebby fabric of gossamer silk. Glass beads in every color. Hair pins of ivory, bone, tortoiseshell, and wood. In the trimmings area, Clara was almost giddy at the excess: ribbons and braids, fringe and feathers, cloth flowers and lace cloth. She longed to scoop all of it up in her arms!

Though she felt like an imposter to be in a shop with so many beautiful things, she forced herself not to run out. She tried to pretend like she belonged there. If only she could take home the ribbons and fringe and cloth flowers, she could make over her plain bonnet. She could make it look like the one in Madame Murphy's window. Well, if not exactly like it, then something close. Something better than it currently was. She imagined herself surrounded by this bounty day after day. The things she might create!

She pushed from her mind the thought of sitting at a sewing machine, sewing pockets all day. She was lucky to have the job. It was far better than being separated from Kitty and sent to the country to be someone's domestic servant or farmhand.

"Can I help you?" Hovering nearby was a clerk Clara hadn't noticed.

"Beg your pardon?" Clara had been thinking of the white silk bonnet at Madame Murphy's. The one trimmed with violet ribbons and pink roses.

"Is there something you'd like to purchase?" The clerk looked pointedly at her hands. She'd been playing with a piece of black fringe, letting the short, twisted cords fall across her fingers.

"No, sir." She let the fringe fall back into its box, and the clerk turned away.

She left the store empty-handed, but an idea had taken hold. On her way home that evening she found a more modest dry goods shop upon a recommendation from Polly. There she purchased a length of violet ribbon, some black fringe, and three pink cloth roses. Even at this shop, with materials not as fine, the purchase pushed the limits of her budget. But she was compelled to follow through on her idea and couldn't contain her excitement. She nearly skipped all the way back to the boardinghouse.

That evening, Clara wiped clean her bonnet as best she could and then spent the next few evenings remaking it. First, she removed the lilac ribbon. Then, using Kitty's needle and thread, she sewed the wide violet ribbon across the brim and down the sides, allowing the excess to hang to secure the bonnet beneath her chin. She made a simple bow at the top and fashioned the three pink roses to the bow. Having removed the trimmings from one of her hair nets, she attached the net to the back of the bonnet. She added violet ribbon and black fringe where net met bonnet. Finally, she sewed the remaining black fringe under the brim. She worked well after dark by the light of a candle. Kitty, who'd been watching her sister's efforts with approval, drifted to sleep as Clara worked. To Clara's great relief, she slept peacefully, without coughing.

Clara donned her remade bonnet before leaving the boardinghouse the next morning. When she arrived at Jeffras, Seeley, & Company, she climbed the stairwell to the sixth floor, pausing before entering the workroom. She briefly considered going up to the millinery workroom on the seventh floor. Did she dare? She imagined walking in, talking to the overseer, showing him her work. But then she imagined him looking at her bonnet, laughing, and turning his back on her. She felt the full humiliation as if it had already happened. Her heart pounding, she told herself she didn't have to do it, and she was greatly relieved. The spark of excitement at the idea quickly faded. It was like Polly said, she didn't have the seniority and wouldn't be promoted over women who'd been here longer, no matter how well she'd remade her bonnet. Who was she to think she'd be an exception? She opened the door to the undergarment sewing room, put her hat on a peg, found her spot at her sewing machine, and began to sew pockets.

All morning, she argued silently with herself. First, she'd tell herself it would've been pointless to ask for a millinery job, despite her lovely remade bonnet, for they would not promote her over operatives who'd been here for years. Then, she'd argue against that argument, telling herself that it wouldn't have hurt to at least try. The millinery supervisor, in seeing the bonnet she'd made in her spare time, might applaud her determination and ingenuity. You never knew for certain until you tried, wasn't that right? But then she'd argue against that, saying that other operatives would see what she'd tried to do, and they would mock her or hate her for trying to put herself ahead of them. Back and forth she went in her own mind.

When it came time for her midday break, she fetched her bonnet and went outside. She'd brought an apple and a piece of bread, and she ate them as she walked along Fourth Street. When she found herself approaching Madame Murphy's Fashionable Millinery, she finished her apple, tossing the core into the road where it would eventually be snatched up by a hog or some other creature. She stopped to check her reflection in a storefront window. Straw material aside, her bonnet now looked not so unlike the one in Madame Murphy's window. Clara touched the roses and thought of her mother, of winter evenings spent by the hearth, her mother teaching her how to weave a straw bonnet, how to trim it with whatever they had: dried flowers, scraps of ribbon, roses made of salvaged cloth.

Spurred on by her failure of nerve that morning, Clara was determined to prove to herself and Kitty that she was no coward. Despite what Benjamin may or may not think, she would, today, standing here on Fourth Street in Cincinnati, Ohio, admit to herself that, yes, she wanted to be a milliner. If she was going to humiliate herself, she might as well humiliate herself by the best. She approached Madame Murphy's. The door opened to let out a customer, and Clara walked in.

*17*

The moment had an unreal quality. Here was Clara, standing inside Madame Murphy's after weeks of walking by the fashionable millinery and peering through the storefront window as she passed. Now, among the elegant hats and custom-made bonnets, she felt a little outside herself. Like part of her still stood out on Fourth Street, looking in at herself through the shop window.

Now she had a better view of the white silk bonnet that had inspired the remaking of her own. She stepped closer while hoping to settle her nerves from the excitement of having dared to enter. As she reached out to touch the bonnet, she caught a reproving look from a bespectacled woman who must have been Madame Murphy herself and quickly withdrew her hand. A few feet away, two well-dressed women with dark hair graying at the temples spoke to one another as they moved toward the door. Clara pretended to look at other bonnets while waiting for them to leave. The smaller the audience, the better.

"Is he still insisting on going to the rally?" said one of the women as she tied a black bonnet under her chin.

"Sadly, yes," said the second woman. "I just hope it doesn't get violent."

"There's always that danger. Men are more riled than ever. My husband will vote for Lincoln, but I fear if that man is re-elected, there will only be more violence."

Her companion nodded, bumping right into Clara without so much as a glance, let alone a *beg your pardon*. "That's the long and short of the matter. My husband says—"

"Ladies." Madame Murphy interrupted the woman, her manner solicitous. "I can't recall if I mentioned it, but your bonnets will be ready a week from Monday."

The woman who'd been talking looked annoyed for a moment, then confused, as if she didn't know what she'd been about to say. Her companion said they'd return a week from Monday and then, to her friend, "Oh, I almost forgot. I have to go by my dressmaker and see to her progress. You know how it is if you don't check in on them."

"I'll walk with you as far as Vine," said the other, and the women left the shop.

Clara, who'd moved to a chestnut bureau displaying a selection of winter hats, ventured, "Pardon me, Madame Murphy?" Then, when the woman didn't correct her, "My name is Clara Douglas. I was wondering if you needed any help. I— I can make hats." Even as she spoke, she feared she sounded ridiculous.

"Is that so?" Madame Murphy peered over silver spectacles.

Clara regarded the woman's embroidered, lace-edged collar and full under-sleeves. Covering a small stain on her left sleeve with her right hand, she fought the urge to flee. "Yes, ma'am. This one I'm wearing, I made it myself."

"I see." Madame Murphy shot a grimace at Clara's hat before turning to the nattily dressed woman next to her as if to make sure the woman was as amused as she.

Clara's face warmed. As she'd feared, she was being made a fool. What choice did she have but to continue? To flee now would only make it worse. "Yes, ma'am. It needs cleaning and pressing, but it's solid made."

"I'm sure it is. You hail from Tennessee?"

"Georgia, ma'am."

"Well. My girls are highly skilled, from good Cincinnati families. You may dabble in hat-making," she said, eyeing Clara's bonnet with scorn, "but you lack true millinery experience. If you want to make hats, I suggest you look at one of the wholesalers. There are women who don't mind buying a hat that a hundred others own if it means saving a few dollars. But those are not my clientele." She turned to the woman next to her and smirked. "Mine are more discerning. And thank goodness for that!"

Hushed giggles bubbled up from behind a velvet curtain at the back of the shop. A lump formed in Clara's throat. Tears wouldn't be far behind. "Yes, ma'am," she squeaked.

Nearly tripping over the threshold in her haste, she fled the shop for the anonymity of the Fourth Street crowds, nearly falling off the curbstone and into the road. Stepping back a few paces, she pressed a hand to the brick building for balance. She took deep breaths to steady herself while dabbing at her eyes with her sleeve.

What had she been thinking, going in there? She may be far from the Roswell factory, but anyone could tell she was used to factory work, and that was all anyone would let her do. That she wasn't from a "good Cincinnati family" would forever block her path to a millinery career. It was folly for Kitty to have encouraged her to strive for something more. Clara would never forget this humiliation.

"I beg your pardon, but I overheard what Madame Murphy said to you in there." A woman with a warm, open expression approached. Clara noted the rich fabric of her dress, the fine trimmings of her hat. At first, Clara didn't realize the woman was talking to her. Had this woman been in the shop just now?

"Pay her no mind," the woman said, gesturing to Madame Murphy's. "She loves to insult those of modest means, and I've long suspected"—she leaned in conspiratorially—"I've long suspected she acts that way because she's not as high-born as she would have her customers believe. People secure in themselves have no need to get the run upon others like that." The woman eyed Clara's bonnet. "Your bonnet is lovely. I can tell from a glance that it's well made. Perhaps you're not ready for Fourth Street just yet, but with proper training, I don't see why you mightn't be someday."

"That's awful kind of you." Clara felt she might start crying all over again at this concern from a stranger. "But what Madame Murphy said is true. I don't belong in a shop like that. All I know is factory work."

"If I could offer you a bit of advice, don't let others decide for you what you can be." Then she did a most unexpected thing. This woman told Clara about a milliner on Sixth Street. Madame LeClair's Millinery offered hats at more reasonable prices, the kind woman said, and her customers included people of varying means.

Sometimes she took on apprentices. "You might go and inquire about an apprenticeship. Tell her Mags sent you." And with a smile, the woman disappeared into the throngs on Fourth Street.

Tears welled again at the stranger's benevolence. It was the first gesture of goodwill she'd experienced since Mrs. Holmes brought them to Longworth House and one of a scant few throughout the whole frightful journey. But Clara could not imagine walking into another millinery looking for work. Not with this humiliation so fresh in her mind.

The next day, the last Saturday in September, Clara's sewing machine broke. Mr. Loomis sent her home early, without pay, while admitting the malfunction wasn't her fault. Regretting the loss of income but not sorry to be free on a beautiful autumn day, with sunshine and temperatures so pleasant that the air felt neither warm nor cool but rather in perfect harmony with her own skin, Clara took a longer route back to the boardinghouse.

She passed the Fifth Street Market House, which stretched an entire block down the middle of the street. The market house bustled with Union soldiers who, Clara later learned, were fed and entertained, courtesy of Cincinnatians, as they passed through the city. She thought about her sister, back at the boardinghouse doing piece work. The girl must get restless. If Kitty was feeling up to it, maybe they would explore the city or walk down to the river. As she approached a confectionery shop, on a whim, Clara went inside to smell the sugary air, maybe even buy a treat for herself and Kitty. To make amends.

They'd had an argument the night before when Clara told her about the disgrace she suffered at Madame Murphy's. Kitty had insisted Clara take Mags's advice and try for an apprenticeship at the more modest Madame LeClair's Millinery. But Clara refused to consider it, and Kitty had told her she was wasting her talents. "You're too chicken. You'll stay in that factory and make pockets for the rest of your life, just like we'd have stayed at the cotton mill if it hadn't burned. You could do something else, but you're too afraid to try."

Clara, who thought the accusation unjust, considering she'd already tried and failed to follow her dream, had responded by saying that everything she did was to keep Kitty safe, and that Kitty didn't appreciate her efforts. Kitty claimed she could take care of herself. At that, Clara had laughed scornfully. "You'd have followed that woman all the way to the brothel!" she said, referring to the woman who'd offered them bread upon their arrival in the city. Kitty retorted that she knew what the woman was and would've followed her only for as long as it took to eat the roll. They'd both gone to bed angry.

A treat from the confectionery shop would help set things right. Inhaling the scents of caramel and chocolate, she delighted in the jars of brightly colored candies that filled the shelves behind the counter. Stick candy, gum drops, jujubes, lozenges, rock candy. If she had the money, she'd have bought two of everything.

A few penny candies would have to do. Having made her purchase, she left the shop and turned toward the boardinghouse. Across the street walked a girl, smiling and talking, beside a man about ten years her senior. It was something, how much the girl looked like Kitty: tall and slim, with the same ash-blond hair plaited and—it *was* Kitty. Clara hadn't expected to see her sister outside the boardinghouse, walking about the city, let alone with a man Clara didn't know. She thought Kitty told her everything; there weren't supposed to be secrets between them.

At a distance, she followed them all the way back to the boardinghouse. The man she now recognized as another boarder, a new one, although she couldn't recall his name. Oliver? Clara waited across the street while Kitty and the man went inside.

Several minutes later, Clara opened the door to the boardinghouse. At the scent of peach pie warm from the oven, she was a child again, back at the farm, her mother putting a warm pie on the sill to cool. Charlotte stepped out of the kitchen, wiping her hands on her apron. Her black hair was all but hidden in a colorful checked kerchief, which was tied in a bow at the top of her head.

"It's Mrs. Bell's birthday," she said when Clara shared her memory. "Now I know she don't want a fuss, but these days I think we ought to celebrate what we can."

"Ain't that the truth." Clara moved toward the stairs, then stopped. "Charlotte, did you see Kitty come in a few minutes ago with one of the other boarders? A man. Oliver, I think his name was?"

Charlotte frowned. "There's no Oliver staying here. You're thinking of Otto. The one that's got a little boy?"

"Otto, that's right. He and Kitty—have they gone for walks before, do you know?"

Charlotte dipped her chin. "That's a question for your sister. I don't get mixed up in other folks' business."

Clara said she understood and climbed the staircase to the third floor, a little unsettled. Clara had always thought she and

Kitty told each other everything. Maybe the truth of it was there'd never been much to tell. Until landing in Cincinnati, they'd lived their days in tandem: working side by side at the mill, eating meals together, spending their Sundays in the vicinity of Mill Street.

The door to their room creaked open. Kitty, who'd been standing at the washbasin, her back to the door, whirled around. It was gratifying, Clara had to admit, to see her sister's surprise at her early return. Hanging her hat on a nail, she explained that her sewing machine had broken and then asked (with a sharper tone than she'd intended) where Kitty had been.

"What do you mean? I've been here."

"It's no use lying. I saw you out for a walk with Otto."

Kitty, recovering quickly, waved away Clara's concern. "Before you ask, he's a friend—not a suitor. I tutor his son in English. And I'm helping him with his."

"I didn't know you were tutoring."

"I was going to tell you. I only started this week."

"Reckon it's all right, so long as you're up to it, but you should have told me straight away. And don't tutor in his room—or ours—only in the parlor. And I'm not sure it's good for you to wear yourself out wandering the city."

"The fresh air is good for me. I'm feeling stronger every day." Kitty looked at Clara as if to gauge her mood. "I don't want another argument, but you should try at the other millinery shop. Who knows unless you try?"

Clara was shaking her head before Kitty finished her question. "No way I'm going through that humiliation again. It was dreadful. Even the girls behind the curtain were laughing at me. No, I'll sew pockets for a year before I try something like that again."

"You have talent, heaps of it, and you shouldn't let those awful people make you think you don't. You can do more than you think. We both can."

Flopping onto the bed with a sigh, Clara wondered where her sister's confidence came from. As she lay there, staring at the whitewashed ceiling, a thought bubbled up from her subconscious. Something else troubled her, something more than Kitty not giving her a full accounting of her days. It was seeing Kitty with Otto. The man's modest stature and bouncy gait had reminded her of Orton. More specifically, it had brought to mind that day in the weave room when Orton stood too close to Kitty. The day he'd sent Clara down to Ivy Mill.

"This may seem out of a clear sky," she said, unable to keep the unsettling scene to herself, "but did you know Orton fathered Mabel's daughter, the younger one?"

"Doesn't surprise me."

"Did he—" Did she dare ask? "Did he bother you in any way?"

Kitty laughed, to Clara's immense relief. "Orton was no match for me. Look what happened to him!"

"I'm not fooling around! You've got to be careful. You can't count on men like that drinking themselves off a ledge."

"No, you sure can't." Kitty put her hand on Clara's. "Sis, Otto's a kind man. And he's just a friend, anyhow. We went for a walk, that's all. I like getting out of this room and seeing the city. It's good for my spirits and my health. I'm feeling much stronger, I promise."

"All right, then. Just don't overdo it." She'd said enough. She would think about this another day. Right now, she was too tired to argue. She lay on the bed to rest, the penny candies still in her pocket.

After peach pie was served and birthday wishes bestowed, Mrs. Bell left the boardinghouse to attend a Union demonstration in the business district. A large crowd was expected; the Secretary of the Treasury was to speak.

Later that evening, Clara and Kitty and other boarders heard echoes of the rally from where they sat in the parlor, playing crambo and drinking cider. Their curiosity piqued, Clara, Kitty, and several others left the boardinghouse and made their way along Elm to see it for themselves.

The business district had become a riotous party, the likes of which Clara and Kitty had never seen. From sidewalks, windows, and rooftops, Cincinnatians cheered for Lincoln as an immense procession went by: hundreds of torches and colored lanterns; martial and brass bands; wagons filled with young women dressed in white and singing patriotic songs. Clara was deeply moved by the display of people proudly proclaiming sentiments that harmonized with her own. Back at the mill, only Kitty and Benjamin shared her views. If others had been likeminded, they'd kept it to themselves.

When more than three quarters of an hour had passed, and the procession still continued, Clara and Kitty left the spectacle to return home. They were followed not long after by Mrs. Bell, who—in spirits as high as Clara had ever seen—was convinced that with the tremendous enthusiasm she'd seen that night, which transcended anything of the kind ever seen in that city, Lincoln would surely be re-elected.

No sooner had she uttered these words than the streetlamps went dark. Clara, Kitty, and the others went to the window overlooking Elm Street to see what the matter was. Gunshots rang out. They rushed from the window toward the back of the boarding-house. They huddled in the kitchen until the gunfire ceased.

# 18

On Sunday, the papers reported that there'd been a riot in the Fourth Ward the night before:

*The Kentucky delegation passing through it on their way home found the gas turned off and the streets dark. They were assailed with boulders and several knocked down by roughs hurrahing for Mc-Clellan... Finally, revolvers were drawn, and firing with small arms became lively. Two men and one woman were instantly killed, two men were seriously stabbed, and several more or less injured... Two persons were accidentally killed, one crushed under an overturned omnibus and one by the kick of horses.*

Mrs. Bell read the article at breakfast. Clara wondered aloud if the city was the best place for Kitty. But Kitty argued that they couldn't live in fear (a point of view seconded by Mrs. Bell), and anyhow, she wasn't going to hide out in the boardinghouse. In fact, that very morning, she hoped Clara would come with her to see one of the sights she'd discovered on her walks with Otto. Though there was an autumn chill in the air, the sun shone in a cloudless sky, and so, after a look out the window to ensure the city was indeed calm, Clara agreed to the outing.

They'd been walking for a quarter-hour when, upon turning down a street, dozens of hogs rushed toward them. Huge and muddy and moving in a swarm, the hogs scrambled past, spurred on by drovers yelling and swiping. The sisters pressed themselves against a building lest the hogs knock them over or soil their skirts with their muddy snouts. The drovers seemed to care not a whit about what might be in their path as they swarmed down the street on their way to the slaughterhouse.

They arrived at the bottom of Mount Adams, one of the many hills that encircled the city. Near the base of the hill, a foul-smelling red stream flowed toward the Ohio River. They lifted their skirts and carefully crossed the nauseous creek of blood and bile and then followed a path up the hill, climbing until they were out of breath, stopping partway to rest on the treeless slope. Clara was gratified to note how well Kitty handled the vigorous exercise. She'd been so careful not to push Kitty, but clearly her sister had been telling the truth about regaining her strength. Continuing their climb, the ground leveled again. A stand of trees partially covered the hilltop like a wig askew.

"Isn't the view glorious?" Kitty said, clearly proud to be offering this scene to her sister.

Clara agreed that it was. Down below, Cincinnati spread out in a grid, the streets like warp and weft, church spires sprouting up at intervals like needles. Using the tall white spire of St. Peter's as her guide, she searched for "221"—as they'd begun calling the boardinghouse; then Jeffras, Seeley, & Company; and on Fourth Street, she guessed at the location of the haughty Madame Murphy's. To the south, the Ohio River flowed past the public landing, a hive of activity: a dozen steamboats puffing black smoke, passengers embarking and disembarking, hogs scrambling about. The hogs were a shifting mass, narrow as they were herded off a steamboat, widening on the landing, and narrowing again as the herd funneled onto a street.

Kitty pointed to a shady spot to their left beneath a grand tree, its massive trunk and crooked branches and golden leaves providing a welcoming place to rest. Clara sat down with a sigh.

"That was a sigh, sure enough," Kitty said. "What's troubling you?"

"Oh, nothing." Even as she enjoyed the fresh air and the breathtaking view, she felt the minutes ticking past, a sinking feeling in her chest. Soon it would be Monday morning, and she would be back in the undergarments workroom. "I wish this day could last. At the wholesaler, all the days pass the same." Clara didn't like to complain, but the fresh air had loosened her tongue.

"I don't know why you won't go to Madame LeClair's like that kind lady Mags told you to."

"Sewing pockets may not be amusing, but it don't matter. The pay is good enough, and I won't be there forever. Maybe not even a year." Clara stood and stretched her legs. She was tired of Kitty pestering her. Clara was no milliner. When would Kitty see that making hats was only a hobby? Clara picked up a fallen leaf and traced its veins with her fingertip.

"We shouldn't plan our lives around Benjamin," Kitty said. "He may never find us here."

"Of course he'll find us. You know how clever he is." A gust of wind blew the leaf from her hand.

"I said it wrong." Kitty looked up at her sister, holding a hand to shield her eyes from the sun. "What I meant was, he won't find us. Not ever. He can't."

"What do you mean, *can't*?" Something in Kitty's solemn expression made her knees weaken. "What are you getting at?"

"I need to tell you something. I can't keep it to myself any longer. Maybe you should sit down." Then, when Clara refused to sit, "It's about Benjamin. I'm sorry to say it, but he's dead."

Clara stood there on Mount Adams, numb and nauseous as if the hilltop vibrated with the force of a thousand looms. She could not go on standing, she felt so faint. She might have tumbled down the hillside and landed in that stream of blood and bile. Steadying herself against the tree trunk, she asked, "Why would you say such a cruel thing?"

In a gentle voice, like a mother might use with a young child, Kitty said, "I'm telling you because it's true. I'm sorry, Clara."

"It's not true! What's true is you don't like Benjamin. You never wanted to go to Nebraska with us, and now you want me to believe we never will!" Clara backed away from her sister. "How would you even know?"

"There's something I need to show you." Kitty reached into her bag and pulled out a pocketknife. She stepped closer, opening the knife.

Clara knew what it was even before she saw the initials "BSL" engraved on the blade. This sterling silver pocketknife, a gift from Benjamin's late father, had meant a great deal to him. It never left his pocket.

"No! Get away from me!" Clara swatted at her sister and the knife and turned away as if to stop herself from seeing what she'd already seen. Down the hillside she ran, following the path up which they'd come. Her legs struggled to keep up with her descent, and she nearly toppled to the bottom of the hill. At last, the ground leveled and her pace slowed, and she leaped over the red stream. Through the city she fled, dodging carriages and hogs and pedestrians, and not caring that she'd left Kitty alone on the hill. *Let her fend for herself!*

When 221 came into view, Clara slowed her pace. After wiping her forehead with her sleeve, she climbed the steps and went inside. She was dimly aware of Mrs. Bell, who was in the parlor talking to a boarder. Mrs. Bell called out, asking if she was all right. Clara waved a hand in reply and, now very tired, trudged up the stairs and down the dark hallway to their room. She collapsed onto the bed but refused to cry. If she cried, that meant it was true.

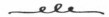

Sometime later, Clara awoke to footfalls in the hall. The rectangle of sky beyond their small window had turned a purplish blue. The door opened, and Kitty appeared with a supper tray. "You should eat something." She placed the tray on the chair.

"I'm not hungry." It took a while for Clara to summon the courage to ask what had happened to Benjamin. What Kitty *thought* had happened to him. An accident—farm equipment or a runaway wagon or unsafe river crossing. Or an illness. She would listen to what Kitty had to say, if only to judge its plausibility. Her supper was cold by the time she sat up in her bed. "Reckon I got a letter, then, and the knife with it. And you kept it from me. How long ago was it?"

Kitty shook her head. "There was no letter. I've known for a few months now." A pause, then, "Orton told me the day you went to work at Ivy."

If Kitty had said President Lincoln told her, Clara would scarcely have been more surprised. "Orton? What does he have to do with Benjamin? He couldn't know anything about Benjamin all the way out in Nebraska!" Kitty *had* been deceived, after all.

"That's just it." Kitty sat on the bed. "He never made it to Nebraska. He never left Georgia."

Her sister was talking more nonsense by the minute. "Sure he did," Clara said. "Benjamin wouldn't lie to me about that!" He'd planned to file his homesteading intentions at a land office in Brownville, Nebraska. A friend had sent him a newspaper clipping with a notice of available lands and the location where applications would be received. She'd seen it herself. "It was his dream—"

"Could be he didn't lie. Could be he meant to leave, but he got caught up in the fighting... He—"

"No, no, no! Don't you see? Orton would've said anything to get us to go with him and Eli when the Federals came. Orton wanted to have his way with you; I didn't see it then, but I see it now." She recalled what Orton had said days before the Federals stormed into Roswell. *You don't have Benjamin here to protect you, and who knows when he'll come back. If at all.* At the time, she thought Orton had been attacking Benjamin's character. Not hinting at his death.

Clara's thoughts shuttled between two possibilities: Orton had lied to Kitty—and the fact that he would tell such a lie meant he was even more hateful than Clara had come to believe. Or, Orton had told the truth, and this explained why she'd never heard from Benjamin after he left.

"Tell me everything Orton said. Don't leave anything out."

Kitty began to explain what she'd kept to herself for months. Eli and his men had been looking for those responsible for the arson attempt on the Roswell mill. They found Benjamin near Acworth, where he'd been living with a band of Southern Unionists hiding in the North Georgia mountains. When Eli came upon Benjamin's gang, there was a fight. Benjamin was shot and killed.

"Benjamin's gang was responsible for the arson attempt?"

"That's what Eli told Orton. I don't know if it's true."

"And when did this happen?"

Kitty shrugged. "Orton had only just learned of it when he told me. Eli took Benjamin's knife and gave it to Orton. And I took it from Orton when he wasn't looking."

Clara sat there on her bed, stunned. Could Kitty's story be true? All these months, she'd envisioned Benjamin in Nebraska, working his land. She still believed that had been his plan, that he'd joined the Unionists only by happenstance. Given his hatred of the Confederacy and all it stood for, it wasn't unbelievable that he'd take up arms for the Union if presented an opportunity. "Can I see it?"

Kitty pulled the pocketknife from her bag and handed it to Clara. She traced the engraving with her finger. Her sorrows of this morning—the workroom tediousness, Kitty's daytime wanderings—all fell into the far-away distance of the forgotten past. Her present anguish eclipsed all else. "Why didn't you tell me?" How could Clara not have known Kitty hid this horrible truth?

"I wanted to. I almost did that first night. But then the Federals came and burned the mill and took us away, and I worried what another shock would do to you. You needed to believe he was alive. It gave you hope. And strength." Kitty put her arm around Clara. "But it's time you knew the truth. He's not coming. It's just us from now on."

A fresh wave of sorrow. For years, the sisters' future had been in Benjamin's hands. He had tended to it and watered it, and now that he was gone, the future on which she relied, upon which she had gazed every single day for years, would wither and die. Feeling suddenly very heavy, Clara lay back down. She fell asleep with the pocketknife clasped in her hand.

# 19

Clara did not go to the undergarments workroom the next morning, the prospect of losing her position only a distant concern. She could not see past her own sorrowful regrets and stayed in bed, wishing the past two years had gone differently. If only she and Kitty had gone with Benjamin when he left Roswell, then he wouldn't have gotten caught up in the fighting, and the three of them would be in Nebraska now, living as a family and working to improve their 160 acres. Why hadn't they joined him? She couldn't recall it ever being discussed.

Benjamin had been a good man, smart and generous and noble. She tried not to imagine his last moments. But the more she tried, the more forcefully the terrible images came. Benjamin, mortally wounded and lying on the ground. Eli, robbing a dying man of his most treasured possession. And then Eli, hands bound, marching at gunpoint into a Louisville prison.

She steered her thoughts toward happy memories, like the time she and Benjamin picnicked on High Rock Ledge, overlooking the Chattahoochee River: the rushing water and the cool forest and the taste of the strawberries he'd brought. But her thoughts worked against her, and soon, her picnic flooded with images of gunfire and blood and bodies. Her only escape was sleep.

But even sleep was treacherous. That night, she dreamed she was crossing Roswell's covered bridge when the bridge erupted in flames behind her. She ran toward the Chattahoochee's south bank, where Kitty was standing, but the bridge kept stretching and expanding, and the flames spread close behind her, and no matter how fast she ran, she could not reach Kitty, who cried out inconsolably, arms outstretched, and the square of daylight at the end kept receding.

The following morning, she awoke feeling stronger, if not quite strong enough to venture outside. She would lose her position at the wholesaler, but so be it. Maybe it was for the best. If she returned to Jeffras, Seeley, & Company, her weeks sewing pockets would turn into months and months into years, and she would spend her whole life in the wholesale undergarments workroom. There was truth to what Kitty had said: Without Benjamin, Clara might have stayed at the cotton factory forever.

It's not that she thought poorly of herself. She knew she was a competent, hardworking, and loving person. But she took a practical view of life, and the truth was, there was much she didn't know about a whole heap of things. Clara often found the world outside of Roswell incomprehensible and overwhelming, and in the face of uncertainty, she clung to what she knew. "Better one safe way than a hundred on which you cannot reckon," as the fable went.

That Benjamin viewed the world differently was one of the reasons she'd been enamored of him. Ideas came to him like lint to a piece of cloth. He knew how to talk to people, how to make his ideas happen. When the Douglas sisters worked in the low-paying spinning room despite having the talent for more, Benjamin spoke to Orton, and before long, they were weavers. Benjamin got them the best provisions at the company store thanks to his rapport with the clerk and his knowledge of delivery schedules. Before leaving for Nebraska, he'd voiced a fear that Clara couldn't survive without him. Instead of taking offense (as Kitty said she should have), she'd been inclined to share in his doubt. He left her a supply of firewood and cornmeal and told her to ask the Summerhills if she had any trouble.

Who was Clara Douglas, now that she was no longer Benjamin's betrothed, a future homesteader? She was a Georgian who lived in Ohio. A weaver who sewed pockets. All that remained of her old life was Kitty: She was still her older sister, still responsible for her well-being. For this, she was grateful.

Clara woke Wednesday morning no more certain about what lay ahead than she'd been the night before, but determined to move toward it nevertheless. The future she'd long assumed was hers was now gone, and it would do no good to cling to its memory. She would not lie abed feeling regretful another day. Cincinnati was no longer a way station; it was their new home.

She would dress and go down to breakfast, and once her belly was full she would think about what to do next. She glanced at the wall, to the nail where she'd hung her favorite bonnet. But it was gone—as was Kitty, she noticed for the first time since waking. What was her sister up to? Another outing with Otto?

Minutes later, the door opened, and there was Kitty as if summoned by her thoughts, holding her bonnet. The bonnet looked different. Brighter. Kitty tossed it on the bed, pointed, and said, "I got it cleaned for you at a shop on Pearl Street. You're getting up, and you're going to Madame LeClair's. Today."

Cleaned at a shop on Pearl Street? Lying in bed for two days had dulled Clara's thoughts, and though she was surprised by Kitty's ingenuity and resourcefulness, she did not comment on it. She reached under her pillow and closed her fingers around Benjamin's pocketknife.

"I've got to teach an English lesson to another boarder's children," Kitty continued. "Promise me you'll get up. And that you'll go."

Clara pushed herself to a seated position. "I'm up, I'm up." She rubbed the pocketknife handle with her thumb, its smoothness a comfort. "I'll go." Then, when Kitty looked unconvinced, "I promise!"

"Good. I want to hear all about your apprenticeship when you return." She kissed Clara on the head—a maternal gesture, as if she were the elder sister! —and left the small room. The door closed behind her, and it was all Clara could do not to slink under the quilt. But she could not hide in their room another day. If the years ahead were too daunting to think about, then she wouldn't think about them. Not all at once. She would think only of this week.

This day. If things got too terrible… Well, she wouldn't think about that now, either.

Clara rose on stiff legs and readied herself for a visit to Madame LeClair's Millinery. She wet a cloth and wiped her face and under her arms. She put on her dress, the nice one in a checked pattern she'd received at Longworth House. Her own two dresses were the dark calico common to factory workers and would not do. As she went about getting ready, it would dawn on her again and again, each time a fresh pain, that Benjamin was gone. Her eyes would well with tears. She hadn't felt this adrift since her mother died.

A melancholy numbness had settled over her, dissipating any qualms she might have had about repeating the humiliation she'd endured at Madame Murphy's. Indeed, the bite of humiliation would be a welcome reprieve from her current despair. Once she had donned her refashioned bonnet, with its violet ribbon, pink roses, and black fringe—thank heaven for Kitty, for the cleaning had improved it a great deal—she felt more like her old self. A little fog lifted. Wearing a bonnet never failed to give her confidence. A lovely, well-made bonnet was like a piece of armor protecting against the appraising stares of those who might find her wanting.

She stepped into the hallway and closed the door behind her. That had been the hardest part, getting over the threshold. Spurred on by this small victory, she descended the stairs with renewed spirits. Benjamin probably wouldn't believe what she'd managed to do these last few months: survive the Louisville prison, make her way to Cincinnati, find work, and put a roof over their heads. If she was honest, she could hardly believe it herself.

She stepped outside 221 and squinted in the daylight, mustering her courage. *You've got heaps of talent.* Kitty's voice echoed in her ear. *Madame LeClair will be lucky to have you.*

Reciting Mrs. Bell's directions quietly to herself, Clara continued east, then north, walking slowly so as not to sweat, and watching for speeding wagons as she crossed the street.

*If you reach the Mechanics Institute, you've gone too far.* Her heart sank when she saw the institute up ahead, a grand four-story building topped with multiple spires on all four sides, giving the impression of a crown. Turning around in order to retrace her steps, she noticed the shop window she'd missed. She'd been standing right in front of Madame LeClair's Millinery. She darted past the window to avoid notice and touched the brick building for support.

Her head spun with naysaying thoughts. *You're just a factory girl. A penniless foreigner. You're no craftswoman.* Clara let these thoughts come and go.

With a sense that she floated above herself, a detached observer of her own movements, she opened the door and stepped inside. The shop was simpler than Madame Murphy's. Smaller, with no leather settees. A few tables displayed a selection of unpretentious hats on stands. A counter with a glass display case ran along the wall to the right. At the back of the shop, two women chatted near boxes of trimmings. Clara had practiced what she would say. She would start by mentioning Mags and the compliment she'd received from her. And then she would ask if Madame LeClair needed an apprentice. Alone in her boardinghouse room, Clara had tried to speak more flatly, like a Northerner, but it came out sounding false, and that seemed worse than simply using her own voice.

"Oh, Madame, I tell you," said a ruddy-complected woman standing near the trimmings. "Mr. Johnson can pinch a penny 'til it squeals. Of course, that's only when it's one of the pennies he gives me. Do you know he once spent five dollars on a book? Five dollars! And once you read the thing, of what use is it? But if I ask for five dollars for a bonnet I can wear again and again, he puts up a fuss!"

"It is unfair, Mrs. Johnson," said the other woman, who must have been Madame LeClair, as she pulled several feathers from a box. Madame LeClair could have been anywhere from twenty-five to forty-five, either a young-looking older woman or an older-looking young woman. There was something regal in her manner, a calmness. Her straight eyebrows and tall nose gave her a refined appearance.

"Sometimes I envy you," Mrs. Johnson went on. "How smart you are, not to have burdened yourself with a husband, the useless creatures so many turn out to be!"

Madame LeClair moved to another box and selected some lace. "A good husband is hard to find. Until then, my little business supports me. Did you say you preferred a pink lining?"

Clara, lingering near a display of fall bonnets, bit her lip. Pink? With Mrs. Johnson's ruddy complexion, a pink lining would be all wrong. It would reflect pink onto her face, and she'd look red as a ripe apple.

"Oh, I don't know," Mrs. Johnson said. "I do love pink, as you well know. And yet I wonder if it's the right color. My sister-in-law wears cherry red, and it makes her glow. What do you think?"

Cherry!

"Or green? Perhaps?" Clara blurted before she could stop herself. The women gaped at her as if she wore nothing but a chemise and stockings. Clara took a tentative step toward them. "Forgive me for interrupting. If-if I may...Mrs. Johnson, I think a green lining would be a lovely complement to your complexion."

Mrs. Johnson turned to Madame LeClair. "Who is this girl?"

Madame LeClair frowned. "I haven't the slightest notion."

Blood rushed in Clara's ears. She spoke quickly: "My name is Clara Douglas. I make bonnets and hair nets." She touched her bonnet. "I made this one. And I've been told I have a knack for choosing colors to suit a person."

Madame LeClair let out a sharp laugh. "Well! I'm being lectured by a hobbyist. Pray such quack millinery doesn't take hold!"

Clara, bolstered by her grief, took the snub with equanimity.

Mrs. Johnson looked from Clara to the milliner. An index finger pressed against her lips in consideration. Then, "Have you any green silk in stock?"

A pause. Madame LeClair said she did.

Mrs. Johnson nodded decisively. "Green it is. I believe the girl is right." She adjusted her bonnet's bow. "I'll return Tuesday to pick it up. Now I must be off. If dinner isn't ready when Mr. Johnson comes home, he'll have a conniption fit. As if missing a meal or two wouldn't do him some good!" The woman gave a polite nod to Clara and then left the shop. Clara stood in place, unable to move. How powerful she felt! She'd suggested a color, and this stranger, this woman of some means, had listened to her!

Madame LeClair raised an eyebrow. "Are you looking to buy a bonnet, or did you come by merely to advise my clients?"

Clara smiled, a little surprised, even sheepish, at her own bold behavior. "The truth is, Madame LeClair, I'm looking for a job. An apprenticeship. I met a woman, a friend of yours; her name is Mags. She liked the bonnet I'd made, and she said you might need an apprentice." Clara waited, and when she wasn't pushed out the door, "I'm a hard worker, and I can do whatever you need to help you run your shop. I've made hats for others, back in Georgia, in trade. Straw bonnets and hair nets."

The milliner regarded her not unkindly. "You fled the war, I presume?"

Careful to speak evenhandedly, Clara explained about General Sherman and the Roswell textile mills and their deportation. "I heard something about that." Madame tut-tutted. "I understand Sherman's a magnificent leader. Born in Lancaster, you know, just a hundred miles from here. They say he'll end this war at last, and if he does that, I'll be forever grateful. But what possessed him to send all of you up here is beyond me."

"I need to support myself and my sister. You won't regret hiring me. That is, if that's your choice."

Madame LeClair eyed Clara's bonnet. "You've seen the September issue of *Godey's*, then?"

"Beg your pardon, ma'am?"

"Your bonnet, the way you've trimmed it, bears a resemblance to one featured in last month's issue. Of course, the bonnet itself was of white silk, not straw."

Grateful she could speak intelligently of *Godey's* at all, thanks to Mrs. Hopewell's donations, Clara said she hadn't seen last month's issue. She almost left it at that but then thought it best to credit the source of her inspiration. "There was a bonnet trimmed like this in Madame Murphy's shop on Fourth Street. I thought it was beautiful, one of the most beautiful bonnets I've ever seen. I bought the materials to remake my bonnet in the same way."

"Is that so?" Madame LeClair gazed out the shop window and was quiet for several moments, and Clara readied herself for the inevitable rejection when the woman said, "It is October, and we're into our busy season. I suppose Mags is right—she usually is, but don't tell her I said so. I pay apprentices seventy-five cents a week, and you may have hats for free."

A mix of thoughts: Seventy-five cents was less than what she'd been making at Jeffras, Seeley, & Company. But Kitty was making a little money with her tutoring. And free hats! How could Clara turn this down? She would be doing what she loved, finally able to free herself from factory work. She would find a way to make both ends meet. She would excel at her apprenticeship and be promoted and then they would be secure.

This victory was enough to pierce the bubble of her sadness. She gave a broad smile, resisting the urge to hug the woman. "Thank you, Madame LeClair."

"'Madame' is fine. You can start tomorrow, I presume?"

Now that she was out in the world again, she couldn't bear to return to the dark, tiny boardinghouse room. "If you like, I can start right now."

Madame smiled. "Very well." And then, with a glance at the curtain drawn against a back corner of the room, "I'll introduce you to the girls."

## 20

It was Madame LeClair's belief that all women looked better in a well-made bonnet and that a pretty bonnet, perfectly suited to its wearer, could make her beautiful. Skill in choosing the best combination of color, shape, and fabric for a woman's unique personality and features was what set a millinery like hers apart.

Unfortunately for Clara, advising customers on bonnet selection was not among her current duties. In the hope that one day it would be, she listened in on Madame LeClair's conversations to learn how to consult with clients, who comprised women from across Cincinnati society: wives of coopers and tanners, daughters of brewers, teachers who'd matriculated from the city's Normal School. Some factory workers and domestics were among Madame's clients, as was a sprinkling of well-to-do women who appreciated that Madame's prices were lower than at comparable milliners on the more fashionable Fourth Street.

As an apprentice, Clara's work was of the menial kind: dusting and sweeping, running errands, boxing up bonnets, and delivering orders. Nevertheless, she performed her tasks with enthusiasm and care, for eventually, Madame would teach her the basics of hat-making, and from there, anything was possible.

On the morning of her sixth day, as she swept the work area (a rear corner of the one-room shop hidden by a black curtain), the other two women Madame employed, Sophrania and Trudie, busied themselves at the worktable.

"Fetch me a yard of buckram," Sophrania said to Clara without looking up from her hat block. It was yet another in a litany of commands issued by the nineteen-year-old maker, not once accompanied by a "please" or "thank you."

Clara set the broom against the wall and went to the shelves where the fabric was kept. The bolt of buckram was on the heavy side, and with some effort, she lugged it to one end of the worktable, where she unrolled and measured it.

"I think Madame has a suitor." Sophrania was speaking in a low voice to Trudie. "Last night after you left, I was waiting for my brother and a man met Madame here in the shop! They spoke quietly, so I couldn't hear. My brother came soon after. I only wished I could stay and find out who he was." Sophrania leaned in closer. "What if she's secretly engaged?"

"I shouldn't think so," Trudie said as Clara cut the coarse fabric. "It may have been her brother, home on furlough. I suspect Madame's in no rush to be married."

"You think she doesn't want to marry? It's unnatural if you ask me," Sophrania scoffed. She frowned at Trudie. "Tell me *you* don't want to make hats all your life!"

A lifetime of making hats, if only Clara could! She placed the length of buckram on the table, taken aback by the words of this girl who snubbed her nose at the position Clara sought so eagerly that she was willing to sweep floors for seventy-five cents a week in the hope of one day attaining it.

"Oh! I've just had an idea," Sophrania said, without acknowledging the buckram. "My Johnny has a friend. I could introduce you."

Trudie laughed. "I'm too tall for men's liking."

"No, I'm certain it's not your height," Sophrania said, swallowing the rest of her sentence.

Clara resumed her sweeping.

"Oh?" Trudie said. "Do tell me what it is."

A pause. "It's that you're quite...forceful in your opinions at times, and—"

"And it puts some men off, does it?"

"More than *some*. That's just how men are. You have to go a roundabout way to get what you want."

Trudie snickered. "Roundabout has never been *my* way."

"Suit yourself." Sophrania cut a glance in Madame's direction and lowered her voice. "I, for one, don't plan on becoming a spinster." Wetting the buckram and pulling it over the hat block, she announced, "I think Johnny's going to propose at Christmastime. He's been giving me hints."

Clara continued to sweep while surreptitiously watching her work. She had only ever made hats and bonnets from straw, and she was curious about the buckram, which resembled a stiffened burlap.

Trudie held up an amaranth bonnet with a spoon-like brim. "The customer wants blue for the inside flowers, but she didn't say what shade."

"Maybe a pale blue?" Clara suggested.

Trudie seemed surprised by the interjection, and Clara hoped it wasn't unwelcome.

"Yes," Trudie said, looking at Clara. "Pale blue."

She set aside her broom. "I'll fetch some for you."

"You don't have to do that."

But Clara had already moved to the back of the store where, arranged on wide shelves, were displayed boxes of trimmings customers could purchase to adorn their bonnets: flowers, feathers, ribbons, leaves, fruits, nets. She found several pale blue flowers and brought them back to the worktable.

"Thank you. Let's give them a try," Trudie said. She held them up to the brim. "Do you know, I think these will look lovely!"

Clara felt her face warm.

From the other side of the curtain, Madame told Trudie to finish up the trimmings on the spoon bonnet and told Clara she was to deliver it as soon as it was finished. Clara readied a box, though she wished she could stay and watch as Sophrania molded the buckram to the hat block. The sooner she learned how to make foundations, the sooner she could be promoted to maker. An apprentice's wages weren't enough to live on for very long.

When Clara returned from her delivery, Mrs. Johnson was trying on her new bonnet—with the green lining—and smiling into a looking glass held by Madame. Mrs. Johnson tied the ribbon under her chin and, upon seeing Clara, said, "Madame told me she has taken you on as an apprentice. Good for you! Well? The green was your idea. What do you think?"

"It's lovely on you," Clara said, unable to suppress a smile. She'd been right about the color.

"I think so, too. Maybe Mr. Johnson will be inspired to take me to Wood's. Everyone's talking about 'The Duke's Motto.'" She clucked her tongue. "I'm afraid my husband has little appreciation for the theater. Even with a play full of intrigue!"

"Some men must be coaxed into a fondness for the arts," Madame said.

Clara returned to the work area, letting the curtain fall closed behind her.

"I'm pleased you're happy with the bonnet," said Madame on the other side of the curtain. Then, silence.

Trudie and Sophrania exchanged a knowing look. It must have had something to do with Madame and Mrs. Johnson, and while Clara wanted to know what it was, it seemed almost an intrusion to ask. On the other side of the curtain, Mrs. Johnson settled her account, and the moment passed.

When Mrs. Johnson had gone, and the shop was empty of customers, Madame pushed back the curtain. "Oh, the folly! Mrs. Johnson would prattle on for hours about her husband's short-comings if I let her." She placed her hands on her hips. "Well, we must remember: Many customers come only when they need a new Easter bonnet, whereas Mrs. Johnson we see even in the slowest days of the winter season. Enduring her fiddle faddle is but a small price to pay. Clara, go tidy up the shelves. We had a woman in here with her three little girls, and now it looks as though a tornado has swept through our stock. Young mothers today don't know the first thing about teaching discipline!"

Clara left the worktable to sort the artificial flowers and other trimmings into their proper boxes. The flowers were arranged by type: forget-me-nots, fuchsias, roses, camellias, daisies, lilies of the valley, and so on. She sorted the feathers by color, as she did with the fine materials like lace, velvet ribbon, and tulle. Lastly, there were nets of varying colors of silk, chenille, and velvet.

A rush of contentment flowed through her, just to be among the beautiful trimmings, so full of possibilities. Infinite combinations of color and shape and texture. She would happily count her days in bonnets.

In a prominent spot on the middle shelf, she placed a box of faux autumn leaves and mulberries. For the shop window, Madame had created a bonnet of violet crepe with a wreath of leaves and mulberries at the crown. How Clara longed to create something so beautiful!

"Madame?" Clara turned from the shelves.

Madame was writing something in a record-keeping book. "Yes?" she answered without lifting her pencil.

"I was wondering when I might learn how to make foundations."

Madame put down her pencil and regarded her with mild bemusement. "Why, Clara, you've been here but a week! Patience, my dear. There is plenty of time to learn what you need to know."

"Yes, Madame." Clara, who still held a cluster of faux mulberries, returned them to the box with a sigh.

The millinery did a brisk business as the weather cooled. In her fourth week as an apprentice, Clara was taught how to make bandeaux, the bands sewn into a hat's crown so that it better fits the wearer. Madame had taught her so that Sophrania, who'd been making the bandeaux, had more time to attend to foundations. Clara had learned to make nothing else so far, but at least it was something. As she constructed bandeaux one late October afternoon, Trudie trimmed a bonnet at the head of the table, and Sophrania struggled with a foundation. Clara, determined to befriend the younger woman despite her coolness toward her, asked what type of foundation it was going to be.

"A Marie Stuart," Sophrania said without looking up.

"With the brim that dips in the middle?" Clara had seen Roswell Royalty wear the type. She hadn't known what it was called until she'd seen one in the magazines given to her by Mrs. Hopewell. Then, when Sophrania didn't answer, "How do you do it?"

"It takes a bit of finesse. It's difficult to explain."

Sophrania would say no more. Though disappointed, Clara supposed it was not the girl's job to teach her, and she returned to her bandeaux work. On the other side of the curtain, Madame was presenting a customer with several new bonnets. The customer said the hats were lovely. Then came a pause. At last, Madame spoke. "I believe the price we agreed on was three dollars for the hats and five dollars for the dress bonnet."

"Yes, of course," the woman responded. "And I will pay you. The problem is...my husband lost his job the day I ordered these, and I dare not ask him for the money until he finds more work.

I'm sure it won't be long. He has a promising lead. I will have your eleven dollars for you by the first of the month."

"Yes, Mrs. Williams," Madame said coolly. "That will be fine."

Eleven dollars! Was Madame going to let this customer leave with eleven dollars' worth of hats and not pay? Clara had been an apprentice for three weeks now and had yet to receive any wages. That eleven dollars would cover months' worth of her pay. A scornful look passed between Trudie and Sophrania, and Clara wondered if Madame was late with their wages as well. But she didn't know them well enough yet to ask and didn't want to admit, to Sophrania especially, that Madame hadn't paid her.

"You are very good," Mrs. Williams said. "I must be off. I've an errand near Fifth Street and I want to be finished before that Union rally. I want to avoid any trouble. So many rallies! I shall be glad when the election is over." The door tinkled open and shut, and the shop was quiet, a rare moment in the busy autumn season.

"I hope there's no trouble," Clara said. "It was awful what happened in September."

Sophrania turned to Trudie, revealing a glimpse of tortoise-shell comb, one of several expensive-looking combs that alternately adorned her braided bun each day. "Remember when that abolitionist spoke at the Mozart a while back?" she asked Trudie, ignoring Clara's comment.

"How could I not?" Trudie said and then turned to Clara. "Phillips was his name. There were some idiots in the crowd who didn't like what he had to say, to put it mildly. They pelted him with rocks and eggs—he had to flee for his life!"

Sophrania shrugged. "My daddy says it's Lincoln's fault for stirring up all the hate."

"Well, I'd vote for Lincoln. If they'd let us vote." Trudie gave Sophrania a look that went unnoticed.

"Oh! Why won't this lie smoothly?" Sophrania tossed her foundation onto the table in exasperation. Trudie set down her own work and gave her some instruction.

Clara listened closely until Trudie was finished, then, "What did this Phillips say that people didn't like?"

"That our soldiers should fight for the slaves' freedom."

Sophrania scoffed. "That's when my brother left the army. He said why should he fight for them?"

"Archbishop Purcell says slavery is a sin," Trudie said, "and I—"

The curtain whooshed open, and Madame LeClair appeared. "Girls!" she commanded in a whisper. "That's quite enough talk of politics. I'm expecting an important client this afternoon. And the autumn rush is upon us, and I have no intention of making my shop the site of the city's next political riot!"

Madame let the curtain fall closed, and the three young women continued their work in silence. For Clara, though riots were a concern, the threat of losing her lodgings loomed larger; November rent was due the following week. She worked up the courage to leave the table and talk to Madame before another customer came in. The others would overhear, but she could put it off no longer. Madame, adjusting a bonnet on display, turned and raised an eyebrow in question. Clara's words came in a rush: When would she be paid her three weeks' wages?

Madame, who seemed neither surprised nor troubled by the question, only shrugged. "Until my customers pay me, I cannot pay you."

# 21

On Saturday evenings, in theaters like Pike's Opera House and Wood's and the National, Cincinnatians found a brief escape from the awful realities of war. Madame kept the shop open until nine o'clock on Saturdays to take advantage of theater and restaurant traffic. Working late wasn't optional: "If you don't work late on Saturday, I don't want you back on Monday," Madame had told Clara her first week. Clara didn't mind the extra hours, especially as Madame would bring in tea and sandwiches on those afternoons. At first, she regretted leaving Kitty alone on Saturday evenings. However, she soon learned that Kitty didn't mind at all, for she'd befriended half the boardinghouse. Furthermore, Mrs. Bell often organized social gatherings in the parlor on Saturday evenings.

On the last Saturday in October, with half an hour left until closing, Clara tidied stock while Madame presented a finished bonnet to a customer. From the far end of the counter, Clara watched to see if the customer paid, or if this was yet another one

Madame let settle her account on her own schedule. It had been five days since she'd asked for her wages, and she had yet to receive any. She promised herself she would not leave the shop tonight until she asked once again for her wages. Begged if she had to. She would tell Madame that rent was due in three days. Mrs. Bell certainly did not allow boarders to pay on their own schedule! Clara hated to entertain the thought of returning to factory work, after she'd finally taken steps toward her dream. And finding another factory job could prove difficult. If she and Kitty were kicked out of 221, they were surely headed for the country, for they couldn't return to Longworth House. With the war dragging on and with the weather turning, more refugees needed shelter than ever, and from what Mrs. Bell said, Longworth House hadn't a pallet to spare.

A few feet from where Clara sorted trimmings, Trudie helped a fashionable woman select hers. The woman's elaborate coiffure was ornamented with peacock plumes, and one long curl fell over her shoulder. "I want it to look like this one," the woman said, pointing to a sea-green velvet bonnet on display. "However, I don't want white for the inside flowers. Is there another color you might suggest?"

Trudie furrowed her brow, thinking. "Purple has been popular this season. I saw such a combination in *Godey's* recently." She glanced at Clara, who shook her head slightly and mouthed *pink roses*.

"Or," Trudie went on, "pink roses would be particularly suited to your complexion and hair."

"Is such a combination in style?"

"It's always fashionable to wear colors that work to your advantage, wouldn't you agree?"

The woman did agree, her peacock plumes dancing and shimmering as she surveyed the shop. "My husband and I just came from the National, and we stopped in on a whim." She glanced at a man who stood near the door wearing a top hat and dress coat. "I must tell my sister about this little gem."

When the woman had made her selections and left the shop, Trudie thanked Clara for her help. "Clients expect me to know what will look best," Trudie said. "I can follow the pictures in *Godey's* or *Demorest's*, and I'm comfortable with certain patterns of arrangement, but when I'm asked to improvise, I'm often at a loss." She put a hand on Clara's shoulder. "You, however, have an artist's eye for this work."

Clara could not have been more pleased at the compliment.

"Trudie." Madame approached them, a woman wearing a dark calico dress at her side. "Please help this young lady. She's brought a bonnet to remake for fall."

"Madame!" another customer called, a nattily dressed lady who had just entered the shop. "I've not much time. Will I be helped presently?"

Madame pressed her lips into a smile. "I'll be right with you, Mrs. Price." Then, to Trudie, in a low whisper, "Don't dawdle with that one."

Trudie gave Clara a conspiratorial look. "How would you like to help your first customer?"

A rush of excitement coursed through her. "Me? What about Sophrania?"

"She's got a raft of foundations to make. If you help with this customer, I can finish trimming the spoon bonnet Madame is after me about."

When Clara suggested Madame might object to her helping a customer, Trudie assured her she would not, given that the customer was not a wealthy one and only wanted a bonnet remade. Reassured, Clara happily agreed. Trudie returned to the worktable, and Clara stepped forward to help her very first customer, a young woman who'd just finished her workday at a candle factory. The woman carried a soiled straw bonnet and wanted it bleached and the trimmings refreshed. With the woman's round face (not unlike her own), Clara thought the bonnet's wide brim, while practical, was unfortunate, as it must make the woman's face appear wider still. But there were things that could be done.

"What I recommend," Clara began, "are navy ribbon accents on the brim edge and crown and red roses for the inside." The color would complement her skin, and the abundance of flowers would minimize the wide brim's broadening effects.

"Is it all right if I buy the trimmings myself?" the woman asked.

"Of course. You might try Peterson's," said Clara, who knew the store to have low prices. "Leave the bonnet with me, and I'll get it cleaned and pressed. In the meantime, you can get the trimmings."

The young woman left the shop, and Clara stood still a moment, reflecting on what she had just done and how gratifying it felt. Like she was a true milliner. If only Benjamin could see her now—he who'd feared she couldn't survive in a city! He would have been proud of how far she'd come. Wistful that he would never know of even this small success, she returned to the worktable where Sophrania struggled with a foundation.

"Busy night," Clara said, lifting a roll of silk fabric to carry it back to its place on the shelf.

"We've had busier." Sophrania's gaze remained fixed on the hat before her. In the nearly four weeks since Clara's apprenticeship began, the girl had rarely spoken to her unless Trudie was at the worktable with them. And even then, it was less like Sophrania addressed Clara directly and more like she spoke at her, or, simply, near her. Clara didn't know what she'd done to offend her, and hoped that with a little more time, a little more charm, Clara might win her friendship or at least lessen her dislike. So far, progress was slow as tar. *Slow as tar.* That was how Benjamin used to describe the way she ate a meal. Clara smiled at the memory. What he hadn't known was that her slow eating served a purpose, to ensure Kitty always got her fill.

"Can I help with those?" Clara asked Sophrania after putting the bolt of silk away. "If you explain what you're doing as you go, I can learn by watching."

"I don't need your help."

"But wouldn't you rather—"

"Clara, you're a factory girl." Now Sophrania regarded her directly. "And it's well known that factory girls don't make good milliners. Your hands are used to rough work, whereas we milliners handle fine materials. We serve women from Cincinnati's upper circles." She held up her hand, palm forward, as if to brook any objection. "I mean no offense. I'm simply explaining to you the way it is. You see how Madame only allows you to assist other factory workers."

Clara felt stricken. "It wasn't Madame. It was Trudie who asked me to help."

"That only proves my point. Madame prefers you don't speak to customers at all."

She tried not to let Sophrania's words upset her. She glanced at her hands. Were they too rough? Would customers find her unrefined? Maybe she ought to use these rough, unrefined hands to rip that lovely tortoiseshell comb from Sophrania's hair and toss it onto Sixth Street!

Taken aback by the vividness of the image and the feelings behind it, she reminded herself it did no good to be angry and walked away. She found her place at the worktable, where a small pile of cloth strips awaited their transformation into bandeaux. Disagreeable as the girl was, Sophrania wasn't wrong about how the world worked. It was sheer luck that Madame had brought Clara on as an apprentice. And that may have been both the beginning and the end of her luck. How could Clara rise any higher than an apprentice if the world always saw her as a factory worker?

After the shop closed that evening, Clara cleared the counter of plumes and roses and organdy. Then she grabbed the broom, going over in her mind what she would say to Madame. She must not leave without her wages.

As she swept under the worktable, Madame approached. Clara cleared her throat and was about to speak when Madame extended her hand, presenting several folded bills. "Here you are, Clara."

A wave of relief: Pleading would not be necessary. "Thank you, Madame." Clara rested the broom against the table and unfolded the six bills. But it wasn't enough. Each note was worth only twenty-five cents. "This is—"

"For your first two weeks," Madame said.

Her heart sank. Two weeks' pay was only half of what she was owed! Even with the wages Kitty earned teaching English to the children of other boarders, it would not be enough to pay November's room and board. "When will I—"

"Soon," Madame said. "Keep in mind, many apprentices are not paid at all." Madame handed Trudie her wages and asked her to lock up.

Clara put the money in her pocket and waited for Madame to leave. "Is she always late with wages?" she asked Trudie when it was just the two of them.

"As often as not, I'm afraid."

When they'd finished their tasks and stepped outside, Trudie locked the door behind them. Standing under a gaslight on the shadowy sidewalk opposite a books and stationery shop, Trudie thanked Clara once more for her help in selecting flowers for her customer. Clara said it was nothing.

"It wasn't nothing," Trudie said encouragingly. "You're good at this work. I'm glad you're here."

"I don't reckon Sophrania agrees with you."

Trudie waved her hand dismissively. "She's a dabbler, biding her time."

"Well, she'll be happy to know I'm fixing to leave." Clara swatted away a moth flitting through the light of the gas lamp.

"What? Don't you like the work?"

"Oh, I love it. But if Madame is always late with our wages, I can't pay rent on time. And then Mrs. Bell will tell Mrs. Holmes at Longworth House and then my sister and I will be sent to the country to be domestics. I can't let them separate us. Kitty's still young, and I promised my mother I'd take care of her. I have to look for something else." It had been a mistake to leave the wholesaler job—she wouldn't get it back, not with so many people coming to the city in search of work.

"Please don't go. With your talent, Madame will promote you to maker—"

"She said apprenticeships last at least three months, and it's already been one month, and all I can make are bandeaux! I won't get the chance to be promoted to maker if I become homeless before then!"

"Wait." Trudie put a hand on Clara's arm. "I'll talk to Sophrania. She can show you how to make foundations—"

A rowdy group of soldiers ambled towards them, singing and hooting. Clara eyed them warily and, once they'd passed, explained how Sophrania had refused to help her. "She said factory girls make poor milliners."

"Don't listen to her. She only says those things because she's afraid you'll take her position. And with good reason! I often must rework her foundations before I can trim them. I have to take the fabric off and fix her mistakes. It wastes a good amount of time."

"Why don't you tell Madame?"

"I'm no meddler, and besides, Sophrania's father paid Madame a good sum for her to be apprenticed here, and so here she'll stay. That is, until she gets that proposal she's waiting for."

"I don't understand. Her father *paid* for her to be an apprentice?"

"It's not unusual these days. It says something that Madame is paying you at all, even if it is a pittance. By-and-by only girls from the wealthiest families will be able to learn millinery." A pause. "Never mind Sophrania. I'll teach you myself."

"You would do that? But how? You've got so many hats to trim. You're dreadful busy!"

"I have an idea." Trudie suggested they meet at the shop the next day. The shop was closed on Sundays, and Trudie could show her how to make foundations.

"I can't ask you to spend your Sunday teaching me."

"I'm not being selfless here. Having you as a maker will make my job easier. I can tell from the care you put into making bandeaux that I won't have to rework your foundations. That'll save me precious time. And I could learn a thing or two from you about how to enhance a woman's features with color and trimmings. We'd make a terrific team." Trudie put her palms together as if in prayer. "Say you'll do it."

"I'm grateful for your offer. But I need to find other work, where they pay me on time."

Trudie thought for a moment. "How about this: I'll loan you the money for your room and board. You can pay me back when Madame promotes you."

Clara stared at Trudie as if seeing her for the first time. "Are you sure you want to do that?" Then, when Trudie insisted, "I hardly know what to say."

"Just say you'll teach me what you know about colors and complexion. You have a real knack for it!"

Clara laughed, giddy with relief and joyful she'd made a friend. "Yes, of course I will!"

"Then I'll see you here tomorrow," Trudie said, smiling. "One o'clock."

## 22

"A reminder, girls: Under no circumstances are you to discuss the election." It was Monday morning, the last day of October, and with the presidential election one week away, Madame had been issuing this admonition nearly every morning for a while now. The Union rally the week before had transpired without any trouble, but tensions remained high in the border city and Madame wanted none of the simmering hostility spilling into her shop.

Madame lifted her chin. "Trudie, where is Mrs. Black's winter bonnet?"

Trudie held up a cloth rose she was preparing to sew into a burgundy brim. "Starting the adornments now."

"Only just? Mrs. Black's expecting it first thing in the morning, and then there's also the widow's bonnets that must be done by tomorrow noon. Let's work faster, girls." She raised a finger. "But not with haste."

"Yes, Madame," Trudie said. "We're nearly out of black velvet ribbon."

Madame turned to Clara. "Go to Tingley & Burton's and get two spools. On second thought, you'd better get three." And then, with a sad shake of her head, "This war makes a new widow every hour." The door jingled, and Madame let go of the curtain, which then fell closed behind her.

Clara rose from the worktable and put on a bonnet Madame had recently given her. It had been on display in the window that summer and, somewhat faded, had been put aside to make room for fall designs. Made of green crepe with lilac flowers at the crown, the bonnet had at its front edge a garland of lilac, overlaid with tulle. Wearing it, Clara almost felt like one of the Roswell Royalty. It was, by a mile, the finest article of clothing she'd ever owned. If it was out of season or too fine for an apprentice's daytime errand, so be it.

Tingley & Burton's, a fancy goods wholesaler, was four blocks south of the millinery, on the corner of Walnut and Pearl. It was a fine day for a walk. The temperature was such that it felt like there was no temperature at all. What a difference from Georgia, where October still brought heat and humidity—even more so inside the mill. Clara didn't mind running the errand on a day like this, and she was feeling especially fine, as after yesterday's lesson with Trudie, she felt she was on her way to becoming a true milliner.

Trudie planned to teach Clara how to make the frame of three different bonnet types. She'd started yesterday with the spoon bonnet, which had a wide brim that rose skyward, giving the bonnet the shape of a spoon. "Won't keep the sun or rain off your face," Trudie said, "but it's fashionable, and our wealthier customers are partial to it." The spoon bonnet could be made for all seasons and of any material. Trudie demonstrated with buckram, a popular choice for winter. Fashioning the frame required the utmost care, as the frame determined the hat's angle and shape. Once the fabric covering was placed over the frame, a hat's angle and shape could be changed only with much difficulty.

Clara had enjoyed every minute of her lesson and got the knack of it quickly. Having only ever worked with straw, she delighted in the challenge of learning how to mold the buckram into shape. Next Sunday, Trudie would teach her how to create the covering for a frame. Clara couldn't wait.

Even after two months in Cincinnati, she continued to be amazed at the city's abundance. There were more buildings than she could count, and new ones were being built, even now, with the war going on for almost four years. She was fascinated by the multitude of people, even on this short walk to Tingley & Burton's: shoppers, produce vendors, newspaper boys, and businessmen, and all the horses and wagons and carriages that went with them. This city was *some pumpkins*.

Upon reaching Tingley and Burton's, a four-story building next to a cider and vinegar manufacturer, she passed a man sitting out front. He wore a Union cap, was missing his left leg, and held out a tin cup. It occurred to her then, as it had from time to time, that from there in Cincinnati, the war was so far away. There was no sense of impending doom like she'd lived with in Georgia for so long. At least, not one caused by the war. The feeling of foreboding hadn't disappeared altogether; it had merely changed form. In Georgia, they'd lived reliably, if meagerly, on company scrip while fearing the conflict. In Cincinnati, the war was less a concern, but unsteady wages caused a similar disquiet.

The injured veteran also brought to her mind's eye the sight of Benjamin lying in a forested mountainside. She didn't know if his death had come quickly. It pained her to think he might have suffered long. Had his fellow Unionists buried him? It wasn't clear from Kitty's account how many men he'd fought with and how many of them had perished. She would likely never know. The brutal sight she imagined came to her often, prompted by a war headline shouted by a newsboy or the sight of a wounded soldier or a glance at his pocketknife. Benjamin's death was always there, following her like a shadow.

She pushed down her grief lest it swallow her up. There was nothing she could do for Benjamin now. She must think of the future and do the best she could for Madame LeClair so that she might be promoted and could therefore take care of Kitty as long as Kitty needed her. And right now, that meant acquiring three spools of black velvet ribbon.

Lifting her chin, feigning a confidence that had yet to come naturally—some of the salespeople at Tingley and Burton's were haughty, and she felt them looking down on her as if they knew she didn't belong—she went inside.

Clara waited her turn at the counter, where, after several minutes, she was assisted by an elegant saleslady whose smart black dress contrasted with her silky golden hair in a striking way that made Clara glad she wore a beautiful bonnet. Clara selected three spools of black velvet ribbon and asked to put them on Madame LeClair's account.

The saleslady checked a book behind the counter and frowned. "Madame LeClair has a long account."

"A what?"

The woman smiled condescendingly as if she were talking to a simpleton. "She's past due for payment. She owes Tingley & Burton's over forty dollars. We can extend no more credit until she makes a payment."

Forty dollars! It was an incredible sum. More than what she'd make in a year on her apprentice wages. How could Madame owe so much? "But I must get the ribbon. We've got mourning bonnets to trim. Our customers are expecting them tomorrow. If I return without the black ribbon, Madame will have a conniption fit."

"And if I give away our merchandise, *my* boss will do the same."

What was Madame thinking? She'd paid only two weeks of Clara's wages, and she had a long account at Tingley's... How sound was her business? More pressingly, where was Clara going to find black velvet ribbon? Another concern: With this debt of forty dollars, Madame might decide she didn't have the funds to pay for an apprentice after all, let alone another full-time employee. Clara set the ribbon on the counter. Was there another wholesaler where Madame did not have a long account? And where would that be?

"I'd like to pay for them, if I may." Behind her, a man's voice, soft yet deep. Not unfamiliar, although she couldn't quite place it.

Clara turned to look. The man was just a few inches taller than she, and wore a well-made brown cotton suit, the bottom half of his right sleeve empty and pinned to the upper portion. She recognized those kind blue eyes. The man from the trunk shop.

He'd given her directions to Longworth House when she'd gotten lost looking for work.

The saleslady tried to hide her surprise. "Mr. Dugan, you'd like to pay for the ribbon?" she asked, looking from him to Clara.

"I would. I'll need some fabric as well." He slid a piece of paper across the counter.

The saleslady, moving in the self-conscious manner of someone accustomed to being admired, glanced at the paper and, with a nod, went to fetch the fabric.

Hauley Dugan, that was his name. He wore his handsome looks with a nonchalance that made him all the more attractive. Why would he offer to pay for the ribbon, unless— Clara stood a little straighter and then felt ashamed at where her thoughts had so swiftly traveled, and while she still mourned Benjamin. Though no one but Kitty and Trudie knew of her loss, it was far too soon to think of someone else in that way. And she was being presumptuous, wasn't she? This man's show of generosity had nothing to do with her and everything to do with the pretty saleslady. He could not be romantically interested in Clara.

"That's very kind of you, sir, but I can't let you pay for the ribbon." Even if his interests were not romantic in nature, it would be unwise to be indebted to someone who was little more than a stranger. She didn't let on she knew his name to save herself from the embarrassment of his not remembering he'd met her.

"Please accept it as a kindness from a stranger." He tilted his head and regarded her. He smiled, a charming dimple dotting his left cheek. "Although we're not entirely strangers, are we? We met before. You came into my shop."

A flutter in her chest that he *did* remember. She looked away, suddenly uncomfortable. "Oh, that's right, Dugan Brothers Trunks?" she said as if the memory had just come to her. "You gave me directions to Longworth House." She immediately wished she hadn't reminded him she was a refugee from the South (for maybe he had forgotten); he was clearly a veteran and might wrongly think her an enemy. Well, she couldn't hide her origins. Her manner of speaking gave her away.

"Yes. Was it Miss Douglas?"

Clara felt her face flush. "Yes. I'm not at Longworth House anymore. I'm an apprentice at Madame LeClair's Millinery."

"That's happy news, congratulations!" He leaned toward her in a spirit of camaraderie. "As a new apprentice, I wouldn't want you to return empty-handed."

Though his kindness seemed genuine, and it was true she did not want to return without the ribbon, nor did she want to owe something to a man she barely knew. She repeated that she could not let him pay for the ribbon.

He accepted her refusal so graciously that, at first, she thought he'd misheard her. It was this reaction that changed her mind. "On second thought, maybe I ought to accept." Her cheeks warmed. He must think her foolish, changing her mind so quickly.

"It's my pleasure to be of help," he said, with no hint of mockery.

"Your fabric, Mr. Dugan," the saleslady said upon returning to the counter. "And the ribbon. Shall I put it on the Dugan Brothers account?" Though the saleslady smiled at him and smoothed a stray hair, and nearly sang the words, Mr. Dugan seemed not to notice. The smile he gave her was merely polite, and his gaze did not linger on her longer than the transaction required. He signed a slip the woman held in place and returned his attention to Clara. He nodded warmly at the ribbon.

She thanked him as she collected the spools. "I will let Madame LeClair know, so that she may pay you back."

"Tell her I said hello, and please give her the ribbon with my compliments."

"Do you know Madame?"

He smiled. "She was a classmate of my sister's." Mr. Dugan picked up the fabric and turned to leave. "You'll find that Cincinnati is not as big as it at first may seem. Good day, Miss Douglas."

Clara bid him good day and, still standing near the counter, watched him walk away.

## 23

When Clara returned with the ribbon, Madame was helping two women, a mother and daughter. Clearly a woman of means, the elder wore a green silk striped dress decorated with velvet trim and black pom-pom buttons. Her daughter would soon make her debut in Cincinnati society and required more mature bonnets to reflect her transition from girlhood. With Madame's help, they settled on a dove-gray spoon bonnet with lots of flowers lining the inside of the brim and, for colder weather, a quilted and padded navy silk bonnet with a large bavolet. At the back of the shop, Madame selected the young woman's trimmings. Clara, after giving Trudie one spool of black velvet ribbon, went behind the counter to put away the other two. The mother and daughter stood close enough that Clara overheard their quiet conversation.

"I've long thought it would be fun to work in a millinery," the younger woman said. Her bonnet had few adornments beyond the ribbon tied in a bow. "All the lovely materials. Maybe I could apprentice in a shop like this one."

"Your work is to get an education, and then make the best match you can while you're young and pretty."

"But Mother, lots of girls these days do a little work before they marry."

"You won't meet any suitors working in a place like this."

"And what if I didn't want a suitor? What if I were a successful milliner and able to support myself?"

"Honestly, Amy!" the mother scoffed at the proposition. "Even a successful milliner is a failure if she's unmarried." As the mother spoke these words, Madame returned, arms loaded with flowers and feathers.

"I beg your pardon," the woman blurted hurriedly upon seeing Madame. "I didn't mean to imply—"

"It's quite all right." Madame set the trimmings on the counter, her features betraying no agitation. Then, addressing the younger woman, "Do listen to your mother. While I enjoy millinery, I work out of necessity. My father was a successful Kentucky businessman who fell on hard times. I moved here to make a fresh start. Without a husband, I have no choice but to support myself."

The mother nodded slowly at her daughter. "You see, dear?" Then, to Madame, with a glance around the shop, "You have done well for yourself." She touched a bonnet on display: violet velvet and ribbon trimmed with a half-wreath of lilies of the valley. "Your winter bonnets are lovely. I may as well buy one for myself."

Clara returned to the worktable to box up several bonnets bound for the bleachery. Trudie was sewing a silk covering to a foundation, and Sophrania molded buckram to a hat block while breathlessly recounting the events of an extravagant dinner party her mother had hosted the previous weekend. A card reader had provided the evening's entertainment. "When the reader did mine, she turned over the ace of clubs. Do you know what that means?" Sophrania paused for effect. "It means good news. She also turned over the nine of clubs, which means an unexpected gain. Mother says it's meant only to be a fun parlor game, but I think there's something to it."

"What do you think it means?" Trudie asked with apparent interest, although Clara wondered if she was simply indulging her.

"Why, it can only mean one thing: Johnny is going to propose marriage! That would be good news, and it's certainly a gain."

But hardly an *unexpected* one, thought Clara. By all accounts, a marriage proposal was the primary expectation of the girl's life; she'd mentioned it almost daily since Clara arrived at the millinery a month ago.

"What is it?" asked Sophrania.

At first, Clara didn't realize the question was directed at her. Sophrania repeated her query, and Clara looked up from the box she was tying with string. "What do you mean?"

"You made a face."

"No, I didn't." She hadn't meant to, at least.

"I suspect you're jealous. Well, you needn't be. I'm certain there's a nice factory hand somewhere who'll marry you."

"Shh." Trudie looked pointedly at Sophrania while nodding at the curtain. "There's a customer."

Clara tied the knot, stealing a glance at Sophrania, so full of smug self-satisfaction. Clara wasn't one for self-pity, but it rankled that someone so loathsome enjoyed so much: with her fancy hair combs and pretty dresses and her talk of parties and proposals.

Meanwhile, Clara couldn't get Madame to notice, much less care, that she would soon be able to make foundations, too. And do a better job of it. Clara hoped the card reader was right and that Sophrania would get the marriage proposal she'd been waiting for. The sooner she quit the millinery, the sooner Madame might promote Clara to maker.

That afternoon, an hour before the shop closed, Sophrania complained of a headache and went home early. Clara seized the opportunity to confide in Trudie. All day long, she'd wanted to share what had happened at Tingley and Burton's, but she hadn't wanted the recounting spoiled by whatever scornful remark Sophrania surely would have made.

"The saleslady wouldn't sell me the ribbon because Madame owes too much," Clara told Trudie. "Forty dollars, she owes!" She spoke in a whisper so that Madame, on the other side of the curtain and in conversation with a customer, could not hear.

"Then how did you get the ribbon? Did you go to Calvert's?"

"I didn't know where else to go." She paused; this was the good part. "What do you know about Mr. Dugan of Dugan Brothers Trunks?"

"I know there are two brothers, and that they both fought in the war—one may still be fighting—but I don't know much about either. Why do you ask?"

"Hauley Dugan was at Tingley and Burton's. He overheard the saleslady refuse to sell me the ribbon, and he offered to pay for it."

"You're fooling!"

"I'm not! I couldn't believe it, myself. At first, I said no, but he was so obliging, and I didn't know what else to do. I was afraid to come back without the ribbon."

"Does he know Madame?" Then, without waiting for an answer, "I suppose all the tradespeople must know each other to some degree, even if only by reputation."

"He said his sister went to school with Madame." Then, watching Trudie closely, "He must know her well enough to want to help her out."

"Or"—Trudie widened her eyes—"he wanted to help *you* out. To be your knight in shining armor."

Clara smiled to herself; it was the conclusion she'd hoped Trudie would come to. But she shook her head as if Trudie were joking. "He is a likely man, though." And then, a pang of guilt and her smile faded.

Trudie put a hand on hers. "Benjamin wouldn't want you to be on your own forever."

"Hauley Dugan is not interested in me."

Trudie only shrugged.

"He's probably married."

Trudie smiled playfully. "Why don't you ask him when you repay Madame's debt?"

"Ha!" Then, more quietly, "I haven't told Madame. I'm worried she'll be upset with me for letting him pay."

"I understand, but you must tell her. Today. Best to be direct in these situations."

"Even if he said he was offering it with his compliments?"

"Even so, she needs to know." With this decided, the conversation drifted away from the subject of Hauley Dugan and back to their work, and Clara felt a twinge of disappointment at that.

Upon arriving at the millinery Thursday morning, Clara asked Madame if she ought to pick up the bonnets she'd taken to the bleachery on Monday. "Oh, and I can stop by Dugan Brothers Trunks while I'm on Pearl." She said the latter part casually, as if the idea had just occurred to her.

Three days earlier, when Clara had told Madame about Hauley Dugan coming to her rescue, Madame had seemed embarrassed and insisted on repaying him before the week was out. But it wasn't until that afternoon that Madame gave her the money owed for the ribbon, and Clara left the shop. She headed south on Walnut Street, pausing at an intersection while several carriages passed. Above her, buildings stretched to the sky, some as tall as seven stories. The sky's brilliant blue and cloudless beauty echoed her own good spirits. That morning, she'd pinned a violet ribbon to her dress. Kitty, who'd been writing in a journal given to her by her friend Otto, which she used to keep track of her lessons, had asked about it.

"This? Oh, it's just a remnant from the shop. The other girls sometimes do this, and I think it looks nice."

"Is that all?"

"What else would it be?"

Kitty narrowed her eyes in a look that said she didn't quite believe her but that she wouldn't press the matter. "Well, I have a busy day myself, thank you for asking. I am tutoring two children this morning, and then, because Otto has told his friends about me, I'm tutoring another two children this afternoon."

"In the parlor?"

Kitty nodded. "Mrs. Bell doesn't mind, even though the afternoon children aren't boarders."

"And they're all paying you?"

"Yes, of course! That's the idea. We need the money."

"Just don't take on too much. I don't want you ruining your health."

"I'm much better, Clara. Better than I've ever been. I swear, the mill burning down is the best thing that's ever happened to me."

"Kitty!"

"Well, it's true! Tell me you don't like it here."

Despite the difficulties—the constant fears over money, feeling like a foreigner, and trying to keep Kitty safe in a city—it surely was better than the Roswell, Georgia, weave room. It was true that Kitty's night cough had all but gone away. And that, despite suffering the measles that summer, she seemed no worse for it now.

A herd of pigs scuffled by, filling the street and dodging whatever obstacles might be in their way, and Clara waited until their drover had passed before crossing over to Pearl. She decided she would see Hauley Dugan before picking up the bleached hats. Just after turning down Pearl, distracted by a woman's particularly fine hat (white feathers whispering down the brim like clouds, a sky-blue curtain at the back), she collided with the broad chest of a man walking in the opposite direction. Her forehead scraped against his wool suit, and she caught a whiff of cigar smoke.

"Watch where you're going!" he bellowed.

Clara stumbled backwards. "Beg pardon, sir."

"A *secesh*, eh? Back to Georgia with you!" The man spat on the street before brushing past her.

Clara's eyes blurred with angry tears. She tried to blink them back before she reached Hauley's shop. Needing a moment to collect herself, she ducked into an alcove away from the sidewalk traffic. She wiped her tears on her sleeve, then opened her eyes wide and blinked several times.

As she stood in the alcove, a man walked past, holding a placard: *Elect McClellan and the Whole Democratic Ticket: You Will Defeat Negro Equality, Restore Prosperity and re-establish the Union!* Across the street, another man's placard supported the president: *The Union Forever, Hurrah Boys, Hurrah! Down With the Traitors, Up With the Stars!*

The city bustled with nervous energy. It was neighbor against neighbor, as Madame had said recently. How must Hauley feel, having lost his right arm in the war, to know that among his neighbors and customers were some whose sympathies lay with those who'd started it? She thought again of Benjamin, and what he had risked and lost. Clara waited until the placard man was far down the street, and then, recovered, she continued to the trunk shop, two doors down.

It took only a moment among the scent of wood and leather inside Dugan Brothers Trunks for her heartbeat to slow to its normal pace. Hauley was with a customer; something about his manner, cheerful and calm, made her feel at once lighter. He acknowledged her with a nod and a smile and then a flash of concern. He assisted the customer a minute longer, the customer deliberating between a trunk with a flat top and one domed, before excusing himself and coming to Clara's side.

"Miss Douglas, this is a pleasant surprise," Hauley said. "But you look troubled. Is everything all right?"

"Yes, thank you." Clara smiled to prove she was fine. "I'm here because Madame insisted on repaying her debt." Then, when he looked dubious, "I collided with a man on the street. The way he sneered at me; it was with such hatred. He thinks I'm the enemy." She didn't want to say what the man had called her, for the shame of it stung. She took a deep breath. "I may be from Georgia, but I don't cotton to the idea that one race is beneath another. It's hateful, greedy men like the one that owned the mill back in Roswell who started this war, and they care for nothing but their money and power, and I hope they lose it all." Hauley looked at her thoughtfully, and Clara, somewhat embarrassed by her outburst, reached into a pocket and found the banknotes. "Anyhow, Madame LeClair is grateful to you for coming to my—to her—rescue."

"She needn't have done that, but please tell her thank you for me," Hauley said. A pause, and Clara thought maybe she ought to leave, but then he said, "How is the millinery business treating you?"

"Business is good, I only wish there was more millinery in it for me. Madame hired me as an apprentice, but I'm more of a maidservant. I clean the shop and run errands."

Hauley looked thoughtful. "Apprenticeships do take time."

"Yes, I should have considered that." Clara ran her hand over the smooth top of a domed trunk. "I don't mean to complain. I'm happy to be learning a trade. And I love hats."

"There's no harm in wanting more. My advice is to make yourself indispensable."

"I'm trying to do that. The trimmer, Trudie, is teaching me how to make foundations."

Hauley brightened. "That's good! See, you don't need my advice. You can handle yourself just fine."

"Oh, I don't know about that." It was out of habit that she put herself down to a man she admired. For the first time, she felt a pang of regret about it.

At the sound of the customer clearing his throat, Hauley glanced over his shoulder. "I'd better get back. Please give Madame LeClair my regards." His attention alighted on something beyond the shop window, and Clara turned to see the two placard-holders trying to outshout the other, each surrounded by their side's supporters. "Be careful out there," he said, his tone somber. "Tensions are as high as I've ever seen them, and whichever way the election goes—and let's pray it goes to Lincoln—but whatever the outcome, there will be men in this city bitterly aggrieved by it."

She assured Hauley she would be careful, and left Dugan Brothers Trunks for Queen City Bleachery, deeply touched by his concern.

## 24

The Saturday following President Lincoln's reelection was a busy one at the millinery, and when Madame finally closed the shop at half past nine o'clock, Clara was anxious to return to the boardinghouse. It was Kitty's sixteenth birthday the next day, and Clara had made her a white silk bonnet with a crown of Azurline blue velvet, both the inside and the crown trimmed with blue daisies and grasses. If Kitty was still awake—she tended to go to bed early—Clara would give it to her tonight. She couldn't wait, pleased as she was to give her sister such a fine hat. Kitty was going to love it.

Outside the shop, she said goodnight to the others. Sophrania left with her brother, Madame started her short walk down Sixth, and Trudie headed north toward the canal, beyond which she lived with her parents and younger siblings, not far from the brewery where her father worked. There would be no millinery lesson with Trudie on the morrow, for Clara had promised to spend the entire day with Kitty.

Carrying the birthday bonnet, she hurried through the cold, dark city, first along Sixth Street, and then down Vine, passing the familiar places now quiet—the jeweler, the fire insurance company, the plate and sheet glass warehouse—when she came to a halt. Something up ahead had caught her attention. A stream of men flowed down the front steps of a stout gray building and pooled in the dimly lit street. Gas lamps cast yellow light on some of them, while others remained shadowy figures in the dark. She felt a tingle of alarm: all these men amassed in the middle of Vine, and she was a lone woman carrying nothing but a hat.

Without taking her eyes off them, she stepped backwards toward Sixth Street.

Then, a curious thing happened: The crowd began to sing. Not only men's voices but women's, too. *My country 'tis of thee,* they sang. *Sweet land of liberty, Of thee I sing.*

Clara relaxed. This was not an angry mob. This was a joyful crowd, out on a chilly November evening to celebrate the election results, which had been announced two days prior. Torches were lit, and Clara now saw the women with their wide skirts intermingled among the men. More voices joined in the singing until the spontaneous chorus filled the night air.

A sense of awe came over her. Even though she was an outsider, even though the revelers might look at her as the enemy, as the cause of their troubles, she felt a pull toward them. Lincoln's reelection was a momentous occasion, and her proximity to this rejoicing crowd made her feel a part of it. Lincoln would end the war and abolish slavery for good. With a smile, she imagined the look on Barrington King's face when he heard the election returns. Now his mill was gone, and his slaves were gone, and when Lincoln ended the war on the Union's terms, King would lose even more. For a man who treated his employees with far less care than he did the machinery, it was no less than he deserved. She thought of Eli Enson, a much poorer man but equally hateful; a lowlife who'd taken up the rich man's fight as his own, killing Benjamin in the process. When the fighting ended and Eli was freed from the Louisville prison, he would have little to go back to, and it served him right.

Another verse began, and Clara hummed quietly along. She'd approached the edges of the crowd without anyone noticing. *My heart with rapture thrills, Like that above.* She looked up at the clear night sky, at the grand buildings towering over her, at these joyful people toward whom she felt a sudden warmth. It may have been the music's effect on her, but in that moment, she was, for the first time since learning of Benjamin's death, optimistic about what lay ahead.

*O Land beyond compare, We love thee best!*

The song ended, and she was reminded of Kitty and the late hour. She ought to be getting home. The throng filled the street, and it wouldn't be easy to push her way through. Once again, she considered returning to Sixth Street and continuing westward. Just then, the revelers filling Vine Street, who now numbered several hundred, started to move. Away from Clara they drifted, south on Vine and toward the river. Torches bobbed among the crowd like fireflies.

Now that they were moving, she would follow them as far as Second Street, where she would cross over to Elm. She was already imagining how she would describe all this to Kitty.

But the parade didn't make it that far. As the procession passed Fourth, terrible roaring voices cut through the joyful ones. Clara was trying to figure out where the voices were coming from and what they were shouting when gunshots pierced the air, and the once-orderly procession turned into chaos.

A cold fear surged down her limbs. People were fleeing in all directions, and she watched them, momentarily frozen. At last, she spun around and ran up Vine in the direction she'd come. She turned left at the nearest cross street. In her terror, she was vaguely aware of people around her, also running.

Gunshots blasted from somewhere close behind and a man, who was running not far ahead of her, fell to the ground. Clara felt a jolt of terror: The man had been shot. She glanced behind her. Darkness obscured the gunman. The acrid stink of sulfur brought her back at once to Roswell and the skirmish over the Chattahoochee.

Two heartbeats later, the fallen man scrambled to his feet and continued running. Afraid she couldn't outrun the danger, that if she stayed in the street, she, too, would be shot, she ducked into an alcove. Her heartbeat pulsed in her ears. In her haste, she'd dropped the bonnet. It lay overturned on the sidewalk. She reached for it—

"Filthy Lincoln-lovers!" a man shouted, his footfalls getting louder. Clara snatched back her hand as if burned. "Despots!" cried another. Their voices betrayed such rage it nearly brought tears to her eyes. These men had gone mad with hate. One ran past Clara, a brick in each hand. Then another man, this one pointing a gun. Crouching against the shop door, making herself as small as possible, she held her breath.

Another gunshot. One block away, maybe two. Glass shattering.

Tucked in the shadows, Clara covered her head, pleaded for quiet, and waited. The shouting and gunfire grew more distant and then ceased altogether. She lifted her head, waited another minute, and when the violence didn't return, she peered out from the alcove.

The street was eerily silent.

Glancing left and right, she stepped onto the sidewalk. With shaking hands, she picked up Kitty's birthday bonnet and sprinted toward Elm Street, trying to make her footsteps quiet and light. A few blocks and she'd be safe. *Please let me get to Kitty.* She was cutting across a corner to make her way south on Elm when she almost tripped over a man leaning against a storefront. He was in a seated position, slumped over. A beggar. After passing him, something made her stop and turn around.

This was no beggar. She knew this person!

"Mr. Dugan!" Clara retraced her steps and knelt beside him. His left arm was limp and pressed against the inner side of his left thigh. In the light of the gas lamp, she could see a darkening of the pant fabric near where his arm touched it. "You've been shot!"

"It would appear," he said, grimacing, "that someone wants to see if I can manufacture trunks with no arms at all."

"Let me help." Clara took the scarf from around her neck and wrapped it snugly around Hauley's arm. Trudie had teased her for wearing a woolen scarf in what she considered mild weather. Now Clara was grateful for her "thin blood," as Trudie put it.

"I'll be all right. The bullet only grazed my arm."

The horrible excitement of the gunfire and the rioters' chilling hatred, combined with her heart-pounding sprint, gave her a new boldness. "Can you stand up?" she heard herself say. "Come with me. My boardinghouse isn't far. Mrs. Bell can help you."

"I need only collect myself before I walk home."

"And how far is that? Mr. Dugan, if you bleed to death, it will be on my conscience."

"Hauley."

"It'll do you no good to argue, *Hauley*." She heard the determination in her voice and was pleased by it.

He looked at her anew. "Yes, Miss Douglas. Upon further consideration, I would be grateful for your help."

Clara helped Hauley to his feet, then bent down to pick up the bonnet, which she had placed on the sidewalk and now hoped hadn't gotten soiled. Together they walked the four blocks to the boardinghouse. Clara's entire body trembled with nervous energy, and she was unable to make any conversation. Hauley, for his part, seemed less shaken but alert. He admitted to no pain. In his fortitude she found a measure of reassurance. By the time they arrived at the boardinghouse, her nerves had begun to settle.

Upon opening the door, Mrs. Bell looked at them with surprise and then wariness, and then, upon seeing the scarf wrapped around Hauley's arm, resoluteness as she ushered them inside.

"I heard the gunshots," Mrs. Bell told Hauley, leading him to the dining room table and pulling back a chair. "I served as a nurse in the government hospitals here in the city early in the war—after Fort Donelson—and I've kept the medical supplies in the house just in case. I'll fix you up right." She asked Clara to make tea while she saw to Hauley's wound.

Clara wondered if tea was truly needed at this hour or if it was for propriety's sake as, with a glance from the kitchen, she saw that Hauley had removed his shirt—though his undershirt remained, and this Mrs. Bell cut with scissors just above the elbow. Clara heard Mrs. Bell confirm that the wound was not deep, that the bullet had only grazed him.

She heard Hauley explain that he'd lost his right arm early in the war and that this evening he'd come from a rally at Mozart Hall, where Treasury Secretary Chase had given a rousing speech. "'Union under the old flag, floating everywhere,'" Hauley quoted, "'and freedom for all men, so that wheresoever the flag may float, it will float over no master and no slave.'"

"Amen!" said Mrs. Bell.

When Clara emerged from the kitchen with tea, Hauley's wound was dressed. She set a cup on the table in front of him, unsure how he was going to lift it with his arm wrapped tightly at the elbow. She placed a second cup near Mrs. Bell.

"Thank you, Miss Douglas," Hauley said.

"Call me Clara, if you like." Then, "Do you know who it was that shot you?"

Hauley shrugged. "I don't know. Knights of the Golden Circle, maybe. Random Butternuts."

"I'm dreadful sorry." She looked at Hauley's tea, untouched. With the last of her boldness (for she felt it seeping from her), she asked, "Can I help you with your tea?"

A pause, then, "That's kind of you, yes."

Clara sat in the chair next to him and lifted the cup. Her hands shook a little, and she hoped he didn't notice. The cup reached Hauley's lips, and she tipped it gently toward him. When he had taken a sip, he looked at her, and she set the cup down, conscious of an intimacy that had not existed a moment before. She looked to Mrs. Bell for her reaction, but the woman's back was turned as she put away her supplies.

"And you were right-handed?" Clara asked in a tone meant to show she was undaunted by what may or may not have just passed between them.

"Sadly, yes. But I've gotten rather adept at using my left. It'll never cease to amaze me, what we can achieve when we have no other choice."

"Well put, Mr. Dugan," interjected Mrs. Bell.

There was a pause in the conversation, and Clara feared Hauley would leave, so she filled the brief silence. "Your name, I've never heard it before. Is it common in the North?"

Hauley chuckled to himself. "My Christian name is Michael, but my parents pronounce it 'MEE haul.' We came to America from Ireland when I was four and my sister Margaret was five. She used to call me 'Hauley,' and the name just stuck."

"My sister Kitty couldn't say 'Clara' when she was little. She called me 'caca.' I'm thankful *that* didn't stick."

Hauley laughed, a genuine laugh that seemed to have taken him by surprise. It made Clara feel powerful and she tried to think of something else to say that he'd find clever. Nothing came to her.

Mrs. Bell returned to the table. "Will you be all right to walk home? Mrs. Dugan must be worried about you."

Clara disliked Mrs. Bell in that moment, even as she understood the rightness of what the woman was doing.

"I'm sure my mother is sound asleep." He pushed back from the table with a smile at Clara as if they were sharing a joke. "But I am well enough to walk home. Thank you both. I'm in your debt."

Mrs. Bell turned to Clara and said with maternal authority, "I put Mr. Dugan's coat in the parlor. Would you fetch it, please?"

When Clara returned with Hauley's coat, he was standing near the door. Clara approached him, but Mrs. Bell took the coat and deftly helped Hauley into it.

"Mrs. Bell, you're a credit to the Union," he said. Then, to Clara, with a return to formality she hadn't expected, "As you may have guessed, Miss Douglas, I don't like asking for help. I appreciate your perseverance."

Their brief intimacy had ended. With an ache of disappointment, Clara wondered if it had existed at all. She watched him leave. Elm Street was silent, and his footsteps echoed in the empty street as he walked away. After a moment, Mrs. Bell said something about the cold and moved to shut the door.

Clara thanked her for her help, gave her a tired smile, and climbed the stairs to their room on the third floor. To her disappointment, if not her surprise, Kitty was asleep. The room was cold, and after placing the birthday bonnet at the foot of Kitty's side of the bed, Clara climbed in and pulled the blanket up to her sister's shoulders. She lay in the darkness, her thoughts abuzz with the events of the evening. It was some time before she fell asleep.

## 25

"Don't forget, we're having dinner at Trudie's tonight," Clara said as she donned her dress for work Thursday morning. Then, when Kitty didn't respond right away, "I told you about this days ago."

Kitty rolled over in bed. "You'll have to go without me. I have other plans."

"But you don't tutor Thursday evenings, do you?"

"There's more to my life than recuperating from measles and tutoring children."

Clara whirled around. "You have a suitor. Is it Otto? Another boarder?" Kitty was sixteen now, and while that was still young, it was no use denying that the right match would solve most of their problems. Clara wondered who it might be: the young clerk who recently moved into a room on the second floor, or the teacher who always read the *Gazette* at breakfast? "Whoever it is, I'll need to speak with him first."

"No."

"Kitty, I insist on it."

"I meant no, it's not a suitor." Kitty looked out the cloudy window as if the answer lay there. "I'm going with Mrs. Bell to a meeting."

"A meeting? With Mrs. Bell?" Clara said dumbly.

"A meeting of the Western Freedmen's Aid Society." Kitty held up a hand. "You needn't repeat that as a question. The group collects and sends food and clothing to freed slaves. They've been doing it for almost two years now, and they want to do more. Not only send necessities but also give freedmen an education and find positions for them so they can earn a living." Then, more to herself than to Clara, "They'll need a heap of teachers."

Clara stared. Since when had Mrs. Bell held sway over her sister? "I don't know about this, Kitty."

"I told Mrs. Bell I would go." Kitty, still lying in bed, propped her head up with her hand. "Haven't you ever wondered what became of the slave men in the pickers room? Or the women and children from the Smith Plantation? Or Barrington's slaves? All of them starting a new life with nothing? The Federals don't have enough resources for everyone."

Clara sat on the bed next to Kitty. "Sure I have. I've thought about Sarah Ann," she said quietly, referring to one of the children owned by the Roswell Manufacturing Company. Sarah Ann's mother cleaned the factory office buildings while she, herself not yet ten years of age, watched over the younger children nearby. Once upon leaving the company store a year or so back, Clara saw Sarah Ann outside with the children. The girl, always quiet and watchful, was now watching her, and Clara sensed she wanted to ask a question. Clara approached, and Sarah Ann pulled a small book from her pocket, opened it, and pointed to a word. Clara told her the word, and Sarah Ann pointed to another, and then another and another, until they heard grown-up voices approaching and she shoved the book in her pocket and turned away.

Clara wondered how Sarah Ann knew she was literate, if perhaps she'd seen her reading the newspaper inside the store. Since that day, Clara would watch for her when she went to buy supplies. Sometimes the girl brought her a piece of bread or another baked good in exchange for the words, which Clara gratefully received and always saved for Kitty. The last time Clara saw her was the day the Federals raided Roswell. Sarah Ann had been walking with her mother north out of town toward the Smith Plantation.

"Let's find ways we can help without you going to this meeting," Clara said. "There could be danger."

"What danger?"

"Only five days ago Hauley was shot, simply for celebrating the election!"

"This meeting's not about the election or politics. It's about helping people. Did you know Charlotte escaped all the way from Tennessee?"

"Mrs. Bell's cook? How do you know that?"

"She told me herself. Said Mrs. Bell had been helping fugitive slaves for years. They'd come here, put on a servant's uniform until they were ready to move on. Most continued north and up into Canada where the Fugitive Slave Law couldn't reach them. But Charlotte wants to go south and find family after the war." Kitty sat up. "You know I never got on with Benjamin. I thought he was full of himself. But if it was his band of Unionists that tried to burn the mill, then I applaud him for it."

"Whether he did or didn't, he's dead on account of it!" Clara, sensing Kitty bristle, softened. "I know you're older now, and you got your own mind. But please wait. Wait until tempers have cooled. Men are so riled up with the election and all. You should've heard the anger and the hatred in their voices the other night. If those same men found out about this meeting, I fear what could happen."

"Well, I ain't afraid." Kitty hugged her knees, resting her chin on top. "Don't you ever want to be part of something? To help take care of others? Mrs. Bell says we—"

"I'm trying to take care of *you!* We've been lucky compared to some, but we're barely getting by."

"I told you I could find regular work. I saw an advertisement for sewing girls and—"

Clara shook her head. "You're not ready for twelve-hour days. You don't know how sick you were, in that prison hospital. I thought I might lose you. And your cough is gone for weeks now. I don't want you tiring yourself out, or it might could come back."

"I'm fine, sis."

"No."

Kitty slammed her hand on the bed. "You don't want me to do anything! You say I'm too sick. Or I'm too young. And now that I'm older and healthier, the things I want to do are too dangerous. Why don't you say the truth: You prefer I stay locked in a room! It must vex you that I wander as far as the parlor! Or, heaven forbid, go for a walk!"

"Don't be daft." Even as she said this, Clara wondered if she *was* holding on to Kitty too tightly. But the girl wasn't ready to be on her own. She was too young and foolhardy, bold for boldness' sake and never thinking of the consequences. Kitty had once mocked Orton behind his back, much to the delight of the other weavers. But if he had turned around and seen her, he'd have thrown them out of the mill. And that was before Clara had met Benjamin! At that point, both their parents had passed, and the mill was their only future, and Kitty had imperiled it with her childish antics. Kitty's ideas about the freedmen's society might be well-intentioned, or maybe she was just trying to assert her independence, to prove something. And while Mrs. Bell's heart may have been in the right place, Clara hadn't given her permission to pull Kitty into work that could attract the kind of violence that, Clara was learning, was not uncommon in this city.

Kitty threw up her hands. "Why do I even need your approval? You're not my mother!"

"Please listen to reason, Kitty." She placed her hand on Kitty's shoulder.

Kitty ducked her shoulder out from under Clara's hand. "I can take care of myself."

Clara laughed at her sister's audacity. "That's quite the claim! When I'm the one who's been taking care of you since Mama died. You wouldn't know where to begin!"

"You have no idea what I am capable of doing," Kitty said.

Clara sighed in exasperation. "Look here, if you want to find other work, I can ask Madame or Trudie if they know of anything. But don't go to that meeting tonight. We'll find another way to help. We can sew. I could ask Madame about donating winter hats. But come with me to Trudie's."

When Kitty at last shrugged her consent, Clara felt relieved that the issue was settled, at least for now.

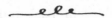

In the weeks that followed, Clara, as promised, solicited a donation from Madame of a quantity of warm quilted hats, which she gave directly to Mrs. Bell. Kitty organized a sewing circle comprising several of Mrs. Bell's boarders and friends as well as Charlotte, and a couple nights a week, they gathered in the parlor to make clothing, the material for which was provided by an anonymous supporter of the Western Freedmen's Aid Society. Kitty asked to attend no more meetings of the society, much to Clara's relief.

To her dismay, she heard nothing further from Hauley Dugan. She recalled, with some embarrassment, the thoughts she'd entertained in the days following the attack on the pro-Lincoln procession: her grand notions that Mr. Dugan would become a suitor and then a husband. The tidy home they'd occupy in a leafy part of the city.

She had, more than once, considered visiting his shop under the pretense of checking on his injury. Each time, however, the impulse was checked by her pride. And thank heaven for that. It was mortifying how thoroughly she had misread the situation. She'd thought they'd shared an intimacy, an understanding, when clearly it had been an illusion brought on by the evening's terrible excitement and nothing more. She was grateful she'd never spoken of her feelings to Kitty. The humiliation could remain a private one.

Throughout November Clara redoubled her efforts to improve her millinery skills. She'd become increasingly worried about money. While Madame had been paying her employees' wages more regularly of late, at only seventy-five cents a week, it wasn't enough. If it weren't for Trudie's financial help, supplemented by Kitty's tutoring wages, she and Kitty wouldn't even be able to stay in the boardinghouse. Clara needed a promotion to maker, and soon.

On Sunday afternoons, her lessons with Trudie became more advanced. Trudie taught her how to create the covering for various types of frames. The trickiest part was learning how to make a covering lie smoothly across a frame's curved areas. The key, Trudie said, was to know the bias of the fabric, for the fabric was more elastic in the bias direction. In return for Trudie's instruction, Clara shared with her all she instinctively understood about color and complexion and how to enhance a woman's features, whether they be plain or exquisite.

In the evenings, when there wasn't a sewing circle, Clara studied the *Hand-Book of Millinery*, which she'd found under the counter at the shop. Madame was happy to let her borrow the dusty volume, even as she dismissed the idea that it would do Clara any good. Madame was against book-learning, convinced as she was that the only way to learn the craft was to work for a reputable milliner such as herself. That was the way she had learned millinery, and in her opinion, there was no replacement for personal instruction from a woman who knew her craft. Nevertheless, Clara found that by supplementing Trudie's lessons with what she read in the book, her skills improved quickly.

By the end of November, Clara could make buckram foundations for the empire and spoon bonnets, and with more practice was certain she could master the capote. She practiced her trimming skills on the bonnets she'd made during their Sunday instruction. On one bonnet, a spoon bonnet with a square brim, she'd fastened black velvet ribbon inside the front and carried it to the center of the crown where it finished in a point. From there, she hung clusters of grapes and foliage. She'd kept the trimming simple, in part because she favored simplicity and because Trudie had purchased the materials with her own money, a favor Clara vowed to repay as soon as she could prove to Madame she was worthy of promotion.

An opportunity to do so came on a blustery December morning in the form of Mrs. Stevens, a woman who had the money to spend on fine hats but took almost no pleasure at all in wearing them.

# 26

The Christmas season was almost upon them, and despite the war and its hardships, there were plenty of Cincinnatians ready to purchase new bonnets for the coming holidays. One Tuesday in early December, Clara was preparing several deliveries, when from the other side of the curtain sounded a throaty voice, like its owner was recovering from a cold. The woman asked for a simple silk bonnet. "All these on display have too many gewgaws for my taste. I must cover my head, yes. But must it look as though I've planted a flower garden in my bonnet?"

"Of course, we can make whatever you like, Mrs. Stevens," Madame said. "We put the more elaborately trimmed bonnets in the window to catch the eye of passersby. May I suggest violet silk?"

Clara, wearing her spoon bonnet with the square brim—the one she'd made during her lessons with Trudie—and carrying the boxes to be delivered, pushed past the curtain hiding the worktable from the rest of the shop.

"What about this one?" Mrs. Stevens said, and it took Clara a moment to realize the woman was talking about hers.

"Come here," Madame said, and Clara approached.

Mrs. Stevens, who wore a brown dress and sparingly trimmed straw bonnet, squinted at Clara's hat. "It's understated, with only the black ribbon and small bit of foliage for adornment. I like it."

"Thank you, ma'am," Clara said.

"Did you make this one yourself? You must make one for me. Only perhaps a different color."

Clara considered Mrs. Stevens's hair and complexion. "A cranberry silk?" she suggested.

Madame lifted a hand to interrupt. "Clara—"

"Cranberry! Yes, I would like that."

"I do apologize, Mrs. Stevens," Madame said, a hint of agitation in her voice. "But she is only an apprentice. She doesn't make bonnets."

Mrs. Stevens looked at Clara. "But you said you made that one?"

Clara was almost afraid to nod lest she upset Madame.

Madame studied Clara's bonnet; if she was surprised by what Clara could do, she did not reveal it. "What I mean to say is that she doesn't make bonnets for customers. Not yet."

Mrs. Stevens frowned. "A pity."

There was a prolonged silence, and at last, Madame tilted her head in Clara's direction. "Can you do this?" Her gaze lingered on Clara.

"Yes, Madame, I can!" she cried and then cleared her throat, momentarily abashed by her display of emotion.

"Good," Mrs. Stevens said. "I'll need it Monday morning."

Madame usually asked for at least one week to create a hat, longer when things were busy, and the holiday rush was upon them. As it was already Tuesday, Clara would need to stay late some evenings to be able to complete it by Monday.

"I'll have it ready," Clara said before Madame could object. She could scarcely believe her luck. If she made a bonnet that satisfied Mrs. Stevens, then Madame would surely promote her. She felt dizzy with possibility.

"Very well," Madame said. Then, to Mrs. Stevens, "We'll have your bonnet for you Monday at nine."

This would be the best bonnet she'd ever made. It would dazzle everyone with its simple elegance. She couldn't wait to get started.

*ele*

Over the next few days, Clara made Mrs. Stevens's bonnet with the utmost care, molding the buckram to the hat block to make the crown, wetting the material and tugging on the ends until it had smoothly followed the block's shape, never forgetting that accuracy and neatness were of greatest importance. She covered the buckram in cranberry silk, lining it with the same. Carefully and neatly, she added the trimmings: black velvet ribbon, grapes, and foliage. A mere inch of ruched fabric around the back rather than a long bavolet.

She recalled her Sunday lessons, how Trudie had demonstrated the proper way to drape fabric over the brim or gather it in evenly spaced folds. Whether the fabric was to be smooth or in folds, it was important to work with dry hands, and to make one's stitches invisible. (Sophrania's stitches were sometimes so obvious, Trudie once lamented, that Trudie had to hide them with adornments she otherwise wouldn't have used.)

Clara finished the bonnet on Saturday afternoon. Madame approved, Trudie praised it up and down, and for her part, Clara thought it was the finest hat she'd ever made.

Monday morning, Clara was at the worktable making bandeaux as usual. Her stomach lurched every time the door opened, for each time she thought it was Mrs. Stevens. It was almost noon when she heard Mrs. Stevens's distinctive voice from the other side of the curtain. Madame called for Clara to fetch the bonnet. Before carrying it from the work area, Clara opened the box she'd stored it in and placed her hands lightly upon the bonnet as if it were a crystal ball.

Trudie nodded once and gave a smile of encouragement. Sophrania kept her head down, either deeply focused on her work or willfully ignorant of Clara's opportunity. As if in a dream, Clara carried the bonnet to Mrs. Stevens.

Mrs. Stevens regarded it with a neutral expression. Clara watched her lips for any hint of a reaction. At last, the woman clapped her hands once. Exhibiting a wholly unexpected enthusiasm, she said, "This is exquisite. I love it. Well done." Then, to Madame, "This girl is still an apprentice? I find that hard to believe. What's her story?"

Madame put a finger to her chin and pressed her lips together. "Clara is a widow from Tennessee; her husband died fighting for the Union. She's always had a talent for hat making, and now that her means of support is gone, she has decided to hone her skills so that she might support herself."

Clara looked at Madame and opened her mouth as if to speak. Madame knew she was from a Georgia cotton factory, even if she knew little else about her life. Why was she giving Mrs. Stevens this false information?

Madame shot Clara a warning look and said hastily, "She has real talent, it's true. However, she still needs the proper training."

Mrs. Stevens turned to Clara. "How did you make this, if you've not had training? This is your work, is it not?"

"Yes, ma'am. It is." With a careful glance at Madame, she said, "I-I've been practicing on my days off."

"How very industrious." Mrs. Stevens then smiled at Madame as if to say, *See?*

Madame put an arm around Clara, a maternal gesture. "When the time comes—"

"Some other shop will no doubt snatch her up if you don't."

"Your point is well taken, Mrs. Stevens." But she said nothing more. Then, to Clara, "Box that up, then, and be quick about it."

"Yes, Madame." Her head swimming, Clara returned the bonnet to its box. Upon giving it to Mrs. Stevens, the woman put a hand on Clara's arm. She spoke in a low voice as if sharing a confidence. "In this business, as in any other, you must advocate for yourself. Trust in your talents."

Clara thanked her and opened the door, and Mrs. Stevens, hatbox in hand, disappeared into the flow of passersby on Sixth Street.

Madame approached her. "Your work is very good. But I cannot promote you when I already have a maker. I do hope you understand."

"Yes, Madame. But why did you lie about who I am?"

"Clients like a good story, one that sits well with their need for romance and doesn't make them think you are snubbing your nose at family life. Nor do they want their headwear made by a factory worker, someone they might consider far beneath them." Then, when Clara flinched, "I mean no offense. It's simply the way people think."

"I suppose the story you gave isn't all that far from the truth," Clara said.

"The truth is of little importance. You're still young but you could have a future in this business, and so you may as well create your story now."

"May I ask, was your father truly a successful Kentucky businessman who fell on hard times?"

"That is for me to know, my dear," Madame said with a smile, and Clara returned to the worktable.

"Well done," Trudie said as Clara sat down. She was attaching a flower to a bonnet's brim. "I wish she could have two makers."

Sophrania, who was sewing a silk covering to a buckram foundation, said nothing.

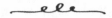

The days leading up to Christmas passed in a flurry of feathers and silk and velvet ribbon. Christmas dinner at the boardinghouse was beyond what the Douglas sisters could have dreamed of: slices of smoked ham, potatoes, hot biscuits with butter, cranberries, chestnuts, and bread pudding. The boarders ate better than they had all year.

Mrs. Bell and Charlotte had outdone themselves. At least, that was what Clara thought at first. As she had neither seen nor heard from Hauley Dugan since the night of the riot, she could not have been more surprised when Mrs. Bell announced that the feast was a gift from Dugan Brothers Trunks in appreciation for her tending to Hauley's gunshot wound the previous month.

Kitty leaned toward Clara. "This is the same man who bought the ribbon?" Then, when Clara confirmed it was, "I'd like to meet this Hauley Dugan," she said, nudging her playfully.

"It isn't like that." Even so, a renewed hope bloomed in Clara's chest. Perhaps Hauley hadn't forgotten about her after all. Maybe he had been out of town or preoccupied with business, and that was why she had not heard from him. Perhaps he'd been waiting for her to approach him, and she should have checked on his well-being after all.

"If you say so, sis." Kitty winked.

Before going to bed that evening, the sisters exchanged presents. "Surprise," Clara said when presenting Kitty with her gift. "It's...another hat." This one was a soft, quilted bonnet for winter, much like those Madame had donated to the Western Freedmen's Aid Society.

"I love it," Kitty said with genuine enthusiasm. She put the burgundy bonnet on and regarded her reflection in the small square of looking glass hung upon the wall. "It will keep me nice and warm. Thank you."

"Our first winter in the North. I hope the cold won't make you ill."

Kitty rolled her eyes. "You have to stop that."

"I can't help it."

"Here, open mine." Kitty handed Clara a small bundle wrapped in brown paper. Inside were two washcloths Kitty had knitted, as well as three crabapple blossom-scented soaps she'd purchased at a shop she'd discovered on Main Street, "Procter and something," Kitty said.

The soaps' scent was so delicious that Clara knew she would be reluctant to use them, to watch them slowly disappear. "I love them. Thank you, Kitty. And your handiwork is first rate."

The sisters readied themselves for bed, and soon Kitty was asleep. As Clara lay awake, she stared at the moon outside their window. She thought about Hauley Dugan and the secret smile he'd given her the night Mrs. Bell tended to his arm. She remembered, with a warming of her cheeks, how she'd lifted the teacup to his lips. She'd already recalled this moment at least a dozen times over the past month. She felt the memory changing in her remembering of it, as if the act of recalling the scene altered it slightly. Nevertheless, it was a delicious pleasure, every time.

When she could wring no more enjoyment from the recollection, her thoughts drifted further back in time to last Christmas, when the factory hands had gathered in Mill Street for dinner. It had been unseasonably warm, and they'd brought their chairs and tables outside to eat, everyone contributing what little food they had. Someone tended a bonfire while the Summerhill men played the banjo and fiddle. It had been a bright spot in a terrible year.

Her memories of last Christmas were interrupted by thoughts of Benjamin, thoughts that were always a weak moment away. During the day, she held them back; his death was too painful to dwell on. But now, late at night, she couldn't help but imagine his last moments on earth. How long after he'd been shot did he succumb to his wounds? Had he been all alone? It made Clara sick to think about it. But she owed it to Benjamin to imagine what she hadn't witnessed, as if her remembering it now somehow made him less alone in his dying.

—— *ele* ——

The next morning, she arrived at the millinery still sated from the Christmas feast. Though she wasn't late, Trudie, Sophrania, and Madame were already there. Trudie, usually cheerful, appeared ashen. Had she received news of her brother, who'd been drafted shortly after he came of age in November? Sophrania worked on a spoon bonnet, her features neutral. She must not have gotten the proposal she'd long been expecting, or surely she would be boasting of it.

Madame rushed to Clara's side and placed a hand on her shoulder. "The winter lull is upon us."

It was a mystery why Madame would announce this in so dramatic a fashion. Clara looked to Trudie and Sophrania for their recognition of Madame's strange behavior, but her coworkers kept their heads bent to their tasks.

"The lull," Clara repeated, as no one else was saying anything.

"Yes, I've explained this to you, have I not? I dare think I had forgotten. Well. January and February are slow months, you see, and I simply cannot afford three employees." Madame went on to explain that most of her customers purchased one dress bonnet and one everyday hat in the spring and did so again in the fall. She didn't have enough of the wealthier customers who were willing to buy distinctive headwear for morning, afternoon, and evening, as well as particular bonnets for walking, traveling, shopping, and mourning. "Had we more customers from Cincinnati's upper ten thousand, I could afford to keep three employees all year long." When Clara said nothing, Madame added, "You may return the first of March when women start thinking about their spring and Easter bonnets. Business will be brisk by then."

It had dawned on her slowly that Madame was letting her go. She'd been disappointed at not being promoted but hadn't thought it could get worse! How was she going to earn a living until March? That Madame could betray her in this way, by giving her no notice at all, offended her deeply. Did Madame think so little of her? Clara felt she might vomit. She still owed Trudie money.

"Most girls find some temporary work, I'm sure there's plenty to be had," Madame said, more to soothe her own conscience, Clara thought, than from any truth of it. "Pray we have a warm spring. Cold, wet weather is bad for business."

Madame removed her hand from Clara's shoulder, and Clara, who had not yet taken off her coat, turned to leave.

"Wait." It was Sophrania. Clara turned back.

Sophrania put down the piece of black velvet she'd started to stitch onto a foundation. "Clara needn't go."

Everyone stared. Clara's mouth hung open.

"We'll all miss her," Madame said, "but you know I have no use for an apprentice in winter months."

"Then perhaps you might promote her to maker," she said, and Clara thought she must have misheard, or that Sophrania was being cruel. But no, she was in earnest. Sophrania, who had all but ignored her these past months, was now recommending her for promotion! A wide smile brightened the girl's face. "Johnny asked me to marry him. We're to have a spring wedding. I may as well quit now."

"I don't know what to say," Clara said. "Thank you for—"

Sophrania held up a hand. "There's no need to thank me. Honestly, I'm tired of fussing over hats. I've got more important things to think about now."

"Congratulations, my dear!" Madame said a little too loudly. "If this is to be your last day, then, yes, I can ask Clara to stay on." She looked at Clara expectantly. "As maker."

Sophrania pushed the partially covered bonnet to one end of the table. "It's all yours," she said, rising.

Clara could hardly believe all that had just transpired. How she'd been standing there, in coat and mittens, dejected, once again uncertain as to how she was going to survive in this city, and now, thanks to Sophrania—someone who'd never shown her any kindness—her position was not only secured but also improved! What a wonder it was that her fortunes could change so dramatically in less time than it took to stitch a rose to a crown.

Aware that her fortunes could just as swiftly change back, Clara hung her coat on a hook and sat in Sophrania's place. She inspected the foundation to which Sophrania had been sewing black velvet. The stitching would need some redoing, but Clara would make it shine.

## 27

"I never thought it would be this crowded." Clara stood with Trudie and Kitty on the bank of the frozen Miami & Erie Canal. The canal, which flowed all the way from Lake Erie, entered Cincinnati from the northwest, extended south to Canal Street, and then cut east to the Ohio River. It was a twelve-minute walk from the sisters' boardinghouse to the stretch of canal where they now stood.

The scene was unlike anything Clara had ever witnessed: scores of people on skates gliding up and down the icy canal with varying levels of grace. Young and old and all ages between. Ladies in fine cloaks, their hands in silver fox muffs. Others in well-worn coats missing buttons. A dog skidding across the surface, following its master. A man pushing a woman on her rocker. Several kids riding in a sled while another dragged them across the ice. "This many people are daft enough to spend their Sunday afternoon in the freezing cold?"

"Wait till you try it," Trudie said.

The canal was about forty feet wide there. Trudie led them down its gently sloping bank and handed them each a pair of skates.

"We'll be lucky if we can stand up at all on these things!" Clara held up the skates. Each had a wooden sole through which leather straps were threaded. A metal blade extended up at the front then curved back toward the skate's wooden sole.

Kitty laughed, pointing at the crowd. "If all these Yankees can do it, so can we."

Trudie showed them how to tie the leather straps around their boots as tightly as they could. The skates, though big, tightened to a surprisingly good fit. Once their skates were on, Trudie stood and helped them both to their feet. Clara and Kitty wobbled at the canal's edge.

"I'm not sure I was meant to slide around on the ice on metal blades," Clara said, "but I'll give it a try."

"That's it, sis," said Kitty.

"It's harder if you stand still." Trudie walked slowly ahead of them. "Just try walking."

The sisters mimicked Trudie's movements, Clara's arms waving frantically to keep her upright. Kitty seemed to have less trouble.

"Point your toes out, like this," Trudie said.

Clara turned her feet as if her toes were pointing at the ten and two positions on a clock face, and that made her feel somewhat steadier. She leaned forward at her waist and waved her arms in backwards circles to offset her persistent wobbling. A young man whizzed past, and she nearly fell backwards. How could he go so fast? Clara was certain that the most she would ever do was this silly-looking duck walk. Well, at least she was upright.

"You're a natural talent!" Trudie called out. Clara looked up and realized Trudie was talking to Kitty, who was already gliding along the ice as if she'd done this many times before.

Trudie skated over to Clara, stopping inches from her skates. Trudie showed her how to push off with one foot and glide on the other. "I'm not ready for that, thanks," Clara said.

"You'll get it. It just takes some getting used to."

Clara didn't want to let Trudie down. It had been kind of her to invite them to skate. Trudie was the only friend she had in this city, and she was grateful for their friendship. She wanted Trudie to believe she was having a good time. But what she wanted even more than that was to sit on the canal bank and watch everyone else.

"You and Kitty go ahead," Clara said. "I'm going to stay near the edge, away from the crowd."

"All right then," Trudie said. "I'll check on you in a bit."

Trudie and Kitty skated away, and Clara retreated to the canal's edge. She wouldn't allow herself to sit down until she had attempted the push-glide technique Trudie had just shown her. She had to at least try. She turned her left foot out, pointed her right foot straight ahead, and pushed off her left foot. She glided on her right for several long seconds, watching the ground speed past, before losing her balance and falling onto the canal bank, catching her fall with her hands and landing on her right hip. She looked around, embarrassed, but no one seemed to notice. She smiled. She had skated for a few seconds!

She tried a few more times—once making as many as three push-glides in a row—before stopping to rest on the bank. As she watched the crowd, a peaceful wonderment came over her. How did she get here? How had she come to be skating on a canal in the middle of winter with her sister and a new friend? It was odd how one thing could lead to another and before long you were somewhere completely unrecognizable from where you'd started.

"Miss Douglas?"

The voice, which sounded much like Hauley Dugan's, came from over her right shoulder. She turned around.

"It is you!" Hauley said, his blue eyes twinkling just beneath a woolen cap in a charmingly boyish way. An actual boy of about eight years of age stood slightly behind him. Was Hauley a widower, and this was his son?

Clara greeted him from her seated position, explaining that she had been taking a short rest.

"Are you here with…?"

"My sister and my friend, Trudie." Clara pointed toward the crowd. "They're out there, somewhere."

"This is my nephew, Sam." Then, to the little boy, "Miss Douglas is the kind lady who helped save my good arm."

"Your uncle exaggerates," Clara told Sam, who was looking at the ground. "He would have been fine without me."

"Don't tell him that," Hauley said in a mock whisper. "He thinks I'm very tough for taking a bullet in each arm."

"Your uncle is tough indeed. Which is why he would have been fine without my help." Then, turning to Hauley, "Oh! I almost forgot to thank you for Christmas dinner. It was the best meal I've had in a long time."

"It was the least I could do. My arm has healed up nicely, thanks to you and Mrs. Bell." Hauley looked at the skates laced around her boots. "Do you like to skate?"

Clara hesitated. "This is my first time. I'm afraid I don't have the knack for it yet. It wasn't a popular pastime in Roswell."

Hauley smiled. "I imagine not. Would you like to try again?" He extended his hand to her.

She felt she could not refuse and wasn't sure she wanted to anyway. She accepted his hand, feeling its warmth through her glove, and he helped her to stand.

"Uncle Hauley! My schoolmates!" Sam pointed to a group of boys his age and, with Hauley's permission, skated off toward them.

"How does he do that, as easy as if he's just running?"

"Trust me," Hauley said. "It's harder to go slower."

"So I've heard."

Hauley nodded toward the ice. "Shall we?"

Clara, still holding his hand, allowed him to lead her further onto the ice. She was aware of her body's every movement and felt clumsy and awkward as she V-walked tentatively over the ice. A pack of boys sped past them, and she stifled a cry. "I know you said it's easier to go faster, but do you mind if we go slow?"

"Of course."

He held her right hand in his left, and they skated the width of the canal and back. Clara, graceless and wobbly, worried she might fall and pull Hauley down with her. Nevertheless, when they'd made it back to the bank, she was invigorated and wanted to go again. When at last she expressed a desire to rest, Hauley led her to a woolen blanket he'd spread near the crest of the canal bank and invited her to sit.

Clara was grateful for the blanket beneath her. "Please don't let me keep you from skating with your nephew."

"He'll want nothing to do with me, not with his schoolmates around. I can watch him from here."

Hauley sat next to her, and together, they watched Sam and his friends chase one another, scooping up snowballs from the bank and throwing them. When Hauley asked about her millinery work, she told him of her promotion and felt herself blush when he congratulated her on her success. She thought Hauley might tease her for it, but if he noticed her cheeks turn red, he said nothing. Or maybe he thought it was the cold. He seemed genuinely interested in what she had to say, and she found herself describing how much she liked her work and why. Not once did she feel like she had to talk quickly in order to keep his interest. If he thought it unwomanly that she enjoyed her work as much as she did, he gave no hint of it.

The truth was, in the weeks since her promotion, she'd begun to feel an undercurrent of hope. She was earning a better wage now, enough to live on and begin to pay Trudie back, and the sense of independence and freedom it gave her was wholly new. Her life was now up to her in a way it never had been before. As a child, she'd been under her parents' rule. From there, she'd gone to work at the mill, where the company oversaw nearly every detail of their lives, from where they lived to what they ate and drank. Paid in company scrip, they could never earn enough money to leave. The mill had kept them alive but little more. Maybe Kitty was right after all, and the mill burning down really was the best thing that could have happened to them.

Lately, she'd even been thinking more critically about the future she had once envisioned with Benjamin. She could admit now that she'd had misgivings about homesteading. About the isolation, the uncertainty, the risks. She'd seen the toll a failing farm had taken on her parents. She'd never mentioned her concerns to anyone; even thinking them had seemed a small act of betrayal. Besides, Benjamin had had enough confidence for them both. Now, however, she saw it as a kind of false confidence, more to do with trusting Benjamin than believing in their plan.

"I love working with beautiful materials," she told Hauley. "And the way a customer's face brightens when she sees her new hat. I think that for many women, a new bonnet is like a chance to start again."

"I know just what you mean," Hauley said. "I feel the same way when a customer is pleased with a trunk we've made. It feels good to put something beautiful into the world."

"Yes, that's exactly right."

Clara asked how he'd found his way into the trunk-making business, and Hauley described how he'd left school at the age of twelve and was indentured for a few years learning the trade, working for various trunk manufacturers after that. He'd volunteered to fight when the war broke out. After losing his arm early in the war, he came home and started his own business. His brother, Patrick, would be his partner when the war ended.

Clara liked the way he talked, the way he saw the world, and felt like she'd be happy listening to him talk about almost anything. When he asked how she'd learned millinery, she explained it was a skill her mother had taught her, and she'd taken to it, and that at the mill, she'd made hair nets and hats for others, sometimes as gifts, other times in trade. "I have this idea that a bonnet is protection not only from the sun but also from the world, in a way. Like armor. With a bonnet, a woman can tell the world who she wants to be." She'd never said this aloud before. "Maybe that sounds silly."

He smiled at her, not in a condescending way but like he understood a truth to her words. "I don't think it sounds silly at all."

"Anyhow," Clara said, "it beats standing at a loom all day."

"You're a long way from home," Hauley said.

"We won't go back." She looked at the crowd of skaters and pointed to Kitty. "This is our home now. I have to take care of my sister. Our parents are gone, and I'm all she has left." This might have been the moment to mention Benjamin and his passing, but she let the moment come and go and said nothing.

"They would be proud of how you've done."

She turned to him. "Do you think so?"

"You've survived a great deal, and it looks to me at least that Kitty is thriving."

"We've been lucky." She'd heard the stories reported from other border cities. She'd read about them in the newspapers Mrs. Bell kept in the parlor. Refugees like her and Kitty found frozen to death in empty warehouses, people starving in boxcars. They'd been nameless in the paper. Any of them could have been from Roswell. They could even have been her friends.

Hauley looked like he was debating with himself what to say next, and then, "If there's anything I can do—"

"There you are!" Kitty called out. She skated over to the canal bank as easily as running barefoot through grass. Trudie skated alongside her. "Sis, I'm freezing. Let's go home!" A glance at Hauley.

Clara made introductions and then excused herself, saying that she ought to get Kitty home lest her sister come down with a cold. Hauley bid her farewell. Having removed her skates, Clara walked along the bank with her sister and Trudie and, upon reaching the street where they would turn, looked back over her shoulder. Hauley watched her. She waved, and he waved back.

"Well?" Clara said to Kitty and Trudie after they'd turned down the street. "What did you think of him?"

"A likely man." Kitty's response was surprisingly tepid.

"Aren't you going to tease me about him?"

"Do you want to marry him?" Kitty said this like an accusation.

"What?" Clara frowned, unsettled by her sister's sudden peevishness. "Never mind. He's a friend, nothing more." Kitty hadn't liked Benjamin much, and Clara understood her objections even if she hadn't agreed with them. But what was there to object to with Hauley? Kitty didn't know the first thing about him.

"I approve of the match," Trudie said amiably. "He's very handsome. And he has kind eyes."

"He does, doesn't he?" Clara said, happy to find agreement. "You can look in his eyes and know he is a good person."

"Does he know how much you enjoy your work?" Kitty asked.

"I did talk about it quite a lot."

"And did he make plans to see you again?" Then, when Clara said he had not, "Well, there you have it. He sees you as a woman with ambition. Not a wife."

"Now, Kitty, he may yet call on her," Trudie said. "And because he knows where she works, who knows? He might stop in one day on the pretense of ordering a hat for his mother."

Clara smiled gratefully at Trudie, but wondered if her friend was only indulging her. They came to the intersection where Trudie had to go one way, and the Douglas sisters another. They bid Trudie farewell and walked in silence to the boardinghouse. Clara wished she hadn't spoken of Hauley to either of them. Kitty's disapproval and Trudie's reassurances both would diminish her enjoyment when she reflected on the afternoon. Better that she had kept him for herself.

# 28

Late one evening in early April, Clara was unable to sleep, a result of various fears nibbling at her. She ought to be feeling at ease. After all, they had survived their first northern winter, and aside from a couple of colds and a cough attendant on both, Kitty's health was intact. The ever-present cough that had plagued her in Roswell had all but disappeared in the nine months since the mill's destruction. Kitty was fuller in the cheeks and seemed of a stronger constitution altogether.

And Clara's financial concerns had lessened. Madame had been paying her on time and at her higher salary. The number of Kitty's pupils had grown to seven, and, though she still talked about becoming a teacher, she didn't speak of the Western Freedmen's Aid Society, much to Clara's relief. Teaching for the society meant returning to the South, which was fraught with dangers and far from Clara's protective care. And it could take a toll on her recovered health. A teaching job in the city, in Clara's opinion, was a much safer aspiration.

Despite the many reasons for optimism and hope, at this time of night, Clara was susceptible to the haunting visions that swam deep in her subconscious and now came up for air. Tonight, her fears took the following shape: What if Kitty became ill tomorrow? What if those Butternuts had shot Clara and left Kitty all alone? What if Orton had hurt Kitty, and Clara hadn't been able to stop it?

The only way to rid herself of dark thoughts like this, Clara had discovered after years of affliction, was to crowd them out with happier ones. Happier thoughts like those of hats: their shape, design, color, and trimmings. Tonight, she considered a hat ordered by Mrs. Johnson for her daughter. It was a newer style, a fanchon, which resembled a half-handkerchief. Clara had recommended it because Mrs. Johnson's daughter was partial to elaborate hairstyles, and the fanchon allowed room for such hairstyles worn at the back of the head. As Clara contemplated the brim (low), the length of the curtain (short), and the color and trimmings (undecided but perhaps sky-blue), her nervousness settled, and she relaxed into a near-sleep...

Bells rang out.

At first, she thought she'd only dreamed the sound. But now she was fully awake, and still, the bells rang.

Believing them to be fire bells, Clara went to the window and threw up the sash to smell for smoke. She detected none. The bells clanged a short distance away, from the Third Street Baptist Church on the next block and the engine house two blocks over on Vine. These were joined by bells pealing at a distance—everywhere, it seemed, bells were ringing. Kitty sat up, groggy-eyed, and Clara tossed her her coat, and they hurried downstairs.

Mrs. Bell was in the parlor, moving toward the front door.

"Is there a fire?" Clara asked.

"I don't know. I think not. I dare hope—" She reached for the door handle. "It must be..."

Other boarders appeared from the stairwell and, in a cluster, followed Mrs. Bell to the door. A rush of cold springtime air greeted them. Clara, Kitty, and the others gathered on the stoop. Up and down Elm Street, people emerged from their homes, expectant and uncertain. Bells were still pealing.

Scores of people now filled the streets, and they began to whoop and holler. A woman skipped by, and Clara asked what the commotion was all about. The woman grabbed Clara's arms and, grinning from ear to ear, said what Clara hoped to hear: "Lee surrendered! The war is over!" And then the woman ran off down the street.

"I knew it must be!" Mrs. Bell said, overhearing. "At long last!"

"At long last!" Clara echoed, throwing her arms around Kitty. At times over the past four years, it had felt like the war would go on forever. What a tremendous relief it was that the Union had been restored, the slaveholders' rebellion defeated. Benjamin's death had not been in vain.

Soon the city was drunk with joy. A couple blocks away, in the middle of an intersection, a bonfire lit up the night. A man played a fiddle, and people danced in the firelight. Clara thought of the Summerhills and wondered where they were now. Men and boys ran up and down Elm, cheering and carrying torches that illuminated houses and storefronts as they passed. The Douglas sisters sat on the steps of Mrs. Bell's boardinghouse and watched the excitement. Judging from the sound rising up from the streets into the chilly night air, celebrations had erupted all over the city.

Four years of worry and heartache and suffering transmuted into joyous relief before her eyes. And though the war had ceased to loom large in the sisters' lives since their arrival in the Queen City, Clara was overcome with emotion. It was too late for Benjamin, but Trudie's brother would come home, and so would Hauley's.

Hauley. Clara wondered where he was at that moment. Was he celebrating in the street, dancing near a bonfire? It had been three months since she last saw him, when they'd skated on the frozen canal. While she hadn't stopped thinking about him altogether, she had given up any hope of affection on his part. She told herself it was for the best, that she had her millinery work to put her attention to.

Kitty rose and said it might be fun to stand near the bonfire and fiddle player two blocks away. Clara, concerned about angry Butternuts and drunk men of any political leaning and the late hour, said it was best they do not wander from the boardinghouse. Perhaps because Kitty was tired, she didn't argue, and sat back down.

Soon after that, at half to midnight, they returned to their room, and Kitty fell fast asleep. Once again, Clara lay awake, this time not due to anxious thoughts but to the rapturous noise that penetrated their single-paned window well into the night.

———ele———

Cincinnati celebrated all week, with newspaper headlines declaring "Glory Hallelujah! Lee surrenders!" and "Grant Dictates

Terms, The End Draws Nigh!" Victory celebrations culminat-
ed in a jubilee on Friday, April 14. With most businesses and
shops closed, including Madame LeClair's Millinery, Clara and
Kitty spent the day wandering the city, taking it all in. A brass
band played in the park, and crowds sang "My Country, 'Tis of
Thee," and there was a two hundred-gun salute at noon, and
city officials gave speeches. Street vendors sold popped corn and
hot sausages and gingerbread and pies. A woman with a cart sold
ribbon rosettes in red, white, and blue; another offered wreaths of
flowers with ribbons trailing down.

"Kitty, look at this," Clara said as they came upon a man standing beside a pushcart, upon which were displayed roses forged
from metal. She pointed to a rose in full bloom. Each concentric
circle of petals was a separate piece of metal, hammered to give the
texture of a rose. "I've never seen anything like them."

"I made them from my vest." The man wore a soft cap with a
stiff brim. A military hat.

"Your vest?"

"I wore a metal vest for protection." He lifted his chin, squared
his shoulders. "I fought with the 5th United States Colored Cav-
alry."

"Did the vests stop the bullets?"

"Sometimes. Mine saved my life. Others weren't so lucky. My
vest came home with me when I was discharged. I'm a blacksmith,
see, and I thought I could do something with it."

"You've made something beautiful from something terrible,"
Kitty said, and the veteran smiled.

"Could these be painted?" Clara asked.

"I don't see why not."

Kitty nudged her sister. "You're thinking of hats, aren't you?"

Clara didn't answer; she was absorbed by the possibilities of this singular metal rose. She asked the blacksmith, "Could the stem be shortened, maybe curved a bit?"

"Sure enough," he said, handing her a card: *Albert Dickson, Blacksmith. Horse-Shoeing, Plows, Harrows, Wagons, Edged Tools, &c, 74 E. 3rd.* "That's east of Lock. Come by my shop tomorrow, and I'll have it shortened for you."

Clara thanked him and promised to come to his shop the next day. Already the design of the hat was taking shape in her mind. She would create a buckram foundation and cover it in white silk. The metal rose, painted red, would sit atop the crown, and she would use wire to secure its stem. A curtain of embroidered black lace and similar material for the inside. A striped ribbon of blue, white, and red would run across the crown and hang on either side to secure the bonnet. It would be a tribute to the Union, a celebration of the war's end. Perhaps Madame would display it in the window.

------ ❧ ------

That afternoon, a procession flowed through the streets: veterans and city officials, women's aid societies, drum corps and brass bands. The sisters sat on the wide front steps of a church to watch the spectacle. It wasn't more than a half-hour when, along the edges of the procession, came Hauley Dugan.

To Clara's surprise, he broke from the procession and ran in her direction. She glanced behind her to make sure he wasn't aiming for someone else. Satisfied that she was his intended target, she stood to greet him. Upon reaching her, Hauley did a second surprising thing: He put his arm around her waist, lifted her off her feet, and spun her around. Her hands went to his shoulders of their own accord.

He set her down gently, his hand lingering on her waist a few seconds after her feet landed on the pavement. Clara, somewhat reluctantly, withdrew her hands from his shoulders.

"I apologize," he said, taking a step back and looking sheepish. "I got carried away. I'm just so happy."

"Please don't apologize," Clara said. "You have every right to be carried away. We all do."

"It seemed the war would never end. It's almost too good to be true," he said, waving hello to Kitty.

"Your brother will come home soon," Clara said.

"Yes! It might be a few months before he's mustered out, but he's coming home and that's what matters." In a softer voice he said, "And you will have a reunion of your own."

"A reunion?"

He knitted his brow and looked at her. "With your fiancé."

"Oh...no. No, it's too late for that, I'm afraid."

"What?" Hauley looked stricken. "I thought...That is, Mrs. Bell said you were engaged, and... Clara, I'm terribly sorry. I didn't know."

"Mrs. Bell told you I was engaged?"

"Yes, as she was stitching up my arm."

It all made sense now. The way Hauley's demeanor had changed that evening last November. They had shared an intimacy, after all. And then Mrs. Bell had meddled. The nerve of the woman, poking her nose into everybody's business!

"She must not have known yet," Clara said diplomatically. "I'd learned of Benjamin's death not long before that night." She explained very briefly that Benjamin had joined a band of Unionists that was ambushed in the North Georgia mountains.

"I'm very sorry," Hauley said, and it was clear he meant it. "He died for a noble cause."

"Yes." They stood there among the noise and the chaos and the celebrations, not quite knowing what to say. Clara felt as if they were the only two people in the city. "Your parade is getting away from you," she said suddenly, without looking away.

"Yes...I'd better catch up." He didn't move at first. And when he at last stepped away, he quickly turned back. "If you ever need anything, you've got a friend in me. You will call on me, won't you? You've been through a great deal, starting a new life so far away from home. Please, if I can be of any help?"

"Thank you, Mr. Dugan," Clara said, her chest filling with joy. "I will."

"Call me Hauley," he said, and ran down the street alongside the procession.

Clara watched until he disappeared into the throngs of people. Kitty gave Clara a look out of the corner of her eye as Clara sat down.

"What?" Clara said. Then, when Kitty didn't answer, "Speak up, then. You clearly have something on your mind!"

"You don't need him. You're getting on well enough on your own."

"Why don't you like Hauley?"

"It's not that I don't like him. I don't even know him. But I know you. I know who you were before you met Benjamin, and

I know who you became after. You became someone I didn't recognize! Someone who questioned her every decision, if she made them at all. Someone who belittled her own talents. Who tried to convince me she wanted to be a *farmer* in *Nebraska!*"

"We couldn't stay at the mill, Kitty. It would've killed you."

"You act like those were our only two choices!"

"Well, we're here now, in a big city like you always wanted, and we're not going anywhere, so I don't know what you're having a fit about."

"I love you, sis." Kitty spoke more softly now. "I don't want to watch you slowly disappear. Not again."

"I won't. I promise I won't."

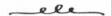

Fireworks lit the sky above the Fifth Street Market House that joyous Friday night. Four hundred miles to the east, President Lincoln went to Ford's Theatre.

The city's jubilant mood collapsed overnight.

On Saturday, the papers reported the president had been shot. In Cincinnati, John Wilkes Booth's brother and fellow actor, Junius Brutus, was scheduled to perform at Pike's Opera House in a production of "The Three Guardsmen." Rumors swirled that Junius's life had been threatened, even though he didn't share his brother's pro-Confederate views. His show was quietly canceled, and he was secreted out of the Queen City.

How cruel it was, Clara thought, that President Lincoln would not live to see the restoration of the Union he had fought to achieve. On her way to the millinery Monday morning, she passed storefront after storefront swathed in black crepe.

Upon arriving at the millinery, Clara saw that Madame, too, had draped her shop window in black. The woman's views of Lincoln were a mystery; whether and to what extent she actually mourned the loss of the president, Clara didn't know. But clearly, the public pressure to grieve Lincoln had surpassed the former necessity of appearing neutral.

That morning, Clara shared her idea of designing a bonnet in tribute to the Union with Madame and Trudie. Clara showed them the metal flower forged from the veteran's vest; she'd already painted it red. Madame loved the idea and decided that each of them would create a patriotic bonnet for display in the window.

That week, the millinery had a visit from Sophrania—her first since becoming a state legislator's wife. Wearing a black ribbon adorned with Lincoln's image and missing no opportunity to refer to her husband's position, she ordered three bonnets for various formal occasions. "Because my husband is a *state legislator*, we must attend all manner of events, and I hate to wear the same bonnet again and again. How delightful to have you make bonnets for me," she said to Clara, "after I've trained you!"

Clara caught Trudie's smirk and forced herself to maintain her composure. Sophrania's chatter no longer rattled Clara the way it once had.

"Married life is wonderful," she said when Trudie asked how she was doing. "I wonder which of you two is next?"

Trudie demurred and, when Sophrania had left the worktable to speak with Madame, said, "Everyone acts as if it's folly to expect to be happy without marriage." Trudie said she'd been raised to believe that every woman was made to be a mother, that children were necessary to a woman's peace of mind. "But I swore off matrimony. I'm an old maid and not melancholy at all. And Madame seems happy enough, and she's older than I am."

"You're not an old maid," Clara said.

"But I am! Twenty-nine come December!"

Mary, the new apprentice, chimed in. "My aunt says she never would touch a baby except with a pair of tongs! She said her sisters were worn to fiddle sticks before they were five-and-twenty."

"Sometimes I think I'd like to be a mother," Clara said, thinking of how well she'd taken care of Kitty. She also thought of Hauley and how he'd twirled her around. (In the days since the jubilee, she had relived the moment more than once.) "But then again, I don't know."

On Sunday, Clara and Hauley climbed Mount Adams and laid a quilt under a sycamore tree. There was a shiver of early spring in the air, made cooler by a breeze, but the sun shone in a near-cloudless sky, and Clara wore a capelet Kitty had knitted; these, along with her bonnet and Hauley's presence, were more than enough to keep her warm. Other Cincinnatians wandered atop Mount Adams that early afternoon, strolling and talking and being happy in the new era of peace. The Mount Adams battery, with its three cannons pointing south across the river, stood silent.

Clara sat on the quilt and adjusted her capelet, quietly pleased with herself. Two days earlier, she'd mustered her courage and come up with a pretense to visit Hauley at his shop. His face had brightened immediately upon seeing her, and she knew at once that the pretense wouldn't be necessary. He hurried to her from behind a display of carpetbags, almost as if he'd been expecting her. They'd spoken for only a few minutes when he alluded to his having no plans on Sunday, and she echoed the same; he mentioned Mount Adams, and she expressed her interest (without a word about her previous visit, that terrible day she'd learned of Benjamin's passing). He pointed out the likelihood of warm weekend weather, and she remarked having read as much in the local weather observer's report. His way made perfectly clear, he invited her on a picnic, and she accepted, and all of it was as easy as winking.

While she hadn't forgiven Mrs. Bell for her meddling, she was too happy at present to wallow in regret over the time they wasted those months when Hauley thought she was still engaged.

Now, as they sat on the hillside with the Queen City spread out before them, Hauley seemed nervous in a way he never had before. It was apparent in the way he spoke faster than usual and seemed intent on avoiding any silences. "Upriver there," he said, pointing, "they built a pontoon bridge early in the war, a line of coal barges that stretched all the way across the river. As you can imagine, it was much faster than ferrying men and supplies. Now that the war's over, we may soon see that much grander one finished," he said, referring to the suspension bridge under construction. It was to be the longest of its kind in the world, he said, although war and other issues had delayed construction, and what existed at present were two massive stone towers at either bank. He pointed upriver to the Marine Railway boatyard, where four dozen civilian steamboats had been converted into tinclad gunboats for the Union Navy. One of these gunboats, the USS *Tyler*, had seen a great deal of combat, he said, some of the most of any gunboat, up and down the Mississippi River and its tributaries at Shiloh and Vicksburg and Hickman, Kentucky.

Clara found herself feeling nervous, too, but with the opposite effect: She didn't know what to say. And so she tried to keep Hauley talking. Had the fighting ever come this far north, she asked. Quick to answer, he said that in 1863, Morgan's Raid had threatened the city, and thousands of militiamen gathered to defend it. There'd been a skirmish twenty miles or so from there, near Camp Dennison, but the fighting never came to the city itself—unless you counted the fighting between the residents themselves.

When she asked about his service, he said he'd enlisted within three days of President Lincoln's call for seventy-five thousand men willing to volunteer for three months. "Three months—that's how long they thought it'd take to crush the rebellion," he said with a wry smile. After that, he enlisted for the three-year service. On April 6, 1862, he was wounded at the Battle of Shiloh, struck by a musket ball in the right arm. "The very first battle I took part in, I was wounded in less than twenty minutes after its commencement." He confessed he often felt he hadn't served long enough to be a veteran of the same standing as men like his brother Patrick, who'd served for years.

"But you mustn't think that. You're as much a veteran as anyone else. You gave your right arm to the cause! No one could ask for more."

"I wanted revenge. I tried to reenter the service, but they didn't need me."

"Is that when you started your business?" When he said that it was and that he looked forward to his brother joining him, "How nice to run a business with your brother," Clara said. "To spend your days together. Kitty doesn't enjoy millinery, but even if she did, she likes to do her own thing. Rarely something of my choosing. And then she thinks she knows what's best for me and that I shouldn't be..." Clara stopped herself; she was saying too much. "It doesn't matter."

"Is she unhappy that you're here with me?"

"It's nothing to do with you in particular. Honest! She has this idea that— Oh, I don't know how to explain it. She thinks back in Georgia I wanted to be a milliner and that Benjamin discouraged it, and..." Clara shrugged.

"Did you?"

"It's not that I didn't, it's that I never considered it as something I could do. It was only when we got to Cincinnati that millinery became a possibility. A necessity, even. I don't think I would've dared try it otherwise."

"And you love it?"

Clara hesitated, unsure if she ought to tell the truth. Would his affection for her lessen if he thought her ambitious? She decided she wouldn't silence that part of herself anymore. "I do. I love my trade. I love helping people find just the right bonnet. I love making and trimming them. Each day is different." She studied his expression, eager to know his response.

"And your sister is worried that if you marry, you will give up what you've worked to achieve." Then, when Clara nodded, "I understand your sister's concerns," he said. "A woman who knows what she wants and who sets about achieving it is undoubtedly the most frightening thing many men can think of."

"And you? Does it frighten you?"

"Me? Not at all. I reserve all my terror for circus clowns."

"Circus clowns?"

"Why, yes," he said, laughing, "don't you find them terrifying? The makeup, the wig, the strange expressions." He pretended to shiver, and Clara laughed with him. Then, after a moment of quiet, "Did you know this used to be called Mount Ida?" he asked. "When President John Quincy Adams came here to dedicate the observatory, they changed the name in his honor."

"Is that so?"

"I was a kid at the time, but I remember what a grand event it was. The lens came all the way from Bavaria. It was the largest refractor in the western hemisphere."

"You're like an encyclopedia." She nudged him with her elbow.

"More like a pamphlet, in truth."

She laughed. "Have you ever been there? To the observatory?"

"It's magnificent. It made me feel small and inconsequential, but in a way that was comforting."

"I'd love to see it sometime."

"Then we'll make a plan to do it." He looked at the basket he'd brought. "Are you hungry?"

She said that she was, and he emptied the basket of its provisions. They ate their bread and fruit and sausage and cheese in comfortable companionship. The wind cooled them, and the sun warmed them, and somewhere to the east, church bells chimed. It was early in the afternoon, and the hours spread out before them like an unspooled bolt of cloth.

## 29

One pleasant-weather Sunday in late June, Hauley and the Douglas sisters arrived at Washington Park in the northern part of the city. They passed beneath an arch at the park's entrance and followed a gravel path that wound along under the shade of tall trees. A brass band, a military-turned-civic ensemble, had begun to play. In a grassy area within view of the musicians, they spread a quilt.

Clara leaned back on extended arms, closing her eyes and tilting her face toward the sun. She'd never been more content. First, there was the music: the weighty sound of the trombones, the trumpets' bright, powerful notes, the rustling, metallic snare drums. Then, there was the company: her sister in good spirits and health; and Hauley, whom she'd seen almost weekly since the jubilee celebration in April, and whose company, whose good-natured, cheerful calmness, she always enjoyed. Finally, she had the satisfaction of a trade she loved which allowed her to take care of herself and Kitty. In short, there was nothing more to be wished for. The mill and its many troubles seemed almost like a life lived by someone else.

A pang of guilt struck. It'd been two-and-a-half years since Benjamin left Roswell, never to return. Sometimes, to her dismay, she couldn't conjure up an image of his face. She wondered how Mabel and her daughters were faring in Indiana and whether they planned to return to the South. What had become of Nan and her family, who'd hid in the hills during the Federal occupation? Maybe Barrington King had returned, and they were working to rebuild the mills.

Were Temperance and Eli doing the same? By now, Eli must have been released from the Louisville prison. Had he learned of his brother's death, and Temperance's accusations against Clara? Hateful as Eli was, he would surely know Temperance was full of gammon, that Orton was a drunk who fell to his own death. Clara wouldn't let those old fears bother her anymore. It was all long ago and far away.

Shortly after they arrived at the park, Hauley offered to get them some popped corn. "I won't be long," he said. "I'll be back before Johnson can pardon another traitor."

As soon as he left their sun-dappled quilt, Kitty turned to Clara, her expression all seriousness. "I have something to tell you, and you won't be happy about it."

"What is it? Are you in some kind of trouble?" A hundred fears passed through Clara's mind.

Kitty shook her head. "I'm not in any trouble. I want to be a teacher for the Western Freedmen's Aid Society." The society sought teachers to send to the South, she explained. If she was selected, she would leave that summer.

·

Clara felt like she'd been punched in the stomach. "What! When did you decide this?"

"I applied two days ago."

"And you're only telling me now? You waited until we were in public, so I wouldn't make a fuss! So, this is what you meant when you said you wanted to be a teacher. You can't do it. I forbid you."

"You can't forbid me anymore, Clara. I'm old enough to go my own way. I can take care of myself."

"You don't understand how dangerous the world is. You're a beautiful young woman. That alone makes you vulnerable. There are more men like Orton out there. If he hadn't died—"

"You're the one who didn't know what Orton was about. And he died—" Kitty closed her mouth as if to stop the flow of words, and then blurted— "Orton died because I saw to it!"

"What in heaven's name are you on about? Orton fell off the dam!"

Kitty's expression was resolute. "Not on his own, he didn't."

Clara would have sworn Kitty was fooling, only there was no humor in her expression. "You—? No. Why would you say that? He fell at night. He was drunk. You were at home with me."

"It was an accident. Mostly. It happened so fast."

"I don't understand! You were at the dam with Orton that night? What were you doing there?" Clara looked at Kitty as if for the first time. Who was this girl sitting before her? She tried to recall that night. "We're not moving from this spot until you've told me everything!"

Kitty spoke in a low voice even though no one was close enough to hear, especially not with the band playing. "It was the day before the Federals came, the day Orton sent you to work down at Ivy. He came over to my looms just as they were about to start up, and he said I was to meet him at the dam that night. Of course, I told him no. But then he said if I didn't come, he would tell everyone that Benjamin was behind the arson attempt. And that you and I knew all along what Benjamin was up to. That we even helped him do it!"

"But we had no idea! We still don't know for certain it was him."

"At first, I thought Orton was mad. Benjamin had gone to Nebraska! But he told me he had proof and that he would show me at the dam. If I'd known the Federals were coming the next day and that they were going to send us north, I never would've met him that night."

"I wish you'd told me. I could've gone with you. You must've been afraid..."

Kitty softly shook her head. "I was more angry than afraid. I don't take kindly to threats made against me and my sister, and I reckon in the back of my mind, I thought if he tried anything, I'd be ready to defend myself. I'd found a rock that afternoon by the creek when you were looking for me. Big enough to fend him off, small enough to fit in my hand. So, I wasn't fearing he'd hurt me. Anyhow, I waited until you were asleep, and I got the lantern and the rock, and when I got to the dam, there he was, sitting on the ledge of the overlook. He had one leg over each side like riding a horse. It was hard to see that night with no moon, but he had a lantern set nearby, and sure enough, there was a bottle of spirits next to it.

"That's when he told me Benjamin was dead, that he'd joined up with a Unionist gang, and that Eli had killed him. I didn't believe him at first. So he showed me Benjamin's pocketknife. I set my lantern on the ledge and asked to see it. He handed me the knife, and I took a step back to look at it in the light of my lantern. I could tell right away it was Benjamin's. Orton just laughed. I felt such a rage then. He told me to come closer, that he wanted the pocketknife back, and that I owed him a kiss for showing it to me. When I hesitated, he said I'd better do as I'm told.

Kitty paused. Clara was terribly anxious to know what happened next but sensed the recounting was hard on her sister and didn't want to push. Finally, Kitty continued. "I knew in that moment I'd kill him if I had to. I still had the rock in my right hand; I'd been holding it the whole time without him seeing. I took a step closer. He reeked of spirits. I gave him the pocketknife, and he opened it and reached for the ribbon on my braid. The sky-blue ribbon from Mama's dress. He cut the ribbon from my hair and held it in his hand like a trophy, and then he put it in his pocket. Then he said he was gonna kiss me and that it was no use screaming because no one would hear me over the dam."

"Oh, Kitty!"

"I raised my hand to hit him with the rock. I thought it'd be easy as he was drunk, but he saw it and grabbed my wrist. I yanked my arm away and got my hand free, and there was a moment there where he wobbled, and I knew I could just give him a little push, and he'd go over. A little push was all it'd take. And that's what I did. I pushed on his shoulder, and over he went."

Clara cried out, covering her mouth with her hand.

Kitty bent her head and traced a seam on the quilt with her finger. When she came to the edge of the quilt, she spoke again. "It was too dark to see where he landed, so I climbed down the embankment. I found him lying face down in the creek, near the edge where it's rocky just under the surface. He wasn't moving, and he lay face down in the water, and I knew he was dead. Not far from his body, the pocketknife shone in the light of my lantern. I grabbed it and ran. I never ran so fast in my life."

Clara's head felt thick as if it were stuffed with cotton.

"I didn't mean to kill him. Or maybe I did. I don't know. It all happened in a flash. I can't say I'm sorry how it turned out." Kitty put her hand on Clara's shoulder and gave it an anxious squeeze. "Say something. Say what you're thinking. You think I'm a murderer now."

Clara stared. It was difficult to reconcile this information with the sister she thought she knew. "No. You're not a murderer. You were only defending yourself. If Orton had lived, he would've done great harm to you. He might've had us hang for something we didn't do." She saw then that Kitty was crying. "Oh, Kitty, you've been keeping this to yourself all this time! Why did you never tell me?"

"I wanted to. So many times I wanted to tell you about that night. It haunts me." Kitty wiped her nose with the back of her hand and sniffed. "At first, I didn't tell you because I didn't want you to know Benjamin had died. And then last fall, when I finally told you what'd happened to Benjamin, I didn't want to burden you with the rest of it. Reckon I thought, what does it matter? It's in the past, we're hundreds of miles away, and I didn't want you to think poorly of me."

"You think I would condemn you for fighting for your life? For trying to protect us?" Clara was humbled by how brave Kitty had been. By what she'd endured for the both of them.

"I might've taken this secret to my grave, but I'm telling you now because I need you to understand that I'm stronger than you think. And so are you. You have to let me go."

The civic band continued to play, but now the music was jarring. The people around them went about their picnicking and playing, all as happy as birds. For Clara, the day had become strange, and she had difficulty forming a sensible thought about anything.

All this time, she had thought that she was the one taking care of her sister. When, in fact, it was Kitty who had defended herself. It was Kitty who'd protected them both from accusations that could've gotten them killed. Clara felt a fool for not having known what Kitty had done. For thinking Kitty capable of far less! How much did she know about her sister? About anyone?

Kitty had recovered by the time Hauley returned with a large paper cone of popped corn. He apologized for taking so long, explaining that he'd run into an old friend. Clara told him not to worry, that she and Kitty had had plenty to talk about in his absence.

She wanted to go home, lie on her bed, and forget about everything. Just sleep. But they'd only been at the park for a short time, and she didn't want to disappoint Hauley by asking to leave. When he asked her if everything was all right, she said she was fine but that she was concerned for her sister, who'd just announced her intention to leave Cincinnati.

Clara hoped Hauley would tell her what to do. Hoped he would tell her how to make Kitty stay. That he knew of a convent they could send her to, where she would be safe. Instead, he sighed in commiseration and said, "It's hard to let go of the people we love."

# *30*

At the millinery three days later, Clara was still reconciling herself to Kitty's revelation. They'd had an argument upon their return from Washington Park, during which Kitty accused Clara of never truly listening to her, of always presuming to know what was best simply because she was older. There was truth in what Kitty said, Clara had to admit—if only to herself. In many ways, Clara still saw her sister as the twelve-year-old girl whose welfare she'd been responsible for since their mother's death. Even now, as Kitty neared seventeen years of age, Clara had been reluctant to think of her sister as someone with her own rightful dreams, someone capable of choosing her own path.

Humbled, Clara had since begun to reconsider her opposition to Kitty becoming a teacher for the freedmen society. Not that she was comfortable with it: The war may have been over, but there were plenty of those in the South who opposed the education of freedmen, and Clara wouldn't be there to protect Kitty from any resulting danger. It was newly clear, however, that there was also a risk, both to Kitty and to their harmony as sisters, in keeping her close when the girl wanted so keenly to venture out into the world.

"We needed help getting on our feet when we arrived in Cincinnati," Kitty had argued. "Without the refugee commission, things could've turned out much worse for us. Try to imagine what it might be like for people who've been enslaved. To start over with nothing! I want to do for others some measure of what's been done for us."

Previously, Clara had attributed Kitty's eagerness to teach freedmen to mere youthful enthusiasm or love of adventure. As if they hadn't had adventure enough! It was becoming clear, however, that Kitty truly saw in the freedmen her fellow countrymen and women. Men, women, and children who deserved an education. And that becoming a teacher was, for Kitty, a calling, not an escape.

And so yesterday, Clara had spoken with Mrs. Bell about all the endeavor entailed (though if she were honest, she was still irritated with their landlady for introducing this path in Kitty's life, this path that would take her so far away). Mrs. Bell described the great need for teachers, not all of whom, as Clara had assumed, were single white women from the North committed to religious reform. Teachers were evangelicals and free-thinkers, male and female, black and white, married and single, Northerners and Southerners. Kitty would find it to be a most absorbing life, Mrs. Bell said. Yet the many unknowns gnawed at Clara: Where would Kitty be sent? Where would she live? Would Clara ever be able to see her? Mrs. Bell admitted that living conditions might be rough, but she claimed it would be nothing Kitty couldn't handle. If Kitty was selected to go, she would leave in August, if not sooner, depending on how long it took for travel arrangements to be made.

The truth of it was, Kitty didn't need Clara anymore. Maybe that's what bothered her nearly as much as anything else.

"Feathers or flowers?"

The customer's question shook Clara from her thoughts. Standing beside the shop's selection of trimmings, she helped a young woman choose adornments for a refurbished bonnet. The color of the trimmings required no thought. They would be black, as would the lining, the bavolet, and everything else. The young woman's husband, a Union soldier, had died in an army hospital earlier that month, weeks after the war ended.

Clara suggested three silk flowers at the crown. As she made this recommendation, two middle-aged women entered the shop and paused to admire the three patriotically themed bonnets displayed in the window. Madame's perched on the tallest stand, in the middle—a blue fanchon trimmed with white lace and red peonies. To one side was Trudie's, a red silk hat with white feathers. And on the other side was Clara's white silk empire bonnet with the metal rose, painted red and perched atop the crown, a striped ribbon of blue and white running across the back.

The taller of the two women admired Clara's bonnet while expressing her disbelief—even after these many weeks—that the war had ended at last.

"Yes," said the shorter one, "but now all these veterans are coming home with guns. It's unnerving. Many are from the lower classes. After years of war, how will they behave without an officer overseeing them?"

"My husband won't hire a single one. What are they good for now, but killing and savagery?"

"Saloon work, maybe."

The taller woman snickered.

In recent weeks, the city had swelled with Union soldiers newly mustered out. Some were returning home, while others came to Cincinnati to board trains or steamer packets for destinations to the west. The young woman Clara attended grew increasingly agitated by the women's conversation. "They might show some gratitude," the war widow muttered, just loud enough for them to hear. The women glanced in her direction.

"Ladies," said Madame, who'd been preoccupied with an accounts ledger, and now approached the women at the front of the shop. "How may I be of assistance this morning?"

The taller woman requested a bonnet in the style of Clara's patriotic creation, including the metal flower painted red. Could she have it quickly made, she inquired, as she hoped to wear it to an Independence Day gathering the following week. "To show my patriotism," she said.

Clara's customer, who must have felt the remark was aimed at her, opened her mouth to respond but thought better of it.

"It will be ready Monday afternoon," Madame said. While the unconventional trimming had been remarked upon favorably by many customers, only a small percentage requested a metal flower for their own headwear. Madame did not keep them in stock, and that afternoon, she sent Clara to acquire another.

Clara was on her way to the blacksmith when, upon crossing Fifth Street, Hauley approached from the opposite direction. She hadn't been expecting to see him, and a smile bloomed on her face at the pleasant surprise.

"I was on my way to see you," he said when they met in the middle of the street, in front of the Fifth Street Market House.

"You were coming to the millinery?" Clara asked. He'd never visited her at Madame's before. "Is something the matter?"

"Not at all. In fact, just the opposite. I wanted to talk to you about Sunday. What do you think about going on a picnic, somewhere new this time? I thought I might take you to Spring Grove Cemetery. It's a beautiful rural setting—with lots of trees and ponds and rolling hills. I think you'll love it."

Clara almost asked if Kitty could join them, as she often did, but something in Hauley's expression stopped her.

"Perhaps just the two of us this time, if that's all right?" Hauley asked tentatively. "Would Kitty be upset not to come?"

"I'm sure she won't mind," Clara said quickly and meant it: Kitty rarely lacked for invitations. And suddenly, Clara didn't want her sister to join them, not this time. There was a sense of anticipation in the way Hauley spoke.

"Splendid!" Hauley said. "I'll pick you up at ten." He stared at her, smiling, as if memorizing her features. "I won't keep you. It looks like you were on an errand."

Clara told him where she was going, and they said their good-byes, and all the way to the blacksmith, the smile remained on her face. Their brief conversation caused her to consider a new possibility for herself, her life, and her future. For what if Hauley planned to propose? They'd spoken in generalities about the future before, like how many children they wanted (maybe one or two) and whether she liked living in Cincinnati (she did). He hadn't asked about her future as a milliner; it must be understood that a woman who marries gives up her work unless absolutely necessary.

But is that what Clara wanted?

She treasured her time with Hauley too much to dwell on any disagreeable consequences. If he proposed, she would accept without hesitation. She would not turn down a life with Hauley. She would find another way to quench her thirst for hat-making—by fashioning bonnets for friends and family, maybe, like she'd done before.

Her love for Hauley surpassed anything she'd felt for Benjamin. Benjamin had been a good man, rest his soul. But her deepest feelings for him were rooted in gratitude. With Benjamin, she realized, with the benefit of hindsight, she'd always been playing a role. Always trying to anticipate what he wanted and how she was supposed to act. She'd thought that's just the way it was in a relationship and that she would get used to it, and eventually, it would feel natural. Now she knew otherwise. And while she'd never admit it aloud, and while his life was too steep a price to pay, it was a relief to know she would not have to live in Nebraska, where she would have played at being a wife and homesteader for the rest of her days.

With Hauley, not once had she felt like she was acting a part. In his company, she felt like herself. Herself, only better: cleverer, prettier, more competent. More the person she'd hoped to be. With Hauley, she could say how she truly felt about almost anything, and he would understand—or, at least, he would try.

Near the blacksmith, she passed an alley, in the shadows of which lay a large sow with a litter of suckling pigs. Clara paused a moment and watched the rapacious piglets. It did sometimes feel like every woman was supposed to be a mother. Well, maybe not *every* woman. Both Trudie and Madame seemed perfectly content to be unmarried. Is that what Clara wanted? Or was her work at

Madame LeClair's only ever meant to be a one-year undertaking? And even if it were, how could she rightly be disappointed? There was too much to be grateful for. Her work had brought her a measure of happiness in a terrible year. She'd made a good friend in Trudie. She was a professional milliner, for goodness' sake—a dream she hadn't dared to dream!

Anyhow, she was getting ahead of herself. Hauley hadn't made her an offer of marriage. He had simply invited her to a Sunday picnic. It was best, she concluded upon arriving at Mr. Dickson's blacksmith shop, to put all thoughts of proposals out of her mind.

# 31

Holding up a small square of looking glass with one hand Sunday morning, Clara adjusted her lace collar with the other. The collar was a recent purchase, the finest she'd ever owned, and not unlike those that Madame's fancier customers often wore. A half-hour earlier, Kitty had left for a sewing circle, the products of which would be donated to the Freedmen's Aid Society. On her way out the door, Kitty had kissed Clara's cheek and told her she looked beautiful. Kitty expressed a hope that Hauley would propose, claiming that not only would it make Clara happy, but it would also give Kitty some room to breathe at last. She said the latter with a smile and a theatrical flourish, and Clara let it pass without comment.

Now she donned a new bonnet she'd made, white silk trimmed with a metal rose, and, full of anticipation, descended the stairs to the parlor. Within a minute of Mrs. Bell's grandfather clock striking ten, there was a knock on the door. Her hand on the doorknob, Clara paused a moment to collect herself, and then opened the door.

Hauley wore a smart cotton suit, the lower empty right sleeve pinned near the shoulder. He looked as handsome as ever, but his expression was all wrong. His smile didn't reach his eyes. He looked as though he were trying to appear happy. Clara felt like someone had stepped on her chest.

She forced a deep breath. Surely everything was fine, and it was only her nerves making her ill at ease. But when he told her she looked beautiful, he said this almost with a sigh.

She crossed the threshold and joined him on the front steps. "Is everything all right?" she asked, closing the door behind her and trying to keep the alarm from her voice.

"Here, I want to show you something." He approached a buckboard and mule tied to a post. Removing a blanket from atop a large object stowed within it, he revealed a beautiful new trunk. "This is for you."

For her? Clara gasped. The lines of the trunk were graceful and curved. Looking at it from one end, it resembled a figure eight or a loaf of bread. She moved her hand along one of its brass bands, which were studded with brass buttons and ran up the front, curved across the top, and down the back. It was a breathtaking gift. Hauley's odd and distracted behavior did not fit the occasion. "Hauley, it's beautiful."

"Do you like it? It's a Jenny Lind, named after the Swedish singer," he said, brightening a little. "I thought the twenty-eight-inch width would be big enough to hold your belongings but not so big that you couldn't carry it yourself when you needed to. I made it from old-growth pine. These brass center bands here are for reinforcement. Do you like the buttons? Oh," he said, reaching into his pocket, "here's the key. Please, open it."

Smiling at his enthusiasm but still unsure what was happening, Clara flipped open the two latches on either side of the lock, then turned the key and lifted the lid. Inside were a tray and a box with a top curved so as to fit neatly inside the lid. "It's marvelous. This is the most beautiful gift I've ever been given. Thank you." Then she waited for an explanation.

But the only explanation that came was that of the trunk's features. "This is a bonnet box, and this is a tray for—well, for whatever you like. Remove them both, and you have the main compartment underneath." The lid was lined with a light-blue floral fabric and decorated with two lithographs, one depicting ice skaters on a canal, the other a view of Cincinnati from across the river in Covington. Clara touched each lithograph in turn.

"I chose those so you don't forget your friends in Cincinnati." There was a wistfulness in his voice.

"Forget my friends? But I'm not going anywhere. Hauley, what's wrong? Please tell me."

"I'm sorry. I've been trying to find the right words, but I suppose there's nothing for it except to show you." Avoiding her eyes, he reached into his vest pocket, pulled out a square of newsprint, and handed it to her. "I saw this in the paper last evening. I'm sorry I didn't bring it to you then, but it was late, and I— Please forgive me."

It was an advertisement: *Seeking the whereabouts of Clara and Kitty Douglas of Roswell, Georgia. Please contact Benjamin Lindley at Spencer House.*

Clara steadied herself against the buckboard. The printed words were strange, like something out of a storybook or a dream. There was her name. And Kitty's. In the newspaper! "I don't understand."

"I don't know how long the advertisement has run. I saw it for the first time last night." Hauley looked to the ground, then at her. "Benjamin Lindley, this is your fiancé?"

"Yes, but..." She read the notice again. It made no sense. "How can he be alive? Kitty told me— She was told he'd been murdered. There was no question..."

Hauley was silent.

"He's at the Spencer House... Where is that? I could go and see him right now?" She couldn't believe Benjamin was not only alive but also in Cincinnati at that very moment.

"It's on the Public Landing. I can take you there if you like." Then, when Clara didn't answer, "Here, let me help you get this inside." He nodded at the trunk.

"Thank you," Clara said, only half-hearing him. She wasn't sure she could go to the hotel, not at that moment. Her head spun with a thousand questions. How could Benjamin be so very close after their more than two years of separation? After she'd thought him dead!

Hauley lifted one end of the trunk, she the other, and together they carried it into the parlor.

"It should come in handy on your journey," Hauley said in what seemed a valiant effort to fill the silence. "That is, I had made it for another purpose, but..."

She told Hauley she loved it and that she would cherish it always.

"You've had quite a shock."

Clara sat in the parlor, the trunk at her feet and a blank expression on her face. Nothing seemed real. The concern in Hauley's voice when he asked if she needed anything was evident, and she shook her head, and there was his gentle goodbye and then the creak of the front door. A moment passed, and she rushed outside.

Hauley stood near the buckboard, staring blankly down the street, looking a little lost. She ran to him and wrapped her arms around his middle. At first, he seemed too startled to respond. Then, he put his left arm around her, his hand pressing lightly on her shoulder blade. She inhaled his scent: wool and cedar and citrus shaving soap.

"I'm leaving for Nashville tonight," he said. "To see Patrick home. We got word that he's unwell."

Clara pulled away. "Will he be all right?"

"I believe so, but I want to be there for him."

Clara nodded, unable to say more for fear tears would spill down her cheeks. Then, in a small voice, "I'll miss you, Hauley Dugan. I thought—"

"I know. I thought so, too."

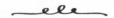

Minutes later, Hauley was gone, and she carried her new trunk up the stairs to her room, ignoring the questioning look of Mrs. Bell, who'd appeared in the parlor. Clara needed to be alone to collect her thoughts. All this time, Benjamin had been alive. When the mill burned, and the mill workers were deported, and when they arrived in Ohio and when she found this millinery job—he'd been alive. He'd been left for dead, and yet somehow he lived. She felt guilty for having given up hope. Guilty for wanting to marry Hauley. Would he see her face and know she had been unfaithful, if only in her thoughts?

She lay on her bed. Could she marry Hauley anyway? Break her engagement with Benjamin, explaining how she'd thought him dead all this time? To do so seemed terribly cruel. No, she would keep her promise and honor her engagement. But she would draw the line at moving to Nebraska. She'd already admitted to herself her misgivings about life on a homestead, and she would not go back to pretending those misgivings didn't exist. Maybe she and Benjamin could build a life in Cincinnati. She must carefully consider how to present the idea to him, for when she spoke with Benjamin, her thoughts often became jumbled, and she lost track of what she wanted to say. Once she'd had a chance to prepare her argument, she would go to the Spencer House.

Benjamin was alive. The news flashed again and again in her brain like a lightning bolt.

She imagined how their reunion would go. She would tell him she'd thought he was dead, and he would explain what had happened, how he'd joined up with a Unionist gang and what they'd done to thwart the Confederates. Maybe he'd admit to the plot to burn the Roswell mill. She would ask him what he thought would've become of her and Kitty had the arson attempt been successful; he would describe his plan for them. He would explain how his gang had been ambushed by Eli and his men and how he'd been shot. Perhaps he'd been left for dead but had been taken in by some kind stranger and nursed back to health. She would be hurt that he'd never told her of his plans to fight for the Union, and he'd tell her that it was for her protection. He'd explain that he did have a claim in Nebraska but that he couldn't leave Georgia without fighting for what was right.

Clara would tell him all she and Kitty had survived: Orton Enson and the Federal occupation and the mill workers' arrest. The Louisville hospital prison and the measles outbreak. Their arrival in Cincinnati and the refugee commission and the search for work. He'd be surprised at how well she'd done in the city. Would he understand how much her position at the millinery meant to her?

Benjamin had traveled a great distance to find her. The Roswell mill workers were scattered like the four winds, and yet he'd found her. She owed him her loyalty, didn't she? If she couldn't convince him to stay in Cincinnati, did she owe it to him to go west? Knowing Benjamin, he was already making plans for the journey: marry in Cincinnati, take a train to St. Joseph's, Missouri. Get supplies and wait for spring and then join a caravan heading out on the Oregon Trail. She saw her whole life before her as if it had already happened.

She'd never convince Kitty to come with her now. And how could she bear Nebraska without her sister?

That afternoon Clara went to Front Street, her stomach twisting with nerves. So much had happened since she last saw Benjamin. In many ways, she was a different person. Would he notice the change? She rehearsed what she would say, all her reasons why they should stay in Cincinnati.

But what was the use? It would be an impossible task if he already had his land. She felt guilty for wavering. It had been their plan; how could she let him down by backing out? How would she feel if she'd stayed in Roswell and he'd never come back for her? He'd kept his promise to Clara, despite all the hardships of the war. He'd survived, and he'd searched for her, and he hadn't given up until he found her. What did it say about her if she did not keep her promise to him?

The Public Landing was a hubbub of activity: stevedores loading and unloading cargo, soldiers arriving and departing, horses pulling wagons of goods into the city. There was Spencer House, on the corner of Broadway and Front streets.

Her stomach twisted in anxious knots. She'd spent two years longing for their reunion, but now that it was mere moments away, she felt almost like she was meeting a stranger.

She went inside and, her legs wobbly, found a solitary chair, its back against a column. To her left, a grand front desk commanded a view of the entire lobby. She watched for Benjamin while summoning the nerve to approach the hotel clerk.

Clara saw in her mind's eye how the day would go. After a tearful reunion, she and Benjamin would have supper at the hotel. Unused to such fine establishments, she would glance at the menu and feel overwhelmed, and he would choose for her, and she would let him. She would remember the girl she'd once been: a girl who found it much simpler to doubt her own judgment than Benjamin's. How easily she might slip back into that person.

And if they went to Nebraska, she would be fully dependent on him. Here in the city, she had her work and friends, and she knew her way around; if they stayed here, she might have a chance at remaining the person she'd become.

After several minutes, her heartbeat slowed to normal. She rose from the chair and approached the front desk. The hotel clerk, who was reading a newspaper, hadn't noticed her yet. The distance between them narrowed, and it felt like someone was pressing on her ears, blocking out all sound.

## 32

The hotel clerk, a young man not much older than Clara, had a neat mustache and smoothly combed hair parted in the middle. When she reached the front desk, he did not look up from his newspaper. Clara waited and, after nearly a minute, decided perhaps she was supposed to speak first. "Excuse me, sir?" He still did not look up, but what was there to do but to keep going? "I'm looking for Benjamin Lindley. I believe he's staying here?"

The clerk slowly closed the paper and minced over to the register. After checking the guest records, sliding his index finger down the page and up again, he looked at her with indifference and said, in a dignified tone, "I'm afraid you are mistaken."

When she asked him to please check once again, he gave her a withering look and returned to his paper.

Stunned, Clara drifted outside. She took several steps toward the river, turned around, and, shielding her eyes from the late afternoon sun, checked the name of the hotel, wondering if she'd made a mistake. But there it was: SPENCER HOUSE. Or had she misremembered the name altogether? She was beginning to doubt her own mind. Reaching into her pocket for the newspaper advertisement, she found it wasn't there. She must have left it at the boardinghouse. Though she swore this was the hotel, she would go back and check the advertisement again.

As she passed through a quiet side street on her way home, someone behind her called her name. Clara turned. A woman stood on the narrow sidewalk about ten paces away. Though the figure was familiar, it was all wrong for the setting.

"Temperance?"

Temperance Enson was a skeleton of her former self. Her dress was filthy. "Well, don't you look charmingly!" She spoke with surprising energy, given her appearance. "I must look a fright to you. I've been living on ash-cakes day in, day out."

"What are you doing here? I thought you stayed in Roswell."

"I come to enemy territory looking for you! You're just the linthead I wanted to see."

Clara's blood ran cold. "Me?"

Temperance took a step closer to her. "Wasn't easy. But I ain't as dumb as you think. I got myself all the way to Louisville. Asked around and learned about the prison hospital they put y'all in. They said most of the Roswell folk went to Indiana looking for work. But when I got to that Hoosier mill, and you and Kitty weren't there, someone said you might've come here. I knew they must be right. I had a suspicion you'd look for something other than mill work—you and your sister always did think you was above it."

Clara stared.

"But this city is tremendous big. I didn't see how I'd ever find you." She tapped her temple with her index finger. "Then I got the idea to put an ad in the paper."

Suddenly dizzy, Clara squinted her eyes, trying to keep the world from going out of focus. "That was you? Pretending to be Benjamin?"

"Cost me as much as I had. But it was worth it!" She turned and spat.

Clara's limbs were shaking. "What do you want from me?"

"Don't act like you don't know. The war may be over, but my countrymen will never forget the *savagerous* actions of the North. And you and Benjamin, you're as bad as any of them. Worse, you're traitors." A watermelon rind lay in Temperance's path, and she kicked it in Clara's direction.

"I did nothing—"

"That's a mighty fine hat. You make that?"

"Why come all this way, Temperance? We have no fight."

"I disagree. You killed my cousin. No! Don't try to deny it. And with Eli not fit to travel, I'm here in his place."

"What happened to Eli? I saw him in Louisville." Clara sought to delay. She wasn't far from the hotel, but Temperance blocked the way. There was a vacant brick building to her left. To her right and just behind her, an alley.

"He ain't well. Not that you care."

"What—what about the mills? Are they rebuilding?"

Temperance scoffed. "All the good that'll do me. They won't hire us back, any of us that was there when the Federals came. Barrington blames us for not defending his factories. Don't that beat all? Says we're responsible for the destruction. He wants a whole new set of workers."

"I'm sorry, Temperance. Truly I am. But look here, I had nothing to do with Orton's death."

Temperance reached behind her back and pulled out a pistol.

Clara's legs buckled, and she braced herself against a barrel for support. "Temperance, no!" she cried, and then, in a voice she tried to make calm, "Don't do this. Let me help you. What do you want, money? I don't have much, but I can get you some."

"I don't want your money. You took Orton's life. You owe us yours."

A lone hog came wandering down the street from the direction of the Public Landing. If only it were a soldier instead. Someone armed. Clara put up her hands, palms forward. "There must be something—"

"She didn't push Orton off the dam. I did."

Kitty?

Her sister's voice came from behind Clara, and a second later, there she was, standing beside her.

Clara put an arm in front of her sister. "She's lying! I did it. It's just like you said. I pushed him!"

Temperance shrugged. "I don't mind shooting the both of you. Reckon I prefer it." She pointed her weapon at one sister, then the other.

Oblivious to the danger, the hog ambled toward the watermelon rind near Clara's feet. She kicked it away. The hog pivoted and, rushing toward the rind, knocked into Temperance, causing her to stumble.

The pistol fired. Kitty screamed.

A terrible pain pierced Clara's skull. Three thoughts flashed in her mind—Temperance pulled the trigger! She wasn't all bluster. People never failed to surprise you—before the packed dirt road rose up to hit her, and everything went dark.

—————ℓℓℓ—————

She awoke to singing. Kitty's voice, her lovely voice. How long had it been? Clara watched as Kitty braided her hair, singing that old song the Summerhills used to play. When Kitty finished her braid, she turned and saw that Clara was awake.

"Oh, Clara!" Kitty hurried over to her and gave her a careful embrace. "How do you feel? You must be parched! I'll fetch you a glass of water. And maybe some broth?"

Clara tried to sit up, but her head throbbed, and so she lay down again and pulled the quilt up to her chin. "Were you accepted?"

Kitty studied Clara's face, stared into her eyes. "How are you feeling?"

"I'm all right." Then, when Kitty looked dubious, "My head hurts a little. But tell me the truth, were you accepted to teach? Is that why you're singing?"

"I'm singing because I'm happy. And I'm not going anywhere until you're better. I'm taking care of you, for once." She went to the wash basin and returned with a damp washcloth, which she placed on Clara's forehead.

"You *were* accepted then. When do you leave? I won't stand in your way. Or lie in your way," she added with a weak smile. "Not anymore."

"The doctor said your brain is concussed. You received quite a blow. Two blows, in fact: one from the bullet and one from the ground. You've barely spoken a word of sense in twenty-four hours. I can't in good conscience leave until you're feeling better."

"I'll be fine. And there's Mrs. Bell."

"You let me fret over it. But, sis? Do you mean what you said? That you'll let me go?"

"Yes, of course." Clara's eyes welled up. "You're old enough to decide for yourself. Even though every time you go out into the world, I fear what might happen to you."

"Sooner or later, you'll have to trust me."

"I trust *you*. It's the world I don't trust. I only ever wanted to protect you, but you don't need me to. You can protect yourself." The white silk bonnet she'd worn the day before hung on a nail. "Can I see it?"

Kitty brought her the bonnet. The metal flower was dented, the red paint scraped off near the middle. "The doctor said if the bullet hadn't hit just there... Well, I don't even want to think about it."

"Did they catch her?"

"Not exactly. A couple of soldiers chased her down to the landing. She tried to escape onto a riverboat. When they cornered her on an upper deck, she jumped into the river."

"No!"

"She never came up. Imagine they'll find her body downriver somewhere."

Clara was quiet for a while. "I couldn't believe I was going to see Benjamin again." She removed the damaged flower from the crown. "Why didn't he tell me he was going to fight for the Union?"

"You know why. He wanted to protect us."

"When he left without us, I thought it was because he didn't think I would be any good at homesteading, at least not in the beginning when there's so much to be done." Clara turned the bullet-struck flower over in her hands. "He would've been right."

"Hush, you're good at everything you set your mind to."

"I wanted to believe I could live that life. Truth is, I feel more at home here in Cincinnati than I have anywhere else."

Kitty turned the washcloth on Clara's head to the cooler side. "I always said we should move to the city."

"I should've listened to you. I was scared. I couldn't imagine me, Clara Douglas, living in a city. I couldn't *see* it, you know?"

"I think that for some things, you just have to do them before you can imagine doing them."

Clara closed her hand around the flower. "I felt so guilty yesterday. I thought Benjamin would see it, plain as day, that I was in love with someone else. I was going to try to put those feelings aside. If I could."

"You got nothing to feel guilty for. You were never unfaithful to Benjamin. And you know what else? I don't believe he ever truly appreciated you."

"You shouldn't speak ill of him. Not now."

"I'm not. I'm only saying he never acknowledged all the things you can do. All your many talents."

"Suppose I'm guilty of the same with you," Clara said, and Kitty smiled. "You were so brave yesterday, telling Temperance it was you who killed Orton. You risked your life to save mine. I don't know how I can ever thank you for that."

"Well, I couldn't have you pay for something I did, could I?" Kitty sighed. "What a turn the day took. When I came home yesterday and saw that advertisement on the bed, I was terrified you were going to leave for Nebraska. I thought I was coming to save you from a life of homesteading—not from Temperance Enson!"

"You came to stop me."

"I did."

Clara took Kitty's hand in hers. "I was never going to go to Nebraska. Not without you."

## 33

It was a Thursday morning in late July, and Clara and Kitty waited on the Public Landing. More than a dozen steamboats lined the northern bank of the Ohio River in various stages of arrival and departure. Kitty's packet was still being loaded with cargo.

"Promise me you'll write as soon as you arrive," Clara said. "Let me know you've made it safely."

"I promise."

"And if it's dangerous, promise you'll come home." When Kitty did not make such a promise, instead reassuring her sister that she would be fine, Clara knew better than to press the matter. "It's hard to believe it's only been a year since we arrived at this very spot. I was terrified. I didn't know how we were going to survive."

"Sometimes it feels like we've lived a lifetime in the last year." Moments later, a whistle blew. "They're starting to board." Kitty turned to her sister. "I never said thank you."

"For what?"

"For taking care of me. For all you've done for me since Mama died. It can't have been easy, having everything on your shoulders like that. And I surely didn't make it any easier on you."

"I was happy to do it," Clara said, wiping a tear. "You're my little sister. Well, not so little anymore." She laughed, a laugh that was almost a cry.

The sisters walked down the landing toward the river, moving slowly to forestall their separation. "I was hoping I could see Hauley before I left," Kitty said. "To give him my blessing. Reckon you two will be married next time I see you."

Clara smiled in spite of herself. "Oh, I don't know. He never actually proposed to me, even though I thought he might." Still, in unguarded moments Clara liked to imagine their wedding. A small gathering with his family and her millinery friends. They would have water ice flavored with strawberries, served in small glass dishes.

Kitty adjusted her bags on her shoulder. "I should get in line."

Clara pulled her sister into a tight embrace, her eyes spilling tears. "I'm going to miss you heaps. You do know how proud I am of you, don't you?"

"You're proud of me?"

"Of course I am! You're the bravest, kindest person I know."

Kitty pulled back so she could look Clara in the eye. "Don't stop making hats, will you promise me that?"

"I promise. Go on, then. You don't want to miss your boat."

Clara followed Kitty to where the line of passengers ended. Standing to the side, she watched as Kitty crossed the stage and boarded the packet. There she went: a piece of Clara's heart walking around outside of her body, vulnerable as anything. No, that wasn't right. Clara reminded herself that Kitty was stronger than Clara knew.

For a moment, Kitty disappeared in the crowd of passengers and crew, a minute later reappearing at the railing on the upper deck. Kitty waved, and Clara waved back.

It wasn't long before the whistle blew, loud and deep, and the steamboat pulled away from the bank. It passed between the two towers of the suspension bridge, which was still under construction. They'd recently begun laying the wire ropes across. When the bridge was finished, someone had said, the whole population of Cincinnati could get on it without danger of being let down into the water. She wondered if that was really true or if it was bluster.

Clara kept waving even after she could no longer make out Kitty's figure, stopping only after the steamboat disappeared around a bend. Even though it pained her to watch Kitty leave, it felt good knowing she was doing what she felt called to do. Clara wiped her eyes with a handkerchief.

Her stomach growled. She found a vendor, bought peanuts, and walked the length of the landing, looking once more for Hauley's boat. Someone at his shop had given her the name of his packet and the arrival time, which had coincided with Kitty's departure. But his packet must have been delayed, for it wasn't there. She ought to get back to the millinery. Madame had given Clara her blessing to see Kitty off but not to wait all afternoon for Hauley Dugan.

She finished the peanuts and ascended the landing.

When she reached Front Street, there was Hauley—but with no luggage and no brother. He stood alone, casting his gaze up and down the landing. Upon seeing Clara, his entire expression lifted.

She ran toward him. "Hauley! When did you get back? I was just looking for your boat."

"We were early. I've already been to the shop, and they said you'd asked about my arrival. They gave me your letter. Clara, what you've been through! I should have gone with you to Spencer House to make sure you were safe. I'm so sorry. I should have made certain."

"It's not your fault! Put that out of your mind. And I'm fine now. Just a knock to the noggin. But your brother, is he well?"

"He's much better, thank you. He's at home, resting from the journey."

They stood there a moment on Front Street, each smiling and looking at the other.

"Are you hungry?" Hauley asked. "I know a place that serves a delicious chicken potpie."

"Oh, I'd love that. But I have to get back to the millinery. Would you walk with me? There's so much I want to tell you."

"I would like nothing more."

He offered her his arm, and she took it, and they started along Main Street together.

# AUTHOR'S NOTE

If you find yourself north of Atlanta, Georgia, where the "Yankee overseers" live (as I once did), and if you enjoy local history, I recommend a visit to downtown Roswell. A number of the town's 19th century residences remain, and several, including Barrington Hall and Smith Plantation, are open for public tours. A trail along Vickery Creek (also known as Big Creek) leads past the Roswell Manufacturing Company's original machine shop, the company's only remaining structure. Continue along the trail and you'll find the waterfall created when the creek was dammed to provide waterpower for the cotton mills.

A block east of the town square stands a monument dedicated to the memory of the 400 mill workers, most of them women and children, who were arrested and sent north by Federal forces in 1864. While some eventually returned to Roswell, the fates of most remain a mystery.

Clara and Kitty and the other mill workers depicted in this novel are purely fictional, but the events they endure are based on historical record.

# ABOUT THE AUTHOR

Kinley Bryan's debut novel, *Sisters of the Sweetwater Fury*, inspired by the Great Lakes Storm of 1913 and her own family history, won the 2022 *Publishers Weekly* Selfies Award for adult fiction. An Ohio native, she now lives in South Carolina with her husband and three children. *The Lost Women of Mill Street* is her second novel.

www.kinleybryan.com

# ALSO BY KINLEY BRYAN

*Sisters of the Sweetwater Fury*

https://mybook.to/l8h2

Made in United States
North Haven, CT
20 May 2024

52720568R00182